"[KIERNAN O'SHAUGHNESSY IS] A NEW CHAR-
ACTER, FUNNY AND AUTHORITATIVE."
—*San Francisco Chronicle*

"A FEMALE 'QUINCY,' WHO APPLIES HER
KNOWLEDGE OF FORENSIC MEDICINE TO THE
ART OF CRIME SOLVING . . . With two highly ac-
claimed detective series, Susan Dunlap has carved out
her own territory in the mystery field, the policewoman
procedural. Now she has created her third and most
fascinating." —*Mystery News*

"O'SHAUGHNESSY IS VERY MUCH A NEW
BREED OF INVESTIGATOR . . . AS EXCITING
AN OFFERING AS WE'VE SEEN ALL YEAR."
—*The Plain Dealer* (Cleveland)

"SUSAN DUNLAP IS ONE OF THE BEST OF THE
NEW CROP OF MYSTERY WRITERS."
—*The San Diego Union*

"A FASCINATING TALE OF DEATH AND DECEIT
. . . A TRUE PUZZLE . . . OF THE SORT THAT
THE LATE JOHN D. MacDONALD'S TRAVIS Mc-
GEE MIGHT HAVE ENCOUNTERED."
—*The Muncie Star*

* *Murder ad lib*

OTHER BOOKS BY SUSAN DUNLAP

PIOUS DECEPTION

SUSAN DUNLAP

A DELL BOOK

Published by
Dell Publishing
a division of
Bantam Doubleday Dell Publishing Group, Inc.
1540 Broadway
New York, New York 10036

ISBN: 0-440-20746-0

Reprinted by arrangement with Villard Books

Printed in the United States of America

Published simultaneously in Canada

October 1990

10 9 8 7 6 5

OPM

For my cousin Marge, with love and thanks

ACKNOWLEDGMENTS

With thanks to Chief Deputy Coroner Tom Siebe, Sonoma County, for his expertise, his patience, and his understanding of the requirements of fiction.

To Dr. Winfield Danielson, John Arndt, and Beth Edelstein for their special expertise and suggestions.

And to Bernadette and Douglas Croy for their unique observations.

PIOUS
DECEPTION

1

LIKE A TOMATO on a grill. That's how the sun looked. And that's how Auxiliary Bishop Raymond Dowd felt.

Seven o'clock at night. A hundred and two degrees. Dammit, where were the clouds? Even the gritty swirls of a dust storm would be better than this—the sun scraping his skin raw, the hot air seething up through the cracked ground, pasting his pants to his ass. Tamarisk plumes, the honey mesquite leaves, the row of palms: might as well be sticks for all the shade they gave. He eyed the cool dark of Mission San Leo fifty yards ahead. Once he would have loped that distance. But thirty years of the priesthood, thirty years of too much good food, too many Christmas bottles, had put an end to that.

He hated Phoenix, the latter-day Wild West. He hated the heat, the sand, the dusty air that kept his throat dry morning to night. But mostly he hated the lack of tradition. Mission San Leo. Look at it: white stucco, plain dark wood, simple mission church of the padres! Ha! The present church was built in 1968! Instant Catholic history! At least in '68 it had stood alone among yucca and century plants and saguaro cacti. Then there had been a chance to imagine the mission as it might have been a hundred years before. Not now. The Phoenician suburbs had sprung up to mock it. Azure Acres Homes—three-bedroom, one-bath, cinder-block shoeboxes—all around it. On the corner a pseudo-Elizabethan shopping mall. Damned bell at the self-service pump rang louder than the one at the church.

They had told him he'd get used to the heat. Ha! Thirty years and it still pressed on his shoulders, on his paun—, his *girth,* as if every degree weighed a pound. Pushing a lock of damp chestnut hair off his ruddy forehead, he slogged on. A familiar acrid smell floated by. Was that incense coming from the church? Was young Vanderhooven conducting a mass in there at this hour on a Wednesday night? *He* had set the mass schedule for all his parishes. Vanderhooven had no business changing it here. Damn uppity kid!

From the beginning he'd known Vanderhooven would be trouble. He'd been suspicious when Bishop Medlin told him his brother's godson wanted to come out from New York. And when Archbishop Groom called from back there—"Got a coup for you, Dowd! Young man with great recommendations from the seminary. Spent a year at Columbia in graduate school—finance. Father's in finance—Vanderhooven and Kline, you know. Good Catholic family"—he knew he'd been thrown a spitter. If Vanderhooven was such a catch, why hadn't they kept him in New York? If Vanderhooven had such a good, *rich* Catholic family, why hadn't he pulled strings to stay in New York? What had been the matter with him? Or, worse yet, who would he be reporting to? How much would he tell them?

Archbishop Groom had ended his call with the clincher: Vanderhooven had the makings of a suitable secretary—*when Dowd became archbishop here* was unspoken, but the implication was clear. Equally clear was the penalty for objecting. Future archbishops were team players. Dowd had accepted Vanderhooven, but he hadn't been fooled.

The breeze picked up, but it did nothing to cool Dowd. He mounted the five wooden steps to the church, paused before the heavy wooden doors, and reached gratefully for the brass handle, noting the scourge of tarnish—another thing to bring to Vanderhooven's attention. If Vanderhooven had spent his time organizing altar guilds and sextons and wardens, as Dowd had told him, the first thing a communicant saw when he came to the mission wouldn't be tarnish.

Dowd pulled the handle. The heavy door moved slowly, as if giving the frivolous time to compose themselves before stepping into sanctified space. He moved through the doorway, into the blessed shade. Sighing deeply, he felt the cool air slap his face and chill the rings of sweat under his arms, the wide strip down his back, and the narrow strip under the tightness of his waistband. After the glare outside, the narthex was dark. He could barely make out the redwood doors that led to the nave. Ought to be a light in here. Some old lady would trip and break her neck and sue the hell out of the archdiocese. Vanderhooven, the financial *wunderkind,* ought to know that. Too dark.

And too quiet. There was no murmur of an illicit mass being

offered—no voices, no creak of pews, no thud as the kneeling benches hit the floor. There was only the acrid smell of incense.

Hesitantly, he pulled open one of the doors and from habit turned immediately to his left, dipped his finger into the holy-water font, and crossed himself, before looking forward to see what Vanderhooven was up to.

There was no mass; there were no parishioners. The pews were empty. Bishop Dowd looked past the low wooden railing up to the altar at the far end of the sanctuary. The gradine was in place behind, the baldacchino cloth hanging above. Nothing out of order. The sepulcher was covered, no sign of the thurible. Where was that incense coming from?

Following the smell of incense, Dowd looked at the side altar to the left. He saw him! Vanderhooven!

Dowd grabbed the corner of the pew in front and braced himself. Then he ran forward.

Five minutes later he stood in the priest's study, sweat running down his cheeks. "Hanging," Dowd mumbled into the phone, "goddamned fool hung himself. I knew Vanderhooven was trouble. Should never have accepted him, no matter what Groom and Medlin said. Trouble from the minute he came here. Christ! Why couldn't they have sent him to Tucson, or Albuquerque?"

"Did you cut him down?"

"Cut? No." Dowd swayed back against the wall. "Dead by hanging. Suicide! A priest in one of my parishes! In this, of all parishes!"

"Are you sure he's dead? You're not a doctor."

"You don't need to be a doctor, *Doctor,* to see that. His eyes are bulging like a frog's. His tongue, it's black."

"You'd better call the sheriff."

"No! His body, Elias, we can't let anyone see it, not like it is."

2

"I DON'T TAKE small cases. I have a decadent life-style to maintain." Kiernan O'Shaughnessy laughed. Living in a duplex on the beach in La Jolla, with an ex-jock as her cook, houseman, and dogwalker, that was pretty darned decadent for a novice in the world of wallowing. At one time she would have been appalled at such self-indulgence, but now, well, she had to admit the transition had been surprisingly easy.

She shifted the phone and ran a hand through her short black curly hair. English racing cap, her hairdresser had called the cut, suitable for a tough little lady. Kiernan had decided to assume that the "tough" referred to her work as a private investigator rather than to the effect of her thick eyebrows and the nose that was just a bit too long for her face. "Little?" It bugged her. But at barely five one there was no way of getting around that. She propped her feet on the deck railing, *her* deck railing, and found herself grinning as she watched the Pacific waves break on the rocky beach.

On the stones below, Ezra, her gangly Labrador/Irish wolfhound, jerked back as the spray hit his snout. He slipped, scrambled for footing, and snarled at the ocean. To her right, where the rocks gave way to beach, a huge former offensive lineman unzipped his wetsuit and waved.

The voice on the phone said, "Kiernan, this case is not small. We're talking the Roman Catholic Church here."

"I don't take cases that don't interest me."

"Don't worry. This one will interest you. If word of it got out it would intrigue half of Arizona. The archbishop is dying. His heir apparent, Bishop Dowd, is an ambitious man. He doesn't want a scandal in the archdiocese. He'll make it his business to come up with the scratch even for *your* fee."

Kiernan pressed a fingertip on her stomach and watched the white spot redden. Time to get out of the sun. That was the problem with the decadent life: you had to be so disciplined about it. With a shrug she leaned back in the chair. Discipline could wait.

"Okay, Sam, why does the Roman Catholic Church of Phoenix, Arizona, need a medical detective?"

"A priest died."

"They should call an undertaker."

"Under suspicious circumstances."

"Okay then, the cops."

"It looks like suicide."

"Whoops. Not a cause of death they'd like made public, eh?"

"Exactly. And that's not the half of it."

Ignoring the fact that she was on the phone, she motioned for him to continue. She had known Sam Chase for years. It was he who had referred her to a local detective, for whom she had worked long enough to fulfill the state licensing requirement. Since then she'd been her own boss, and Chase had referred cases. During those years she had employed that *ciao* wave often, in person and on the phone, and knew he would fill in the silence.

"The priest, Kiernan, was strung up from the altar."

"And they want me to find out why? For that they need a forensic psychiatrist, not a detective."

"Their concern is whether they can bury the priest in hallowed ground."

Kiernan leaned back precariously in the wrought-iron deck chair. It was a game with her to see how far she could go without falling. "Sam, is there any chance the hanging could have been an accident?"

"That's a thought I had. I'm not sure they have, though. Kiernan, this one is *very* confidential. The priest's hands were bound. You get the picture?"

Kiernan nodded. "I can see their predicament. Not exactly a holy way to go. Not the type of thing that makes the parish mothers glad they forced their sons to be altar boys."

"That, Kiernan, is why they're willing to pay you twenty-five thousand dollars—for you to find out what happened. Do it fast and on the QT. They're desperate to avoid publicity. What they need is an open-and-shut case by the funeral Monday."

Behind her the front door burst open. On one leg of the chair, she spun around. The big brown-and-tan mongrel splatted eagerly across the deck and thrust his wet muzzle into her bare stomach. She jerked back and gave his head a halfhearted shove, knowing

Ezra would only press his wiry muzzle more firmly against her stomach and grunt until she scratched behind his ears. She cupped her free hand over one ear and rubbed.

Groaning with pleasure, Ezra let his feet slide out to the side and sank to the floor.

From the doorway came guffaws. A six-four, 240-pound ex-lineman nearly filled the doorway. His wiry sun-bleached hair and deep tan testified to his unfailing morning beach runs. At twenty-eight, two years after he'd been carried off the field with three ruptured discs, he was back in shape physically. He was one of the few men in San Diego who could make the huge dog appear manageable. Walking between the two of them Kiernan, as Sam Chase had said, ridiculous. That amused her. It was why she had chosen Ezra—the biggest, undeniably ugliest puppy in the litter. Brad Tchernak was another story. He might try coaching football, as he threatened almost nightly. Or broadcasting. But the sudden fall from stardom to rehab patient and the discovery that no amount of toughness or determination would ever get him back in an NFL uniform had been devastating. He needed "space" while he reassembled his life, he'd told her when he showed up in answer to her ad. And, he'd assured her, he was a great cook, he'd be a great house*man,* and a lot more diverting to have around than anyone else who might apply for the job. She'd hired him. Seeing the phone in her hand, he made chopping motions and pointed toward his half of the duplex.

"So you'll take the case?" Chase asked.

"I didn't say that. I'd hate to be the one to get the Catholic Church out of a jam. On the other hand I may discover things that are worse than the ones they're worrying about."

"That's their problem."

Kiernan kneaded Ezra's neck. "Okay. Give me the specifics on the deceased—the priest."

"Austin Vanderhooven, priest at Mission San Leo, outside of Phoenix."

"Friction with superiors or other priests?"

"You'll have to assess that yourself. Dowd sounded overwrought. But he pulled himself together enough to avoid that issue."

Kiernan leaned back again, balancing on the chair legs. The air was just beginning to have the briny smell of low tide. "So what Dowd's telling us is there was friction and he figures Vanderhooven was in the wrong."

"You're not jumping to conclusions, are you?"

"I don't jump, Sam, at least not to conclusions." Smiling, she glanced through the French doors at the statuette on the bookcase. The statuette was missing an arm. The inscription read: "State Gymnastics Competition, 2nd prize." She had kept the statuette with her, furious at the "2nd" each time she came across it, yet unable to throw the thing out. It had become her symbol. In medical school in San Francisco there had been plenty of frustrations: hospital rules, the unwritten etiquette of the medical hierarchy, and the reality of pain and death that even modern medicine couldn't cure. After each clash she had yanked out the statuette and flung it across the room. Then, abashed, she would glue its arm back on. During her residency there had been only two or three occasions when she had come home angry enough to vent her frustration on the little chrome gymnast, and in her four years as a forensic pathologist with the coroner's office she hadn't flung the statuette at all. Not until she was fired. Then she hurled it into the fireplace; the arm was beyond repair.

"Sam, if Vanderhooven had been a prize priest, Dowd would have been happy to tell you. If he had been a defender of a just cause, a cause that Dowd subscribed to, Dowd would have told you that. So, it's reasonable to assume neither is true. Maybe Vanderhooven was involved in something Dowd didn't like. Now, what about the body? How long has Vanderhooven been dead?"

"Dowd found him last night."

"Autopsy findings?"

"None. There was no autopsy."

"No autopsy? What are they doing about the authorities? And where do they have the body?"

"Dowd called the doctor, who called the mortician. The body's in his fridge." Chase exhaled slowly. "Kiernan, if you take this case, I want to know as little as possible."

"Really, Sam, on a case you said would intrigue half of Arizona?"

"I nurture professional disinterest. Philip Vanderhooven, the priest's father, is an important financier here and in Phoenix. I've done business with him. I'd like to again. I don't want to know the shade of his family linen."

"What's his relation to this case? Is it Bishop Dowd who'll be my client, or Vanderhooven too?"

"It's muddy. Dowd's paying. But Vanderhooven must have made the referral. Philip Vanderhooven is not the hands-off type. When he hires men he sets strict limits and reacts strongly if they exceed them. He's not a man used to hearing no. But then, neither is Bishop Dowd. What's your decision?"

She gazed at the statuette, recalling the events that had led her to seek escape in gymnastics, practicing back flip after back flip through a haze of fear and anger that never lightened. The events that had led her to forensics.

As if reading her mind, Chase said, "I know the Catholic Church isn't your favorite institution. But the job will only take a few days; it's *got* to be done by Monday, before the funeral. And Austin Vanderhooven wasn't your ordinary priest."

"How so?"

"You may find that in some ways you're not unlike him."

She laughed. "Now what exactly does *that* mean? Did he have fresh bluefish and tomatoes flown in from the East Coast, or a houseman polishing his Triumph?"

"The similarity runs a little deeper than that. I'll leave it to you to assess. There'll be a background packet waiting for you at the airport, if you can tear yourself away from your houseman. He is just a servant, isn't he?"

"I'll leave that for you to assess, Sam." She laughed and gave Ezra one last scratch, pushed his head off her stomach, and stood up. "You know I can't commit myself till I talk to Dowd and see the body."

Chase sighed. "You're booked on American Eagle flight five-oh-four-nine. It leaves at five forty-seven."

3

FROM THE WINDOW of the descending airplane, Phoenix looked like a prospector's pan. Rugged brown hills formed the edges. Shining snakes of blue—canals that brought water from the Colorado River—slithered past the green of lawns and parks. And in one clump, like nuggets of hope, stood the tall buildings of downtown. The Valley of the Sun, they called it.

Kiernan finished reading Sam Chase's report as the plane taxied in to the terminal. She was still pondering it as she hurried through the airport. According to Chase, Austin Vanderhooven, thirty-two, had been born in Manhattan but moved to San Diego early on. There he had attended three high schools—two private ones that had expelled him and one public school whose staff would have liked to. His college career was similar, until his last three semesters, when the Ds and Fs were replaced by As. He'd gone on to graduate school, at Columbia, in economics, finished his first year in the top ten of his class, and left—for the seminary. Why this sudden change? Why had Vanderhooven abandoned rebellion for economics and as suddenly dropped economics to become a priest?

She stepped out into the parking lot; hot dry air seared her skin. At seven thirty at night, with the sun setting, it felt as hot as noon. The rental Jeep was waiting. She checked the map and headed for the Maricopa Freeway.

Chase's report raised another question. The dead priest had had a juvenile police record. That record had been sealed, and the nature of Vanderhooven's crime or crimes with it. But that the son of a man as rich and influential as the elder Vanderhooven had a record at all—now, that was suspicious.

At eight-fifteen she turned off the Pima Freeway at the last exit before the Gila River Indian Reservation and made a left by a blue-and-yellow gas station into a housing development. A left at the next corner brought her outside the brightly lighted palm-lined courtyard of Mission San Leo.

A man hurried down the path toward her Jeep. Bishop Dowd?

In the sharp shadows of the courtyard lights, he looked more satanic than priestly. His ruddy skin had a coating of tan that only years of exposure to the sun could have brought. His reddish hair looked faded, but his thick eyebrows were still dark. As he came closer she noticed hollows in his cheeks, surprising in view of his girth.

"Miss O'Shaughnessy? I'm Bishop Dowd," he said as he opened the gate. "I suppose you want to see where I found Father Vanderhooven." Abruptly, Dowd turned and started down the path toward the white adobe church.

"I will," she said, more sharply than she had intended, "but first there are a few things we need to clear up."

He stopped. She could see his jaw tightening.

"Legalities," she added. "The contract. I understand there are variations in this case. It's always best to be clear from the beginning. Our agreement states that by Monday—"

"The funeral is Monday," he whispered. He glanced nervously around the lighted courtyard. Even though it was clearly empty, he continued to whisper. "I have to know about him before that. He died in a, well, questionable manner, you see."

To ease his obvious discomfort, she said, "I have a general picture of how he died."

Dowd nodded. "I can't bury a suicide in hallowed ground. I have to know how he died. But"—he shook his head sharply, as if to clear it—"this investigation must be strictly confidential. We can't allow this to become common knowledge, have everyone wanting to know how he died, young and healthy as he was, or we'll have a full-blown scandal here. . . . If you can't find out how he died by Monday you won't be any use to us. And at the rates you charge . . ." He glanced pointedly at her silk jacket. A man used to sizing up his adversaries, Kiernan thought, but one less than subtle about it. It didn't fit the picture of the canny, ambitious bishop Chase had painted. She looked at Dowd's hands; his fingers trembled ever so slightly.

"I've altered the contract to state that my fee is contingent on that. I'll start with examining the scene of his death, and his body. If I don't think I can clarify this situation, I won't take the case."

"You don't waste any time, do you?"

"I don't plan to," she snapped.

Her retort seemed to stun him. He cleared his throat, and when he spoke it was with the voice of the canny, ambitious bishop Sam Chase had described. "Now, Miss O'Shaughnessy, I understand you *used* to be a forensic pathologist. That's right, isn't it?"

"Right."

"And that you, eh, *left* the department—"

"I believe the phrase you're looking for is 'was fired'? And the answer is yes. I was fired." She fought to keep her voice from betraying her.

"Surely, you agree I have a right—"

"If you have second thoughts about hiring me, we can settle up now."

Again his brows lifted, but this time his eyes seemed to sink back into his head. "No, we need to get rid of the odious questions about Father Vanderhooven. That's the important thing. You've been a medical examiner. You can look at his body and see what happened."

"Well, sometimes. Mostly, the body just shows me the discrepancies. I don't work miracles."

"I'm not asking for miracles, just to have Father Vanderhooven's name clean." He veered to the left toward a one-story white stucco building. Pulling open the dark wooden door, he motioned her into a foyer. To her right was a shabby room with a rose-print broadloom carpet and old green leather office chairs with sharp edged circular depressions in the seats. Kiernan could feel her shoulders tensing. They were all alike, these rooms where Catholics waited while their priests finished mass or sipped their postprandial liqueur. After the death of her sister, Moira, she had sat in one of those sagging green chairs in Father Grogan's study. She had dug her fingernails into the green leather arm rests, jamming her teeth together as the priest told her to stop lashing out at the Church. She had been twelve years old.

Dowd motioned her down the hall and opened a door to a study, itself a mixture of two cultures—Old Priest and Old West. The chairs obviously had been a tax-deductible gift, like those in the anteroom, but the floor was covered by a Navaho rug with a geometric pattern in black, brown, and white, and on the walls were Indian sand paintings in the reds and oranges of the desert sunsets. Kiernan knew little about Indian art, but the paintings looked like originals. Apparently, Father Vanderhooven had given some thought to this room he worked in and where his parishioners came seeking comfort.

Before Dowd could take the seat of authority at the desk, Kiernan settled herself on the couch. Dowd hesitated, then moved to the other end of the couch and sat down.

She handed him the contract and watched with surprise as he ran a finger down the margin and skimmed the document. She had expected him to look at it, but she doubted he could take much in now. How devastating had the shock of finding Vanderhooven been? she wondered.

Dowd leaned more heavily back into the sofa. His foot tapped an irregular beat. When he put down the contract, she asked, "Have you notified the police yet?"

"No. Of course not. I thought you understood everything, with all the time you've spent putting every fine point in this." He waved the contract.

"I do realize your fears about publicity."

"It's not publicity I'm worried about. It's Father Vanderhooven. I have to preside over his burial. Where am I going to bury him? He can't be laid in consecrated ground if he's a suicide. You know that, Miss O'Shaughnessy. Surely you're a Catholic."

"*Was* a Catholic. But about the police—"

"*I* have to make the decision that stamps Father Vanderhooven's memory. I can't leave that decision to the police. I have to know before I call them in."

Kiernan hesitated. Dowd seemed much more in control now. There was an element of truth in his explanation, but how much? And how much was he just interested in avoiding scandal? She knew the ramifications of a Catholic suicide only too well. "I take your point. Nevertheless, you must notify the authorities immediately. It's a criminal offense to conceal a crime."

His ruddy face paled. "Crime?"

"Suicide's a crime. Attempted suicide, too."

"It could have been an accident," he insisted.

"Bishop Dowd, the only way it could have been an accident is if Father Vanderhooven strung himself up there and couldn't get down."

"Miss O'Shaughnessy!"

Kiernan sighed. She felt a wave of sympathy for the bishop, who was so clearly out of his depth. But sympathy wouldn't help now. What he needed was, alas, a cold splash of reality. If he couldn't take that, better he, and she, know it now. "Bishop Dowd, what we're discussing is a priest found hanging from his own altar, with his hands tied behind his back. It's possible to rig a rope that way but not usual. The other possibility is that someone else did it. That's what the papers will say if this comes out. The papers will have a field day with that."

Dowd gasped.

Could he *not* have considered that? "Bishop, you can be arrested for concealing a crime. We're talking a class-four felony here; that's up to four years in prison and a hundred-fifty-thousand-dollar fine. As a private citizen, you are liable. The doctor you called could lose his license, and I could lose mine. So if you're not willing to notify the police, I'll leave now."

Dowd tapped a finger on the arm of the sofa. His eyes rested on one of the green leather chairs as if for comfort. He seemed to be weighing the alternatives, and the process was taking him a long time. Too long.

She had already had second thoughts about taking this case, twenty-five thou or no. Let the Catholic hierarchy squirm. She could get other cases.

But this room of Vanderhooven's, with its statement of respect for the people who made up the shabby little parish, intrigued her. The contradictory man who had created it intrigued her. The suggestion of similarity to herself had hooked her, as Chase had known it would. And, she realized with a start, she didn't want Vanderhooven banished in disgrace, as Moira had been. A quarter of a century later, the accusation of suicide still stung. "Bishop Dowd," she said, "you don't have a choice about maintaining secrecy. Vanderhooven's burial will involve too many people. The word is bound to come out. The only question is when, and how much trouble it will cause you."

Dowd kept his eyes on the chair, offering no acknowledgment of her statement. Finally, he sighed. "All right; I'll deal with it. But in the morning. One of the men in the next parish is on day shift. I'll report it to him."

She pointed to the contract. When they had signed and taken their copies, she said, "You've talked to Vanderhooven's parents?"

"To his father. I had to call him in Maui. They were vacationing. I didn't get him till two in the afternoon. They're on their way here now."

"Did you tell him the whole truth?"

Dowd winced. "I said young Vanderhooven had been hung."

"Did you mention that his hands were tied?"

There was a hesitation before he said, "Of course not. Telling a man his son died a suicide was bad enough." Absently, he rolled his copy of the contract into a tight cylinder and squeezed it between his hands.

"And how did Mr. Vanderhooven react to what you did tell him?" Kiernan asked, glancing from Dowd's tightening fingers to his tense face.

"Disbelief. Outrage. What do you expect?"

Outrage wouldn't be a parent's first reaction to his son's suicide. And a bishop wouldn't automatically hire a detective. "And he referred you to me?"

Slowly, Dowd twisted the contract. Then with the smallest possible movement, he nodded.

Kiernan didn't know just what Dowd's fears about Vanderhooven's death were, but she could see why he was so unnerved. Her own suspicions were getting clearer. She said, "Show me where you found the body."

4

SHE FOLLOWED Bishop Dowd through the sacristy, glancing at clerical garb on hangers. The white dress the priest wore over the black one, what was that called? Alb. And the black one was the cassock. The purple robe, the flowing outer one, that was the chasuble. Surprising how those terms she hadn't thought of in twenty-five years came back. There was a time in her childhood when setting eyes on the room where priests dressed would have been a coup. How disappointingly ordinary this one looked now. Without the robes and the stole the priest wore around his neck, it could have been any other dressing room.

Dowd opened the far door, reached around it, and flicked on a light.

Kiernan glanced in at the altar. It wasn't at all like the one at St. Brendan's in Baltimore. The pale brown-and-green statues beside the main altar seemed to blend into the gold that covered the wall. Subtle, tasteful, this altar had none of the gaudy blues and magentas of St. Brendan's.

The acrid smell of incense hit her, momentarily obliterating the differences between the altars, erasing the past twenty-six years. She stared with a twelve-year-old's bewilderment, despair, and fury. She could feel her father's hand on her arm, restraining her as she started toward the coffin; she could feel his shaky fingers pressing into her flesh. She could almost see the angry tears running down his cheeks as he looked at the corpse of his beautiful red-haired daughter.

Swallowing, she turned back to Dowd. "Where was Vanderhooven's body?" Her voice sounded sharper than she'd intended.

"Over there." He seemed unable to move. There was no mistaking the sincerity of his reaction. He stared beyond the altar rail to a side altar in the nave. "He was there, hanging there."

"From the altar."

Slowly, Dowd nodded.

She moved down through the opening in the railing toward the side altar. Four painted wooden columns about five feet tall rose from the altar table, framing the statues of three saints and supporting a kind of cornice with an upright carved ornament at each end. The altar table itself was narrow, and the bases of the columns left barely enough space for a man to clamber up and loop a rope around one of those ornaments. But even from where Kiernan was standing she could see where the rope had scraped some of the flaky paint off the right-hand ornament.

Fine place for a suicide, Kiernan thought. And if Vanderhooven had strung himself up here, he certainly had danced on the edge of disaster to get his kicks. Dowd could have walked in any time, as he had Wednesday evening. No ordinary priest, indeed. She could certainly see why Bishop Dowd was so nervous.

She glanced back at Dowd. His ruddy skin had paled and his eyes stared blankly. "Bishop Dowd, how was Vanderhooven hanging when you found him?"

Moving his head slowly side to side, he said, "He was in front of the altar. Here. But not facing it. His back was to it. His feet had slid out behind him, soles up. His toes were against the altar. His body was arched way forward. His knees were almost on the floor. Like he'd been in prayer and then he lurched forward and . . ." Dowd looked beseechingly at Kiernan. "He could just have slid one foot forward, stood up and walked away."

"But he didn't. Or couldn't," she said softly. "Why not? That's the issue, right?" When he nodded, she said, "Now tell me about the rope, how did it go? What kind of knots did he use?"

"The rope? I don't know much about knots. Never was a Boy Scout. Didn't bother with that sort of thing when I was a boy. Don't sail." He shrugged awkwardly. "You can sail in Arizona. There are lakes, plenty of man-made lakes, big ones behind the dams. You'd never know they were man-made. Little ones in the nicer developments. Ornamental lakes. I used to hang around the docks when I was a kid, in Boston, you know. Looked out to the ocean. Never could get up much interest in a lake after that."

Giving Dowd time to stop rambling, Kiernan stared at the altar. Vanderhooven wouldn't have had to climb up there. The ornament was only eight or nine feet above floor level. He could have tossed the rope over it. Lassoed it. Without turning, she said to Dowd, "You were going to tell me about the rope."

"Well, it'll be specifics you're wanting, more than I could tell you, so . . . well, here."

She turned to find him holding out a proof sheet. A photographic proof sheet! She stared in amazement. What kind of man, what kind of *bishop,* would take a roll of pictures of his subordinate, hanging dead *in his own church?* Kiernan struggled to keep the evidence of shock from her voice. "You took pictures?"

"Someone might ask how he was. I knew that, you see," he said quickly, almost stumbling over his words, as if he had rehearsed his explanation and now was trying to remember it. "But I couldn't leave him hanging. From the altar. He was dead. His skin was clammy, and his arms"—Dowd shivered—"were already stiff. His face was gray. It was like all the blood had drained out of his head. Only color was in his tongue." He swallowed. "You can see that from the pictures, even as small as they are."

A cold shiver of horror went down Kiernan's back as she looked down at the proof sheet. Three images on the glossy, dark sheet. Views from the front and both sides. The slight, pale figure, was hanging, tongue distended, eyes bulging. Kiernan held the sheet closer, squinting in the dim light. Another shiver iced her back. The priest's fly was unzipped. The rope crossed there between his legs, extended up his back to encircle his neck and from there—pulled taut—to the wrists.

She had considered the possibility of autoerotic asphyxia, but that did nothing to lessen the shock now that she saw the evidence. It wasn't the act itself that shocked her; she had heard tales of autopsies done on men who had tied themselves up, tightened the noose in hopes of that ultimate sexual thrill, and failed to get loose in time. She had done an autopsy herself on one such case. It was not even that this act had taken place in the church and been photographed there. It was the sudden, clinical betrayal implicit in Dowd's presentation of the photos.

She looked back at the bishop. There was no sign of embarrassment or outrage or even awkwardness on his face. She took a breath and asked, "Did you develop these yourself?"

"I have a dark room. Photography's a hobby of mine. I—"

"How much can you enlarge these?"

"And still keep the clarity?" He took the edge of the sheet, held it closer to his face, and stared down intently. She could see his jaw relax as he contemplated the familiar, the manageable. "I had to use a flash, of course. And it's four-hundred film, faster than what you'd be using for vacation photos. I'd say eight by twelve, maybe eleven by fourteen, but that'll be getting grainy. You'll still see the ropes, all right. Any larger than that, no."

Taking the sheet back she asked, "How soon can you have them for me?"

"In the morning, I guess."

"Fine." She stared back down at the sheet. No wonder Dowd was so nervous. "With his pants unzipped like this, no wonder—"

Dowd gasped.

She looked up at his ashen face. Now he really was shocked. Not at the state of Vanderhooven's body, she suspected, but at the fact that he wouldn't be spared dealing with the consequences. Why hire a detective and then hope she won't see . . . But clients did that type of thing all the time. And Dowd came across as a man who could hope that his detective would somehow solve his problem without ever raising the question he so desperately wanted to avoid. "Bishop Dowd," she said, "we need to be honest with each other. It's not only the question of suicide you're worried about. It's the issue of sex. Autoerotic asphyxia."

Dowd's face went white. He sank back against the pew. "No! He couldn't have . . ."

She peered closer at the tiny photos. "The knot by his hands, was it a slipknot?"

Dowd shook his head. "I told you I don't know about knots."

"Just a knot with a bight—with the tail looped through, so it could be pulled out quickly and the hands released."

"There was. You're—"

"Rats!"

"What?"

"That's one sign of autoerotic asphyxia. When men do this to themselves, they're not planning to die. The idea is to cut off the oxygen to the brain, experience the orgasm, and then pull the tail of the rope and free the hands *before* they strangle themselves."

Dowd clung to the back of the pew. His face was sweaty, his skin whiter than Kiernan could have imagined possible. "You're saying young Vanderhooven did this to himself? No! I can't believe that."

"I'm saying the slipknot and rope like his are essential to the procedure. If Vanderhooven concocted this himself, he would have used them."

Suddenly Dowd smiled. "But Vanderhooven couldn't have done that. With his hands behind him? There's no way."

He was so relieved, she almost hesitated to disillusion him. "Vanderhooven could have stepped through his arms. He could have tied the knot loosely, given himself enough slack on the standing end of the rope between the neck and the hands and stepped through." She squinted at the photo, then shook her head. "Some men can do that, but it doesn't look like Vanderhooven could. Not with the angle his humerus was coming out of his acromioclavicular joint. His shoulders were too tight." She looked back at the photo. If Vanderhooven couldn't pull his hands back there, then someone else did, and left him here, in the church, to become an object of scorn. "Let me see the body."

5

"THE BODY'S IN THE FRIDGE, Bishop. You know where that is. I don't want nothing to do with this. I ain't seen him; I don't aim to. Door three. He's all yours." Leaving Dowd and Kiernan standing in front of an elevator, the sundried little man scurried away over the mortuary's thick carpet.

Kiernan caught Dowd's eye. "That's what I mean about too many people."

"Russ? Don't worry about him. He can be trusted. He wouldn't have his job if he couldn't be. The diocese sends a lot of business here."

Kiernan looked over at Dowd. "Everyone's got his limits. Give Russ a few free drinks, *then* see how discreet he is." She looked at the mortuary elevator. "We're going down, I presume."

Dowd pushed the button and the doors opened. They stepped in and descended in silence. The doors parted to reveal a hallway. Empty coffins on raised tiers stood to the left, their lids opened invitingly. The dead air was laced with an old-rose perfume that screamed "air freshener."

Kiernan followed Dowd down the hallway to an unmarked door. Inside there was no rosy perfume, only the familiar smell of ammonia, antiseptic, and decay. And the cold. There had been ample comments on that in medical school: the icy fingers of death, the frozen-meat section.

She walked forward, rubber heels reverberating on the tile floor. Unlike a county morgue, where there would be rows of metal tables with scales and troughs and microphones, here there were no tables at all. The refrigerator, which filled half the floor space, did not look like a giant filing cabinet where the dead, stacked one upon another in drawers, waited to be slid out and hoisted onto autopsy tables by hydraulic lifts. Rather, the doors in this refrigerator could have opened to a meat locker.

Kiernan reached for door number three. Automatically, she began breathing through her mouth. It was a defense everyone connected with autopsies discovered sooner or later. She opened the door, exhaling against the stench, and pulled the metal table out. The naked body was lying on its side, the arms still extended backward. She had to steady the shoulder to keep the body from rolling face down.

She looked around for Dowd. He stood unsteadily at the hallway door, hand still on the knob, his face gray. "Is this Vanderhooven?"

Dowd swallowed, opened his mouth, then paused as if waiting for the words to come out of their own accord. Mouth still open, he nodded.

"It's okay," she said. "I'll take it from here. You can wait upstairs, or out in the car, if you prefer. I have to go over the body now. It'll take me an hour or two."

Dowd didn't respond. He looked more in control than he had in the church, but still shaky.

She rested a hand on his arm. "Why don't you go out and get yourself a cup of coffee, Bishop. I'm sure you could use it after a day like today." What he needed was a stiff drink, but she wasn't about to suggest that.

"No," he choked out. He was breathing through his mouth, too.

"It doesn't get any more pleasant. And the smell never lets up."

"I can't leave him. I must stay here with you."

"There's nothing you can do here. You'll only be in the way."

Dowd swallowed again. "I'm staying." Eyeing the priest's naked body, he muttered, "I am Father Vanderhooven's superior."

She sighed. "Very well. But the time is limited. It's nearly midnight. I've had a long day and I need to devote all my concentration to him. Find yourself a chair." She took off her jacket and slipped a set of green hospital scrubs over her slacks and shirt. Turning around, she clasped both hands on the side of the metal table and shut her eyes, using the dark to clear her mind. Then she stared down at the body, as she had so often in her years as a forensic pathologist. For a moment the silence in the room was unsettling, she missed the long-familiar sounds of autopsy rooms: the clatter of trays and equipment, the sloshings of fluids, the intermittent whir of the saw.

Allowing herself a luxury she would never have permitted had she been performing an autopsy, she looked down at the face.

What had gone on in the mind behind it? Were these blue eyes and lank blond hair the features of a lonely, frustrated man who had been driven to suicide? Or was it the opposite case? Had he become so sexually jaded in his preclerical or clerical years that the fantasies of bondage and the thrill of anoxia-enhanced orgasm were all that turned him on? Desecrating the church—had that innovation created an exquisitely intense climax? One worth the risk of death? The face Kiernan studied was too distorted to give any clue.

Focusing her attention on what the body could reveal, she began, as she had so often: "Well-nourished Caucasian male, about thirty years old," she murmured under her breath. "Slight cyanosis evident in the face. Tongue distended." And the eyes were open and bulging, the pinpoint red petechial hemorrhages evident in the whites, and throughout the face.

She took hold of the arm and flexed the elbow. "Movement," she said to herself. "Movement at the elbow."

"Rigor mortis is gone?" Dowd asked.

She eased the corpse onto its back.

"How long has he been dead?"

Shaking her head, she withdrew her concentration from the body. "No way to say. Too many factors affect the onset of rigor, the speed with which it moves. Under normal circumstances a person is dead as long as six hours before onset, but if the temperature outside is hot . . ." She shrugged, reached for the leg, and flexed the knee. "Rigor has passed."

"So that means how long?"

"Probably not less than twenty-four hours."

"*I* could have told you that!"

"And you have," she snapped. She took a moment, softened her voice and said, "Bishop, you're going to have to let me work."

With a grunt Dowd crossed his arms over his chest, but he didn't move away or relax his vigil. Red blotches had appeared on his gray skin and despite the cold there was a line of sweat at his brow. He didn't look a whole lot better than the corpse, Kiernan thought.

Returning her attention to the dead priest, she bent closer to the stomach. On the lower right quadrant she could make out a greenish discoloration, the first sign of bacterial decomposition as the microorganisms from the intestinal tract worked their way outward. Putting a hand on the belly, she could feel the swelling from the internal gases. Those signs merely suggested that Vanderhooven had been dead at least twenty-four hours, more likely forty-eight or a bit longer.

Holding his breath, Dowd bent closer. Suddenly he took a step toward the neck. "What's this? The mark from the rope here, it stops at the back of his neck!"

"The ligature was pulled away from the skin there. The pressure was on the bottom of the ligature, not the top. You only need to have the throat constricted to die."

"Oh." It sounded like hope escaping from a balloon. He stepped back.

"There's no indication there was padding under the rope. That's a good sign. If he was in the habit of doing this—"

Dowd gasped.

"Bishop Dowd," Kiernan said in exasperation, "men rarely do this type of thing just once, not unless they make a fatal mistake the first time. Usually they move cautiously. It's carelessness that comes from the false security of months or years of adventures that leads them to forget to make the bight in the rope, or to leave the noose taut a second or two too long. My point about Vanderhooven is that if he were a regular practitioner of this type of thing, he would have put some padding between the rope and his neck. It would have been embarrassing for him if someone had seen rope burns every couple of weeks. I assume he didn't wear a clerical collar all the time."

She could hear Dowd's quick intake of breath. Before he could ask another question, she said, "I need silence to work."

He nodded.

She leaned over Vanderhooven's arm.

"Now what are you doing?"

"Checking for defensive wounds," she said, giving up her attempt to quiet the bishop. "I'm looking at his hands for scratches or wounds, like he would have gotten fighting an attacker. I don't see any. In my bag there's a magnifying glass. Get it for me, will you?" She squatted and, taking the glass from him, looked at Vanderhooven's fingertips. "If there are any particles under his nails, they're too small for me to see, but that doesn't mean they're not there. The police will check."

She stood. "Lividity—blood settled—in the hands, the feet, and in the penis."

Dowd stared at the flaccid penis. His face flushed; he averted his eyes. "But he, um, he had an . . . in the church. I saw it. It—"

"Erections relax after death. What looked to you like an erection was the result of the blood settling to the low parts of the body. Because his back was arched blood had pooled in his penis, and the penis was *hanging* at an angle away from the body. It wasn't erect."

Dowd swallowed. "Then does that mean—"

"It doesn't mean anything. The blood would have settled there whether he'd had an erection or not."

"Oh."

"But there's no sign of lividity on the shoulder blades or the buttocks."

"So he wasn't killed lying down?" Dowd asked, clearly relieved at the change of subject.

"Right, and what the lividity tells us is that either he died arching forward like he was in your photos, or someone hoisted him up almost immediately after death." She bent over the right hand.

"Now what are you doing?"

Kiernan sighed loudly. She found herself feeling more compassion for the bishop than she would have imagined possible. He had had an awful shock. Still, she couldn't allow her sympathy to interfere with her concentration. She yearned for a regular autopsy room where visitors were kept out. She tried one last explanation. "Bishop, if he was murdered, the question is: How did his killer get him into that position? Even at gunpoint no one would calmly allow himself to be tied up like that—the outcome would be too obvious. But there are no signs of struggle, no defensive wounds, no fresh ecchymoses—bruises—unless they're covered by the hair. That's what I'm checking now. Then I'm going to check the body with a magnifying glass for needle marks. He could have been drugged. A needle would leave a microscopic depression." She turned back to the scalp. No discoloration. Starting with the arms, she began the search for a puncture mark, knowing that she couldn't stop even if she found one. After the first, she'd need to know how many. Only if there were none would she check the scalp again. It was a good place to camouflage the mark, but a difficult one to use. In an autopsy she would have deflected the scalp back to expose the skull and checked there, where the signs of trauma would have been clearer. But the pathologist would have to do that, after Dowd reported the death to the police.

As she scrutinized the front of the body inch by inch, she could hear Dowd pacing on the far side.

By the time she had checked the underside of the tongue, her back ached. There was no way to sit, nothing to do but bend over. She started the examination of the back. The chill of the room lay on her skin like a wet towel. At one-thirty A.M. she said, "That's it. No needle marks."

"You mean after all this, there's no way to say how he died?" Strands of his pale chestnut hair hung over his forehead. His black shirt was limp against his stomach, which, itself, seemed to sag, as if his internal stuffing had given way.

"Nothing I'd go into court with."

"But—"

"But that's not what you're paying me for. I can only do an external exam. He could have been drugged orally. The medical examiner can do a thorough toxicological screening, not just for the twenty to twenty-five common drugs. The problem with drugs is that with all the synthetics pharmaceutical houses are turning out, even an expert toxicologist needs to have some clue as to what to look for. Make sure you and Vanderhooven's father demand as thorough a screening as they do here."

"What are we paying you for, if they're going to do the real work?"

"Have you been somewhere else for the past hour and a half?" Dowd blanched.

Bedside manner, Kiernan reminded herself. But bedside manner had never been the emphasis for forensic pathologists. And the bishop had just about run through her meagre supply. "One of the things you're paying me for is narrowing down the possibilities so the pathologist can order the right tests."

Dowd sighed.

But Kiernan didn't share his relief. "We're not in the same county as Phoenix here, are we?"

"No. The line's a few miles north."

"Few big crimes, not much need for autopsies?"

"Coroner's got a graduate he calls when he needs him."

She nodded slowly. "Vanderhooven's father can hire the best forensic pathologist in the country. But that'll take time, more time than you've got. In the meantime, the coroner here will go with his own man. Inexperienced pathologists make mistakes. And chances are, with the rope marks and the hands tied, he'll latch on to the idea of autoerotic asphyxia and he won't be looking any further. Unless I can find something conclusive, chances are Vanderhooven's really going to be hung."

6

WHEN BISHOP DOWD brought her back to begin her search of Vanderhooven's house, Kiernan expected him to follow her inside and dog her footsteps, demanding explanations for every drawer she opened, every paper she picked up. Instead, he announced he was leaving for the airport to pick up the dead man's parents. It was two-thirty A.M.

The shutters had been drawn all day against the sun, but the desert heat had worked its way in. The hot stagnant air seemed thicker than it had when she'd been here with Dowd earlier this evening, *yesterday* evening. Surely, Father Vanderhooven would have had the air-conditioning on, but someone—Dowd?—had turned it off.

Kiernan located the thermostat, turned it on, and began her survey of the house—six rooms: waiting room, study, living room, dining room, kitchen, and bedroom. The living room, dining room, and kitchen could have been rooms in an Azure Acres display model. The study and waiting room she had seen earlier.

She paused at the bedroom door. Looking in she felt the same unpleasant rush she used to have when she had completed an external examination of a body and was poised to make the incisions that would uncover the pathology within. Every time she had felt a momentary nausea, an awareness of the ultimate invasion she was about to launch, to bring to light secrets its owner would never, very possibly *could* never, have admitted. Then, speaking into the microphone, she would begin: "Incising from left acromioclavicular joint to inferior sternum, from . . ." She would block out the humanity of the body on the table and force herself to see it as a cluster of organs to be clipped and severed, lifted off and sliced and tossed into specimen jars.

She felt that same momentary nausea as she looked into Vanderhooven's bedroom. Unlike the other rooms, Vanderhooven's bedroom had forest-green walls and mahogany furniture. A well-worn oval hooked rug waited for bare feet to be lowered over the side of the bed. A della Robbia hung above the headboard. It could have been a bedroom in any cramped house on Baltimore's Rohan Street in the fifties, like the one she grew up in, except for the picture that hung over the table that Vanderhooven apparently used as a desk: a photograph of a herd of wildebeest racing across the barren desert. Fleeing. For her, that photo could have summed up her whole life in Baltimore.

If anything in the house could illumine Vanderhooven's personality, it would be here, in this anachronistic room.

A hodgepodge of volumes filled a scarred bookcase, leatherbound volumes on the top shelf, paperbacks with broken bindings on the bottom. A good third of the titles were in Latin. She had blocked out her childhood Latin and could not draw it back. Medical terminology was no help. The best she could do was to categorize the volumes as religious, and that any fool could have done with no Latin background at all.

When the sheriff arrived later this morning he would seal off the house and she wouldn't be able to get back in, even with permission of the archdiocese. This was her last chance. She turned to a fresh page in her pad and began to list the contents of the room: "Mahogany table, 2½' × 5'—scratched. On it—stack of books." She noted the titles. Two biographies of monks, one book on Arizona history, one on state tax law. She paged through them, but no passages were underlined, no corners were dog-eared. On the blotter under the last volume were two stains, a small round outline and an octagonal one about three inches wide. She fingered the dark marks—a shot glass and a bottle? An unusually shaped bottle. She traced both marks, rolled the paper and banded it, and stood it next to her purse. Vanderhooven's calendar she stuck in her purse. That she'd xerox and return.

"Dresser top—comb, brush, wallet, handkerchief, change, key ring with six keys." She pocketed the keys—just in case.

She put a thin glove on her left hand and pulled open the bathroom medicine cabinet—"razor, shaving cream, Vaseline, aspirin, deodorant, talcum powder, toothpaste—no prescription medication." Nothing out of the ordinary.

The bedroom closet was huge, nearly half as large as the bedroom. She stepped inside and pulled the light cord. Priest's clothes. Jogger's clothes. Hiking boots. Jeans, slacks, shirts. But no ropes, chains, handcuffs, blindfolds, whips, no falsies, padded bras, garter belts, or panties, no pornography hidden in the back, no portable mirrors: none of the normal accoutrements of autoerotic asphyxia. And there had been no book on knots, a necessity for untutored devotees. She hefted a large leather suitcase—empty.

The front door slammed.

She glanced at her watch—3:30 A.M.—then lifted two smaller suitcases. They too felt empty.

"No, I will not *wait in there,* thank you very much!" a woman's voice insisted. The priest's mother?

"You'll only upset yourself, Grace." His father.

"Upset myself! My son is dead; how do you think I'm going to *upset* myself?" There was a note of hysteria in the woman's voice.

Damn, Kiernan thought. Why couldn't Dowd have had the sense to keep them out of here until morning? She stepped out of the closet just as the bedroom door banged open. The scent of jasmine perfume struck her.

The woman, tanned, with monochromatic ash-blond hair, stared, not at Kiernan but into the room. For a moment she made no movement with either her eyes or her head. Then she turned stiffly and methodically moved her gaze around the room, favoring no item with a pause.

Behind her, hand on her shoulder, stood Philip Vanderhooven. The resemblance to his son was striking—medium height, round face, blue eyes, thin faded hair, closer to the white it would become than to the blond it had once been. But there was no softness beneath the pale hair. Horizontal creases cut deep into the forehead and vertical ones between the eyebrows; the troughs beside the mouth were the lines of control. His palm lay on his wife's shoulder, barely curled fingers held stiffly away from the linen of her blue-and-white dress.

Strangely, it was Dowd, in his black suit behind the vacation-garbed couple, who looked out of place. All three appeared on edge, Grace Vanderhooven tottering, Philip holding himself in, and Bishop Dowd clearly exhausted and nervously eyeing the other two.

Kiernan took a step toward the couple. "I'm Kiernan O'Shaughnessy. I'm very sorry for your loss."

Vanderhooven nodded. "The bishop has told us about you. You've seen the body. So what's your report?"

Either Vanderhooven had no qualms about discussing the priest's death in front of his distraught wife, or he was more upset than he appeared. Or, more likely, he was simply accustomed to being in charge. "Not a hands-off type," Sam Chase had said of him. "Not a man used to hearing no." Kiernan hesitated, then said softly, "There's nothing I would take to court without an autopsy. The sheriff will probably need a couple of days to arrange that. What I *think*, from observation, is that your son was set up."

Vanderhooven's entire body seemed to sag, as if he had been holding himself taut for this moment. But his wife gave no indication of having heard; she continued her appraisal of the room. Vanderhooven asked, "Do you have any leads?"

"Not yet. I'm trying to get an impression of what your son was like. I'll have to ask questions that may be painful."

"I understand that."

"I'd like to continue to look through the room while we talk. Time is important."

"Fine. Grace, why don't—"

"No! I told you I am not going to wait out there. Austin is my son." Jerking free from his hand, she started slowly toward the dresser. "What an odd room this is."

"Not like his childhood room?" Kiernan asked as she pulled open the door of the bedside table with her gloved hand. A phone book lay inside.

"This? This is an old man's room. Austin never had a dungeon like this! Not in New York. And when we moved to San Diego he had a bright yellow room, with his posters and his surfboard. His brother and sister fought to get that room when he left."

"It was black then, not yellow, Grace." Vanderhooven turned around the chair by the mahogany table and lowered himself into it in one controlled movement.

Momentarily, Grace Vanderhooven smiled. "Austin painted it while we were on vacation. I thought I would faint when I saw it. It looked like a cave. It was terrible, but it was his room. His rebellion."

Fighting her reluctance to yank them back from the solace of the past, Kiernan said, "Tell me about his rebellion. I already know he had a juvenile record."

"That!" Vanderhooven said. "That has nothing to do with this."

"We can't be sure."

"It was kid stuff, fifteen years ago."

Kiernan shut the drawer and turned to Vanderhooven. "One of the ways I proceed is to get a clear picture of the victim. Then if I discover something out of character I can spot it. Otherwise when witnesses lie—and they will—I'll have no way of judging." Purposely, she hadn't caught his gaze, hadn't made her statement a challenge.

Vanderhooven nodded slowly. "It was nothing serious, a foolish adolescent mistake. Austin—"

Hand on the dresser, Grace Vanderhooven spun to face her husband. "Nothing serious, Philip! You didn't think it was *nothing serious* at the time. The boy was arrested for theft!"

"We've been through this, Grace. It was a misjudgment. He was trying to help those people."

"Help them to property that wasn't theirs!" Grace's voice trembled and rose. Bishop Dowd shifted his weight onto the foot nearest the door.

Catching Vanderhooven's eye, Kiernan let a moment pass before saying, "Tell me what happened."

"The kid thought he was helping a poor family extricate their possessions. The landlord locked them out for lack of rent. Kid should have assessed the situation before he got involved, instead of letting his emotions bulldoze his sense. Learned the hard way. Didn't know he was helping these people take the landlord's possessions as well as their own. He worked the rest of the summer to pay off that fine."

Kiernan glanced at Grace, but she showed no reaction to her husband's words. Neither did she elaborate.

"What else?" Kiernan prodded.

"Else?" Vanderhooven demanded.

"Mr. Vanderhooven, your son wouldn't have had a record for one offense. Any competent lawyer would have gotten him off if that had been his first offense. But it wasn't, was it?"

Vanderhooven shook his head. "Bearer's bonds. Kid got hold of some bearer's bonds. My security at the firm was lax. My fault.

Should have been on top of it. Not that that excuses the kid. But he was only sixteen then. Most kids that age don't know a bearer's bond from a tamale wrapper. But the kid saw the glitch in the security system, knew bearer's bonds were largely untraceable in those days. Headed off for a big weekend in Mexico; *with* his girlfriend." Vanderhooven's face relaxed; the corners of his mouth eased upward. His unspoken admiration was unmistakable. "Didn't think a sixteen-year-old with bearer's bonds might arouse suspicion. He almost got away with it. Had the bank officers down in Mexico nearly convinced. Said he was a special courier; said his youth was protective camouflage. The plan was dumb, but the kid could think on his feet."

"Theft," Grace Vanderhooven muttered.

"So when he was caught with the landlord's possessions later, that was a second offense," Kiernan said. "What happened then?"

"He got thirty hours of community work, hard labor with a shovel," Philip said. "I could have pulled strings, but I didn't. He needed to feel the sting of the law."

Kiernan moved to the dresser. The jasmine scent of Grace Vanderhooven's perfume filled the air, as if marking off territory. Kiernan stooped and opened the lowest drawer. Sweaters, what seemed like a lifetime supply for a Phoenician. "Did he do drugs?"

"Never. Wasn't that kind of kid," Vanderhooven said.

"Alcohol?"

"No."

"Are you sure?" she asked, eyeing the stained desk blotter.

Grace whirled to face her. "Of *course* we're sure. The only time Austin ever drank was on that . . . that *lark* to Mexico. He learned his lesson then."

If Austin Vanderhooven had had a drinking problem, keeping it hidden from parents who lived in another state would not have been difficult. Kiernan turned and glanced questioningly at Bishop Dowd, who stood by the doorway behind Vanderhooven. But Dowd seemed to have tuned out the whole scene.

Kiernan turned back to Philip Vanderhooven. "Were you surprised when your son decided on the seminary?"

For a few moments—long enough for her to turn back to the drawer, finger each sweater, and satisfy herself there was nothing hidden beneath or in them—there was silence. Then Grace said,

"You were, weren't you, Philip? You didn't think Austin cared about the Church. You thought he'd be like you." Her voice was sharp and the undertone of triumph clear.

But Grace's accusation must have been a slice of a well-worn battle between the couple; her words seem to fly past him unnoticed. Answering Kiernan, he said, "Kid could have been a first-rate economist. Had the makings, the temperament. But he had a mind of his own. The boy had his wild moments, boys do, but he pulled himself together. And I'll tell you, Miss O'Shaughnessy, he approached the priesthood as he would a business. He told me he could make a difference there, with his background. He knew their resources were invested poorly. He wanted to be with an institution that stood for something; he knew he could contribute."

So Philip Vanderhooven still saw his son as what he had wanted him to become, an economist, but one working within the Catholic Church. Kiernan opened the middle drawer—underwear, plain white jockey shorts, plain tank shirts, plain white socks, and to one side, six pairs of black nylon socks. She looked over at Grace beside her as she too eyed the drawer. "Were you surprised?"

"Yes."

"What had you thought he would do?" she asked, feeling carefully through the piles, then pushing the drawer shut.

"Finish school, live in New York, marry, I suppose."

"You seem hesitant about his marrying."

Grace pulled open the top drawer and stared down.

"Try not to disturb anything, Mrs. Vanderhooven," Kiernan said softly. "About Austin's marrying, did you think that was unlikely?"

"Marry?" Grace laughed, bitterly. "Why should he have bothered?" Grace ran a hand through her stiff hair, leaving thick ash-blond clumps thrusting out from her head. "That girlfriend of his, that Beth Landau, she lived with him while he went to school, right in San Diego. Oh, I know it's done all the time now, but this was fifteen years ago. This was in the town we *lived* in, where his younger brother and sister lived. If it hadn't been for her there would have been no bearer's bond business. And she was the one who made him move that stolen property." Turning her back to the room, Grace began rooting frantically through the drawer.

Abandoning the effort to restrain her, Kiernan watched Grace snatch up and toss aside an eyeglass case and a rosary, a scapular, a fountain pen, some white handkerchiefs. Her hands shook; the discarded handkerchiefs fluttered into a heap. The smell of perspiration cut through the cloud of jasmine.

"I thought—" Grace stopped, mouth half-open. "I was sure he'd marry that whore." She yanked the drawer forward. It hovered but didn't fall. She grabbed a ball of lacy red nylon, shook it till it hung free—red lace bikini pants.

7

"WHAT COULD HAVE POSSESSED YOU to falsify Austin Vanderhooven's death certificate? *You, a doctor,* Elias?" Sylvia Necri
shouted. She stood, hands braced on thick hips, back to the picture
window and the skyscraper across Central Avenue. Her coarse
dark hair was brushed back in the same no-nonsense style she had
worn it in when she had reached the construction site in the Superstition Mountains at six the previous morning. The furrows in her
forehead and the grooves beside her mouth were the scars from
many an architect-vs.-contractor battle.

She had missed dinner because she'd had to haggle with the
cement contractor. The next hour and a half she had spent on the
phone tracking down the general contractor, finally unearthing
him in a roadhouse ten miles north of the site. She'd reasoned,
cajoled, and threatened till one in the morning before she got him
back to following the plan. It was nearly two when she had headed
home to Phoenix, squinting into the blanketing blackness of the
mountain road, shoulders hunched from anger. The shot of Chivas
at the roadhouse hadn't put a dent in it. She had opened the door
of her condominium at 4:13 Friday morning, looked into her living
room and found her nephew, looking exhausted and frightened.

"What are you doing here?" she'd demanded. "You told me
you'd be in Acapulco, windsurfing. You'd planned it for months."

"I changed my mind."

"Changed—"

"Forget that, Aunt Sylvia. That's not the problem." Then he had
told her about Vanderhooven's body, Dowd's detective, and the
death certificate he had signed twenty-four hours earlier.

It was now 4:54 A.M.

"How *could* you be so *stupid*?" she yelled at him, for once un-
moved by his handsome face.

"What else could I do? Austin was my friend, I couldn't tell the
world that he'd been found, er"—Elias dropped his gaze—"unzipped, in the church. People would never forget that."

He wasn't lying about his concern for his friend Austin. He was loyal, her nephew, sometimes too loyal, and he had come to like the priest. But that was beside the point. "This could mean your medical career, Elias, the career I've sacrificed my life to pay for. With the money I spent on your education, I could have bought— no, not bought, *designed* and *built*—a house by Encanto Park, instead of living here in an apartment someone else slapped together."

With a small grin playing under his dark mustache, Dr. Elias Necri looked around the condominium living room, his gaze resting on the handcrafted coffee table, the twelve-by-eighteen Navaho rug she had commissioned, the framed photo of her group of young architects with Frank Lloyd Wright at Taliesen West. He stared at the window that overlooked Central Avenue, center of Phoenix's banking and government. "You're not living in poverty, Aunt Sylvia."

"Stop it!" she snapped. "Don't you tell me that because we were raised poor we should be satisfied with crumbs now. You of all people!" She stared at her nephew, fighting even now the allure of his deep, dark eyes, that earnest, hurt, little-boy look. "What else, Elias? You don't endanger your entire career to protect someone's memory."

"Aunt Sylvia, Austin was my friend. We jogged together three days a week."

"Don't fool yourself. You were his friend because I asked you to be his friend. How many weeks did you go panting around the streets at dawn so you could run fast enough to keep up with him, so you could *happen* to run into him and suggest you jog together? You've always been a liar, Elias—"

"Aunt Sylvia!"

"Don't look so shocked. Even as a toddler you lied." Her voice softened. "It was cute then; you were so transparent. Your mother threatened to beat it out of you; it was I who protected you. You fooled her; you fooled them all, but not me." She tried to read his face, so handsome despite the reddened eyes, the nascent lines of tension, but she couldn't quite get her bearings. She had always been able to read him; the sharpness of his mind had been no hindrance to her. It was only recently that she had been less aware of his dissembling, and more recently that the startling thought occurred that perhaps Elias had learned to deceive her, too. There had been other things like this supposed trip to Acapulco. Pushing that from her mind, she reiterated, "No one knows you like I do. What is it that could make you falsify a death certificate? What did you say on it?"

"Heart failure," he muttered.

"Heart failure," she shouted. "Heart failure! Austin has rope marks on his neck and you say he died of heart failure! An altar boy wouldn't believe that!"

"Aunt Sylvia, what could I say? If I'd said asphyxia, the sheriff would have demanded an autopsy. The sheriff checks all the death certificates." He took a final swallow of his drink. Bourbon, bourbon she kept for his visits. Then raising an eyebrow in question— the boy never forgot his manners; it was part of his charm—he walked to the liquor cabinet.

"You could have said no, Elias."

"No, I couldn't."

"Why not?"

"Bishop Dowd insisted. He was beside himself with panic, terrified that word would get out. When I told him I'd have to do a death certificate he turned the color of . . . this." Elias scanned the liquor cabinet and scooped up a milk-glass bottle. "He said, 'Don't let on about this'—the way Austin died. I asked what he expected me to do. He just repeated, 'Don't let on about this.' "

"So he didn't specifically tell you to falsify the death certificate."

"Well, no." Elias turned and replaced the bottle. "He was in too much of a frenzy to think that clearly. I don't know how he's going to get through this."

"Bishop Dowd can look out for himself. *Believe* me, Elias, I've known the man for years. He's not the one who stands to lose his career."

"He won't be thrown into the poorhouse, if that's what you mean." Elias hesitated, then sat on the pale leather sofa, patting the cushion beside him in invitation.

She didn't move.

He sighed. "Aunt Sylvia, if I had said Austin was asphyxiated, the coroner would be looking at his body right now. There'd be a scandal. Dowd would never get to be archbishop. He wouldn't even remain in charge of Mission San Leo. A scandal would dredge up everything. It would ruin his chances. And ours."

Under his trimmed mustache, his lip quivered infinitesimally. "And?" she prodded.

His shoulders slumped; his head dropped, and a lock of thick, wavy hair flopped over his forehead.

Again she resisted the urge to go to him. "Elias, I don't have all night."

Looking up, he said, "Okay, okay. If I hadn't signed that certificate, Dowd would have fired me. My job with the archdiocese is three-fourths of my income. I can't afford to lose that business, or Dowd's friendship. You, of all people, should know that. I have my mortgage, the payments on the boat, the car, the country club, the golf club, and the Rotary, and all those organizations I have to belong to. You know, Aunt Sylvia, you can only be up-and-coming so long. If I don't make it now, in five years it'll be too late. I can't hang around till *I'm* fifty-two waiting for my ship to come in."

Sylvia fought to keep the signs of fury off her face. Never before had the boy stung her like that. She *had* waited too long before she made her move. Fifty-two, and not one notable commission. She'd assumed competence would be rewarded, because she worked harder than the men around her, because she could be counted on. She'd been a fool. It had taken her nearly thirty years to realize it. And it had taken the boy, what? Three? Or maybe he'd always known. She said, "And?"

Elias flushed again. "I was his friend, Aunt Sylvia, his best friend." He dropped his gaze. Almost in a whisper he added, "If he died like that, what would people think of me?"

"Forget 'people,' Elias. The only person you need to worry about is right here. I asked one thing of you, and you didn't do it."

He glared at her. "What do you mean? I ran fifteen miles a week. I listened to Austin carry on about his goddamned church, about the bishop, about Beth and the blowout they had when he dropped it on her that he was going to throw her out. If it hadn't been for me, you wouldn't have known anything had changed. You would have sailed along blindly."

"But you didn't get me the one thing I need, did you, Elias? And when you were at the church, falsifying the death certificate—

instead of windsurfing in Acapulco, like you told me—did you think to have a look in Austin's rooms?"

"The bishop was right there. What was I going to say? 'Excuse me, Bishop, let me root through Austin's things before I go?' "

Sylvia Necri turned to face the picture window. To the east the sun was rising over Camelback Mountain, coming up over the house of her up-and-coming nephew. It wasn't unusual for her to be awake at dawn. Seeing the clear yellow sun rise in the cloudless sky, so absolute, so perfect in its form, its presentation, renewed her will to face the duplicity everywhere beneath it. But today, though the sun peeked coquettishly over the hump of Camelback, it did not entrance her. She spun to face her nephew. "Elias, we have too much involved to stand back and wait to see what Dowd's detective turns up. She has to be stopped. You have to get me what I need. You understand that, don't you?"

"Yes," he said with a determination she had never heard in his voice, "I understand completely."

8

KIERNAN LEANED BACK in the metal chair. At ten A.M. it was almost too hot to sit outside, even under the restaurant awning. There was an otherworldly quality to this desert city. Despite the carefully nurtured lawns and lakes in development after development and the fountains downtown, it had a space station look. In mid-morning not one person walked along the sidewalk or crossed the street. People were encapsulated in cars or, in the case of this restaurant Stu Wiggins had chosen, behind the plate-glass windows in the air-conditioned interior. "No one else'll chance the patio," Stu Wiggins had assured her as he settled into the chair by the street. "It'll be as private as a conference room." Although Wiggins had had breakfast with some other lawyers three hours ago at seven, he had managed to down two blueberry muffins and half the bacon on Kiernan's plate.

Wiggins had been a courthouse fixture for nearly forty years. "Saf" Wiggins, his cronies called him, the master of "slip and fall" cases. "Tell you what they say about me," Wiggins had announced after closing the first of the two other cases he'd done with Kiernan in Phoenix. "The produce manager in the Hi-Qual market goes on break; a gal he fired comes by the plums and plops one on the floor; a man slips on the plum, and before his knee hits the floor, Stu Wiggins is there." He'd thrown back his head and laughed. "I'm not that fast anymore. But the way I figure is people've got a responsibility to their neighbors. My job is to remind them of that. Getting paid on contingency keeps me honest. And it gives me time off to hire out on cases like yours."

She could picture him in court—a wiry sun-weathered man in a tan suit, tails of a bolo tie splaying out over a budding beer belly, spindly legs so bowed that she could almost see the overstretched external lateral ligaments on the outside of his knees. Before the judge he'd describe the chain of causation between the untended Hi-Qual produce counter and the broken kneecap. Then he'd slouch into the chair beside the crutch-laden plum victim, head thrust forward as if to ferret out the judge's reaction precious seconds before the judge announced it.

For Kiernan, Wiggins served a double purpose. Wiggins had the reputation, according to Sam Chase, of knowing all there was to know about everyone worth knowing about in Maricopa County. What facts he didn't possess he'd make it his business to get. And, although he assisted her on cases, their contract stated that it was she who worked for him, the lawyer; for an out-of-state investigator, that provided an element of legitimacy.

A truck rattled by, sending a gush of hot dusty exhaust across the patio. Aversion to heat was apparently not the only reason Phoenicians steered clear of the patio, Kiernan thought.

Before she could mention that, Wiggins helped himself to her last piece of bacon and said, "So, Kerry, what kind of pretzel positions did you get yourself into this morning?"

No one outside her family had ever called her Kerry, and even the family had stopped doing so, as if by unspoken accord, after Moira's death. But despite the fact that she had worked with Wiggins for less than three weeks altogether over the last three years, coming from him, the nickname seemed right. She smiled at him. "I did back flips, Stu, twenty of them—backbend to handstand to forward bend. *Viparita Chakrasana,* the Wheel, the yogis call it. I figured I'd need all the energy I could get today."

"So that's why you always want a ground-floor room, because you're banging around doing your gym stuff?"

"Sometimes when I'm in really good shape, I get an upstairs room and see if I can do it without disturbing the people below. But I've been known to misjudge." She laughed.

A heavily loaded pickup made its way up the street. The driver's weathered skin and the sand-worn finish of his truck marked them both as desert dwellers. A rusted bumper dangled precariously from the bed, slipping with each movement. Ten yards past the patio it banged to the street.

Kiernan sat back and chewed thoughtfully on a blue corn muffin. "Did Austin Vanderhooven string himself up and die, intentionally or accidentally? Or did someone murder him? And if so, why would he be worth killing? If someone just wanted Vanderhooven dead, why kill him in church? It took time; it was hard; it was dangerous. Why this way?"

Wiggins lifted his chin in question.

"Okay," Kiernan continued. "I asked myself what it accomplished. For one thing, silence. The church is trying their best to cover it up, and the parents certainly aren't going to mention how he died."

"Kerry, I don't know a whole lot about young Vanderhooven, but I'll tell you about Raymond Dowd. He looks like he spends his days sitting in the confession box—or don't they use those anymore?—guzzling hooch, right? But he's got a taste for money; plays golf with the Camelback set—for the most part that's old money around here. And in a business where you don't get promoted till someone dies, Dowd's done right well. He's gotten himself on a heap of boards and committees. He should be in solid. But there's something not quite right about him. Bitter. Must have expected more. He came here from Boston, and the powers in the church here have never trusted the guy. It's like they're afraid one night he'll gather up all those holy bones they keep in their altars and cart them back East."

"But why?"

"That I don't know. You let me check. The lawyer for the archdiocese is a buddy of mine."

"They're all buddies of yours, Stu."

"You know how it is with us old boys, Kerry." A grin crossed Wiggins's thin leathery face.

Brakes screeched as the driver of a beige Cadillac came within inches of the fallen bumper. The big car bounced, and through its closed window Kiernan could see a white-haired woman jolt forward against her shoulder harness. In San Diego or San Francisco, Kiernan thought, all conversation would have stopped and people would have stared. But here there was no one on the sidewalk to do either. The streets were always empty.

"First snowbirds of the season," Wiggins said, pointing to its Ohio plates as the Caddy continued down the street. "Usually the white-hairs from up north don't light here till winter."

"I guess to be a real snowbird you have to have escaped snow, huh? What about the Vanderhoovens? They've wintered in Phoenix for the last five years. Could Austin have been involved in something with them?"

"Possible. Philip's got connections, conservatives with money.

He does some of their investing. I reckon when he settled here that first winter it was easy as slipping a slick hand into an old glove. I've heard rumors he's handled a bit of mob money, all on the up and up. Word is he's too smart and too well entrenched to chance anything shady."

"While you're checking, see what you can find about the archdiocese."

"Right."

Kiernan took a swallow of coffee. It was cold, but not cold enough to mask the weak, bitter taste. Strong fresh-brewed coffee was one of the things she missed most when she traveled. "So, Stu, here's another possibility. Maybe the killer, if there was a killer, chose this method of death to shine light on Austin Vanderhooven's sex life. There was a pair of red lace bikini pants in his drawer."

Wiggins whistled. "How big were they? Can you rule out that he dressed up in them himself? I reckon guys who hang themselves for kicks don't fret about an unsightly panty line."

Kiernan's breath caught. Normally she would have laughed at a comment like that. "When his mother saw the bikinis, she assumed they belonged to a girlfriend."

"Guy's got a girlfriend, too? I thought these guys took vows of chastity."

Kiernan shrugged. "This one's open to interpretation. According to his father, the romance was nothing more than an adolescent fling—well before his son ever thought of the priesthood. He could be right, of course, but, according to the Vanderhoovens the girl lived with Austin in San Diego. She wrote to him when he was in graduate school in New York. And now"—Kiernan paused—"she's here in Phoenix."

Stu raised his eyebrows. "Okay, I'll see what I can find on her. And?" The eyebrows went a notch higher.

"Here's his calendar. Most of it's pretty straightforward: altar guild meetings, a talk at the Knights of Columbus. But there are one or two questions. This, for instance." She pointed to the words "Hohokam Lodge" inscribed in one square of the calendar. "Know anything about that? Apparently he was there last Saturday. And this Saturday, tomorrow, it looks like he was planning to go some place called Cerrito del Oro—"

"Little hill of gold."

Kiernan nodded. "But there's a line through that, and above it he's written 'McKinley.' "

"Anything else? You're looking at a battalion of employees here. I'm glad the Catholic Church is paying."

"These names: G. Hayes, Maria Vasquez, Ann Applegate, Joe Zekk."

He wrote down the names, one under another, then flipped his pad shut and laid it on the table. "Now tell me, with all you've given the boss to do, what is there left for you?"

"The doctor who signed the phony death certificate. Dowd said he was a friend of Vanderhooven's, ran with him three mornings a week. If there's anyone who should be able to tell me about Austin Vanderhooven it should be him."

"You think he will?"

"If he wants to go on practicing medicine he will."

9

BACK IN HER MOTEL ROOM, Kiernan slid a foot into her running shoe and propped it on the edge of the table to tie the lace. It was too hot outside for running shoes but she had no choice. It was too hot for jeans, too, and for her long-sleeved yellow shirt. She held the phone between ear and shoulder. She was at the point of hanging the receiver up—it had rung twelve times—when a harried female voice answered. "Dr. Necri's office. Doctor isn't in. Can I put you on hold?"

"Doesn't he have patients scheduled?"

"I'm rescheduling now. Hold, please." The button clicked and elevator music came on.

Where was Necri? Doctors did not disappear Friday mornings, not with patients scheduled. As one of her professors had said, "Half this business is based on trust. Patients will sit in your waiting room for hours, because they believe in you. But cancel an appointment without good reason and patients will suddenly realize you're merely human. Their implicit trust will be gone. Never again will they automatically believe your diagnosis, or that the medication you prescribe is bound to work. Whatever there is to the placebo effect will be gone. They'll question more, heal slower, and be potential pains in the ass."

So why was Elias Necri making his patients wait now? Had the sheriff gotten to him already?

"I'm sorry to keep you waiting," the woman said.

"When will Dr. Necri be in?"

"At one."

"This is Dr. O'Shaughnessy," Kiernan said, playing one of her trumps. "Where can I call Dr. Necri? Is he at the hospital?"

"Oh, *Doctor,* I'm sorry. He didn't leave a number."

So much for trumps. "Tell him I will be in his office at one." She hung up and dialed Bishop Dowd's rectory, hoisting the second shoe up for tying as the phone rang.

Dowd's housekeeper announced that the bishop had left at twenty to eight, as he did every Friday morning.

Kiernan dialed again.

"Archdiocese of Phoenix, Rita Gomez speaking," a scratchy voice said over a scratchy connection.

"This is Kiernan O'Shaughnessy. Bishop Dowd is expecting my call."

There was a pause before the woman said, "His Grace is out right now. Can I take a message?"

The edginess was evident in her voice. Had Dowd come in at all? Had the sheriff called on him, perhaps taken him to the scene of the hanging? "It's important that I reach him. Is he at Mission San Leo?"

"Oh, no," she said quickly. "He, eh, wouldn't be there on Friday morning. He's, uhm, with the Sheltons at the Self-Help Center downtown."

Deciding to see where this story led, Kiernan asked, "Where is the Self-Help Center?"

"Near Sixteenth and Buckeye."

"Is Bishop Dowd in charge?" That would fit Stu Wiggins's description of him as a man with a highly visible finger in half the local pies.

"Oh, no. They just call him when they have an emergency."

"A bishop? What kind of emergency?"

"Oh, well, the Sheltons. They know they can count on him. Such a good man. With all his responsibilities it's not easy for him to drop everything and run down there. Not many bishops would do that. Not time and time again."

And not thirty-six hours after his subordinate was found hanging in the church! Rita Gomez had relaxed audibly when she talked of the needy Sheltons, as if slipping comfortably into a small pocket of truth. Kiernan asked, "What has the bishop done for the Sheltons?"

"Just about everything there is. He's found them jobs, good jobs. He's gotten them food more times than I'd care to say, even though they can get dinner at the Self-Help Center like all the rest of them. Sometimes he even gets them Knights of Columbus funds, and they're not supposed to go to the same people more than twice in a six-month period. They just don't know how lucky they are to have a man like Bishop Dowd."

"Taking advantage, huh?"

She could almost hear the woman clicking her teeth together, deciding whether circumstances justified the indiscretion pushing to escape her mouth. "He could find them seats in the choir of angels, and they'd complain about the noise."

Kiernan laughed. "It sounds like they've been around for a long time. But there are plenty of deserving poor, so why did the bishop choose to help them? Were the Sheltons in his parish when he was a priest?"

"No, no. In eighteen years I've never seen them in church. They've always been Self-Help people. To tell you the truth, if it weren't for the bishop, those Sheltons would probably have moved on by now. They'd be somebody else's problem."

"Like the Bible says"—Kiernan bit back a grin; if Sam Chase could hear her, of all people, quoting scripture, he'd be laughing himself out of his chair—"the poor will always be with us. And the Sheltons will keep having crises, right?"

Rita laughed. "They'll be moaning when they're lowered into the grave."

"So," Kiernan said, "there's no pressing need for the bishop to spend today of all days with them, is there?"

But Rita Gomez was not bullied. "Bishop Dowd is with the Sheltons," she repeated.

Kiernan took a breath to calm her voice. "Rita, I'm here to clear up the questions about Father Vanderhooven's death. Bishop Dowd hired me. And even if he's too fine a man to think of these things, you and I know that a scandal will destroy the bishop's career. Rita, it's vital to him that he call me. I'm going to leave you my number. And if you think of anything that will help, please call me."

It was hardly a victory, but neither was it suitable for the defeat column. Not yet. But it still left the question *Where* was Dowd? Was he with the sheriff at Mission San Leo? Or was he avoiding her for some reason?

For form's sake she dialed the Self-Help Center. Dowd hadn't been there this morning. Then she grabbed her purse and headed into the parking lot. The scorching air hit her, searing her skin. It was too hot, too dry, to breathe. All around, the sun ricocheted off automobile chrome and mirrors.

The Jeep had to be the hottest place she had ever been—worse than the Maharatha plains of India before the monsoon. She had been there only a few days, on her way to Nepal, four . . . no, five years ago. She hadn't been dressed for the weather then either. But then the error had been due to ignorance and impulsiveness. After she got fired as a pathologist with the coroner's department she'd packed two pairs of jeans and her passport, left northern California for good, and headed west to find the truth—something to replace the truth she had expected forensic pathology to reveal. All her teenage years she had viewed forensic pathology as her mother had the Church; she'd been so sure that if she was familiar with every toxin, if she could discern the minor differentiations in skin coloration well enough, if she could spot the smallest needle mark, then death would be unable to hide its secrets from her. Maybe Moira's death would shed its veils, too.

She pulled into traffic, grateful for the blast of air, albeit hot, through the window. The Valley of the Sun was laid out like a *T*. At the west end of the crossbar was Phoenix proper; at the east, the road to the Superstition Mountains. The wealth of Scottsdale and Camelback Mountain lay at the junction, the suburb of Tempe and her motel below, and Mission San Leo way down at the bottom. And nothing, she thought in disgust, was near anything else.

Kiernan tapped her forefinger hard against the steering wheel, waiting for the light to change. Already the traffic was heavy. Treeless seven-lane thoroughfares ran between walls of stucco block or covered fiberglass whose shade of tan changed from one housing development to the next. For a short distance one of the irrigation canals ran beside the street.

When the light finally turned green, vehicles surged forward like flood waters and raced to the next traffic light, a mile away. In the turn lane to her left, drivers sat idling anxiously; when the green arrow opened their flood gate they sped forward, close as one drop of water to the next.

"Ridiculous," Kiernan muttered. But she, too, pressed hard on the gas pedal the instant the light changed and kept the pedal floored as the automatic transmission struggled to shift.

At least the freeway was empty. But there was no need to reread

Sam Chase's warning about speed. She had closed the window and put the air-conditioning on high; with the drag from that there was no chance of hitting sixty. She would turn it down, she promised herself, just as soon as the Jeep cooled.

But it was still on high when she passed the blue-and-yellow gas station. In contrast, the pale stucco houses of Azure Acres with their green-brown grass or pebble gardens appeared faded. And plopped in the midst of them, Mission San Leo looked like a relic of the forgotten past. Perhaps if there had been patrol cars with pulser lights blinking crimson on the whitewashed walls . . .

There were no patrol cars, no technician's vans. No sign of the bishop's big black Buick. No Mercedes or BMW with M.D. plates, either. No sign of life at all. Where was the sheriff?

This second chance to search Vanderhooven's room was a gift not to be ignored. Vanderhooven must have had an address book, letters, phone bills—something that would lead Kiernan to Cerrito del Oro, McKinley, Hohokam Lodge. Just like an autopsy, she thought. You go in, you observe, you record, you take all the right samples, you close. Then the lab findings come back and you wish you could take another look.

Kiernan rounded the corner and pulled the Jeep to the curb by the alley that ran behind the church and the rectory, Vanderhooven's home. The alley was deserted. Tan walls, like the ones along the main roads, concealed the dwellings on either side. The pavement was almost invisible under the red desert dirt; and tall, brittle, sun-bleached weeds and scraps of paper stood poised as if they had stopped momentarily and would be blown on. But there was no wind. The alley went on, block after block, as far as the eye could see. It had an overexposed look, like a photo forgotten on a windowsill.

Kiernan pocketed her keys, license, and emergency cash, and Vanderhooven's keys. She stuffed her purse under the seat and swung down to the ground, feeling anew the blast of midday heat. The air smelled dusty. She swallowed and began loping down the dirt-covered alley. Halfway, she slowed to a walk. Arizona in July was definitely not loping country.

Behind the rectory, she paused, glad for Vanderhooven's key and the semblance of legitimacy it and her contract with Dowd gave her. An out-of-state private detective couldn't be too careful. Draw too much attention to herself, slip into a merely off-white shade of illegality, and some local sheriff would delight in notifying the licensing authority in California. Her legal arrangement with Stu Wiggins would provide some protection, but only some.

She unlocked the gate. The backyard hadn't been abandoned, not quite. Minimum maintenance, the type you get from a cheap gardening service. Faded grass mowed short but left shaggy at the edges. Minimally watered. The cement patio by the kitchen door was bare—no planters, no chairs, no tables, no barbecue.

She circled to the side of the house and checked the street— empty. If Dowd had contacted the sheriff, he would have arrived by now. And he'd still be here. At the back door Kiernan hesitated. She should call the sheriff herself. She smiled. She should call *after* she went through Vanderhooven's desk again, more thoroughly than she could last night with his mother falling apart, his father trying to foist the woman onto Dowd, and Dowd, with an ingenuity Kiernan hadn't expected of him, squirming out of pastoral responsibility.

She unlocked the door and stepped gratefully into the cool of the kitchen. The air-conditioning was still on from last night. There was an odd smell to the place, or rather, a *lack* of smell—no lingering trace of coffee or toast, of shampoo or aftershave.

She stepped across the hall and paused at the bedroom door, as she had last night. There was no hint of the rush she had felt then, the momentary queasiness. This time she knew where she was headed. She walked in toward the table Vanderhooven used as a desk.

Someone grabbed her from behind. A hand slammed over her mouth.

Cold metal jammed into the base of her skull, jamming her head forward. She froze. Infinitesimally, the pressure at the back of her head eased. Kiernan thrust her head forward and up, pulled her mouth open, and sank her teeth into the fingers that had covered it. The hand jerked away. The cold metal was gone. She heard a grunt behind her. Before she could turn, she felt the blow on her skull. The room darkened, the walls wobbled; hands grasped her shoulders, shoved her forward through the bathroom door, and flung her toward the sharp edge of the cabinet.

10

THE BATHROOM was a blur of light and colors; the sharp corner of a cabinet came up at her fast. Instinctively Kiernan spun to the right—and landed hard on the side of her face. She lay there, stunned. In the distance a door slammed. Footsteps hit rapidly; there was a bang.

Tentatively Kiernan flexed her fingers, then made a fist. The muscles felt weak, but not useless. She moved her head warily. The top of her skull ached. She put a hand to the sore spot, wincing at the pain.

Pushing herself up, she tried the door. Locked. She banged. No response. *Of course* no response.

She tried the knob. It didn't move. She slammed her fist against the nearest panel. The impact sent a wave of pain into her skull. The door was oak, she realized, a door that suited the dark green New England bedroom. It was probably the sturdiest door in all of Azure Acres. She wished she were built more like Brad Tchernak: at least a foot taller with an extra hundred and forty pounds of muscle to slam through that door.

Irritably, she glanced around the small bathroom, typical of a fifties tract house. Door at one end, toilet at the other. The window, two feet wide, little more than one foot high, was over the shower/tub combination about five feet above floor level. It slid along a narrow aluminum track set in a slick, tiled window ledge. Even if she pushed one pane across the other the opening would be too narrow for her shoulders.

She smiled. Tchernak would be up shit creek here. But a tough little gymnast could handle the window. She grabbed the shower rod, pushed off the side of the tub, and swung her feet into the glass. It shattered. She kicked out the remaining large pieces, then ran a towel around the edges, poking it into the grooves till the shards were cleaned out.

There was nothing to hold on to on the slick window ledge. She couldn't slither over it and out head first, not without landing the same way. Going through it feet first would take a taut, slightly arched torso, arms extended overhead, and one solid swing. And luck. Even for her, at barely five foot one and ninety-nine pounds, it would be a close fit. And the chances of coming out without clipping a nipple or nose were slim.

For an instant she remembered the time she had spent in the gym, two hours a day, every afternoon of her junior-high and senior-high days. Two hours of flips on the balance beam, of floor routines that required a balletlike grace she had never quite achieved, of rib busters on the uneven bars that created pain so intense it blocked out the pain of Moira's death, the pain of neighbors' suspicions. On the uneven bars she wasn't "that Moira O'Shaughnessy's sister," she wasn't "that O'Shaughnessy girl who doesn't go to mass," she was the coach's hope for a spot on the state team. Kiernan had worked the bars more than anyone else in the gym, probably more than any other gymnast in the country back in those days, when art and grace were foremost in women's gymnastics and athletic ability like hers was a necessary unmentionable.

She stared at the tiny window now, setting it in her mind. She visualized her swing through. Then she grabbed the shower bar, pushed back off the tub and swung her legs forward and up, skimming the top of the window. Her stomach smacked the aluminum. She fought the urge to bring her hands up, to protect her face. Stretch them back! Head down! Slip right through!

Or almost. Her forehead grazed metal. Then her head was free. Her feet came down planted together, not even a small step required. "Decent dismount," she muttered, feeling ridiculously impressed with herself.

She squinted against the piercing light. Then she looked around the backyard. Greeting the sheriff as she came flinging through the window would have taken some explaining. And it would require more than her legal arrangement with Stu Wiggins to get her out of a situation like that. But the high fence around the yard protected her. That fence would be a burglar's delight.

The yard was empty but the window glass hadn't shattered silently. A neighbor could have called the sheriff. She had no time to lose. She stood listening, but there was no sound of a car, not coming or going. Not yet. Her head throbbed. The heat was making her shaky. She'd have to get some aspirin; it wouldn't help much, but it would be something.

What had there been in the house to draw her assailant back here so soon after Vanderhooven's body was found? Had her own arrival panicked him? Had he abandoned his search and run, or had he already found whatever he wanted and been on his way out when she surprised him? Going back into the house now was a risk. Still, there were no car noises. If she moved fast . . .

She headed across the dry grass to the back door and hurried in, through the kitchen back to the bedroom. The icy air made her dizzy. A wave of nausea rose in her throat; she clamped her teeth. Bracing a hand on the wall she pressed her eyes closed and waited till the throbbing in her skull eased.

At first glance the dark green room looked just as she'd last seen it. The dresser drawers hadn't been turned out, the closet hadn't been emptied, the covers were still on the mahogany bed. The photograph of the fleeing wildebeest hung over the book-laden table Vanderhooven had used as a desk. In the bookcase all but one of the books was in place. That one, the last of the five big leather volumes with the Latin titles, lay on the floor, open and empty. It was a shell, and whatever it had concealed was gone.

"Damn!" she muttered. She dragged out the other four books. They were what they seemed: volumes of double-columned Latin. It said something for the quality of Vanderhooven's hiding place that even a detective had found the books too uninviting to open. And it said something about the thief that he or she hadn't bothered searching anywhere else.

The throbbing was worse. She felt as if the wildebeest were thundering across her skull.

She picked up the hollow book. The space was large enough to hold two stacks of letters side by side. A small piece from the gummed flap of an envelope had caught in the corner.

She dropped to hands and knees and surveyed the floor.

An envelope lay beside the bookcase. It hadn't been there last night, she was sure of that. She picked it up and fitted the portion of flap to it. A phone bill. What kind of man, she wondered, hides his phone bill? Vanderhooven was not your average priest in more ways than Sam Chase imagined. For some reason he had made a call he definitely did not want anyone to know about.

But this was no place to hang around and ponder that. She gave the room one last look, then headed to the study to hunt for Vanderhooven's address book.

Five minutes later she tucked the phone bill between the *M*s and the *N*s and hurried outside. The heat made her head worse. By the time she reached the Jeep she had to clamp her hand over her mouth to keep from retching.

She leaned back against the hot seat-cover till the throbbing lessened, then drove around the block and parked up the street from the gas station, where she would see anyone headed to Mission San Leo.

She laid Vanderhooven's address book on the seat and studied his phone bill. There were eleven Phoenix calls listed, eight to one number, two toll calls to "Wht.Bn.Mtn.," one collect call from there, and two long-distance calls to an area code she recognized as covering the region between San Jose and San Simeon in California. Finding the numbers in the address book could be a major project, and a disappointing one. After memorizing the Phoenix number Vanderhooven had called most frequently, she started through the address book. She'd reached the *N*s before she found it. Elias Necri! She sighed with pleasure. The same doctor who had falsified the death certificate had received eight calls from Vanderhooven in the last month. How many had he made in return?

It was quarter to one. Necri's office was in Phoenix, a good half-hour drive. If she left the air-conditioning off, she could make it in twenty-five minutes.

11

THE TRAFFIC, the clumsy handling of the Jeep, the smothering heat—everything annoyed her. Her head throbbed. The Pima Freeway passed over a canal, then another. The flowing water looked cool but too shallow to be inviting. According to Stu Wiggins the summer monsoon was late this year. When it did come, the canals would run fast and full. Rain would fill the gutters. It would flow quickly over the cracked clay soil and turn the dry washes under the bridges into rivers. Flash floods would send walls of water down mountain streams and arroyos, and, Wiggins added, sweep away out-of-staters who weren't prepared.

All that was hard to picture as she looked out at the dry brown grass next to the doctor's parking lot. Only one space was empty— Necri's. She took it.

Finding her Jeep in his spot wouldn't do much for Necri's mood, but that was fine. She wanted him on edge.

She hurried across the hot macadam to the low white building. Dr. Necri's waiting room was nearly empty. Only one older man and a woman with a young daughter sat on the tan padded chairs. The receptionist looked at her warily when Kiernan introduced herself—as well she might, Kiernan thought. Her short dark hair was matted with sweat, her yellow shirt stuck to her back, and her jeans were streaked where her stomach had hit the window track. Hardly the garb of a visiting physician.

But when Elias Necri arrived ten minutes later, he didn't resemble a candidate for the cover of *Physicians' Monthly* either. His hospital-green scrub pants looked as if they had spent days wadded in the laundry bag and his green scrub shirt was streaked with sweat. Clumps of dark, wavy hair stuck out just a bit above his ears. His tawny skin was grayish; Kiernan suspected the dark circles under his eyes had not been there two days ago. Necri looked like a man worried about whether he had just destroyed his career.

As he crossed the waiting room, he favored each of his patients with a weary smile. Kiernan stood, extended a hand up—the man was nearly a foot taller than she—and said, "Kiernan O'Shaughnessy. You're expecting me."

His face tightened momentarily, then relaxed as he looked down at his garb. "Give me five minutes to change."

"Scrubs are fine," she said as she headed for the hallway door.

By the time he opened the office door he was smiling that weary, winsome smile again, a smile that accentuated his thin but sensuous lips and finely chiseled cheekbones. Motioning her to the patient's chair, he settled himself behind the desk. "Now how can I help you, Doctor? It is really Doctor, isn't it?"

Somehow the question sounded friendly. Necri was going to be a hard man to dislike. But she had no intention of letting him run the interview with that charm. Necri would answer her questions because she knew he'd falsified the death certificate—they both understood that. "Really a doctor," she said. "And really a detective. The first thing you can do is tell me where you were this morning."

He looked down at his streaked scrubs. This time he added a shrug to the smile. "Guess you're better dressed in California. My patients are used to seeing me rush in here from the hospital."

"But you weren't at the hospital this morning."

He hesitated momentarily, his dark eyes half closing. Then he shook his head. "No, dammit. Look, there's no point in my trying to fool you."

The smoothly inserted flattery did not escape her. Giving no acknowledgment, she waited for him to continue.

Still shaking his head very slowly, he said, "I haven't slept since I saw Austin's body. How long has that been? Christ, I don't even know anymore."

"What have you been doing all that time?"

"Worrying, what else?"

"Worrying about . . . ?"

"Austin, of course. I've been over every conversation we had, on every run. How he could have been involved in something as bizarre as stringing himself up, and never have given me the slightest hint? This is not your standard hand job. I just can't believe it. And in the church! Austin was really committed to the Church. He would never have done something like that."

"But you aren't sure, are you?"

He shook his head sadly.

"And you were willing to endanger your career by falsifying his death certificate."

His eyes snapped open. "It was a mistake. Christ! The mistake of my life."

"That's what's been keeping you up, right?"

"Both. My friend is dead, and my entire career is swirling in the toilet. Do you wonder I can't sleep?" Looking directly at her, he said, "I'm counting on you to clear this up." This time it seemed not just flattery but an implicit trust that a woman *would* do whatever she could for him. And Kiernan noted with disgust that her first reaction *was* to rush in and take care of him, she who was not known for her bedside manner. The man was a pro.

"Tuesday night? Where were you then?"

If he was surprised by her tone or the question, he gave no indication. "Tuesday night? The night before Dowd called me. Life was still normal then. Austin was still alive—" Necri's eyes widened. "Or was he? You can't think that I . . ." He sighed. "It doesn't matter. I was up in the mountains, two hours away from here. I had dinner with a friend, Bud Warren. I'm considering investing in an oil shale process he has up in the mountains. Could make mountains of money." He laughed, but the muscles around his mouth stiffened. Kiernan wondered how long the doctor would hold up. His laughter stopped abruptly. He shivered, and in that shiver seemed to pull himself back together. "Sorry. What you want to know is that Warren can vouch for my time."

"Where was the dinner?"

"At Callahan's in Globe. I didn't get home till after two A.M."

"I'll need his address and phone number."

"Of course."

Kiernan took down the information. Leaning back in the chair, she said, "Let's move on to Wednesday night. Bishop Dowd called you when?"

"Seven-thirty, maybe a little before. Dowd was almost incoherent. When I got to the church Austin's body was still hanging. Dowd was a wreck. He looked like a shoo-in for a coronary. He wasn't even in the church proper. He was hanging around"—Necri flinched at his choice of words—"standing by the front door, making sure no one came in. It didn't occur to him that he should cut the body down. He just left Austin hanging there."

"So you took him down?"

"Who else? All Dowd was good for was taking a sedative and going to bed, and he wouldn't even do that."

"How long would you guess Vanderhooven had been dead?"

He shook his head, more and more slowly. As long as he was following his own train of thought, Necri seemed able to function; it was questions, the need to react, to switch gears, that was throwing him.

She repeated the question.

"I don't know. I'm not the medical examiner. Isn't that what you're here for?"

"I'm asking your opinion."

"Well, he was good and dead by the time the bishop called me, if that's what you're asking. His eyes were bulging; the blood had settled in the extremities; they were purple. And his penis! Christ, it looked like a hard-on to last through eternity!" A shrill spurt of laughter escaped. His cheeks reddened. "Excuse me. But you don't know what I've been through. I can barely think straight."

She had assumed the air-conditioning would ease her headache. It hadn't. The hum of the machine was setting her on edge, or was it the underlying sense that Elias Necri, as exhausted as he was, was still hiding something? "Tell me about Austin Vanderhooven. What was he like?"

He stared over her shoulder. His finely etched face seemed to sag under the weight of betrayal. "I was his friend, or I thought I was. We ran together five miles a day, three days a week."

"And you called each other in between, right?"

Necri pressed his fingertips into the desk, but his melancholy expression didn't change. "We were in similar positions. You know how it is, as a doctor you can never be yourself. You're expected to keep up a standard. You're always on. Of course, it's even worse for a priest. I was one of the few people Austin could relax with. Or so I thought."

What he said suited his expression, but there was an edge to his voice that belied both. What was he still concealing? Kiernan took a stab, "Did Austin talk about sex?"

"Only in the abstract."

"What about you? Did you tell him about yourself?"

"Well, yes. I mentioned my dates occasionally."

Kiernan leaned forward. She let the ten years she had on him show in her voice. "Elias, we're both adults. How graphic were you when you talked to Austin Vanderhooven?"

Avoiding her gaze, he said, "Well, I may have described a mammary gland or gluteal protuberance. But I was careful at first. Then, after a while, with Austin there in shorts and a T-shirt like any other guy, I'd forget about him being a priest."

"How did he react? Did he encourage you? Did he press for details?"

"He just listened. If you want to know, I had the feeling that part of what attracted him to me was that he liked being a voyeur on my life, not just my sex life, but the whole shtick of being a young doctor—the car, the trips, the parties, the business deals. He was always interested, I could tell. But he never asked. It was like he was testing himself, only allowing himself to enjoy what I gave him, not demanding more. I'll tell you, once or twice it made me feel uneasy. When Austin died, I realized how little I knew him."

Necri seemed more comfortable, more in command of himself now. His description of Vanderhooven, Kiernan was willing to bet, was not what he was lying about. "It sounds to me," Kiernan said slowly, "as if he censored what he said, but he managed to find out a great deal about you."

Necri flushed. "It wasn't like he was peering through a one-way mirror into my soul," he said angrily. "I'm not that naïve."

So that was Necri's Achilles' heel, worrying that Austin had manipulated him. Manipulated the manipulator. Outmaneuvered him at his own game. And what prize had Elias been playing for? "Did Austin ever mention Beth Landau?"

"Beth? Sure." He smiled, showing his skill at recovery. "Nice woman. Runs the women's center at Self-Help. Austin told me they were friends before he entered the seminary."

"Just friends?" she asked, reacting to the tiny hint of a smirk that he couldn't, or didn't, restrain.

His smirk melted into a self-satisfied expression. "Of course, I guessed there had been more. I've done enough diagnoses to read between the lines. It didn't take a master diagnostician to find it odd that Beth followed him to Phoenix, and then asked him to be on the board of the women's center."

That, she thought, didn't sound like the actions of a long-ago girlfriend. "How did Austin react?"

Necri leaned back in his chair. "He wanted to help Beth. But being on the board of a center that supports the right to abortion, birth control, and divorce would have gotten him in hot water with the Church. Another guy might have felt caught between the two, forced to choose. But Austin found a path down the middle. He agreed to help, but just with the battered women's shelter. You know it's not easy to rent a building to be emergency housing. Those women have irate husbands who could shoot up the place if they found it. Once the landlords realize that, they're not so anxious to rent. So Austin did Beth a big favor. He let her use a building the church owned out of town for her families to hide out in. And the church could hardly complain about it, not without looking real bad."

"How could he do that? Doesn't the archdiocese control church property?"

Necri shrugged. "Probably, but this particular place, Hohokam Lodge, belonged to Mission San Leo. So Austin was in charge. And since no one was using it, why not? It's a couple of hours east of town, up in the mountains, and pretty run-down."

Kiernan could feel her pulse quickening. Hohokam Lodge! "Is there a phone up there?"

"Must be, but Beth was very secretive. I guess she'd have to be. I know she would have been pee-oh'd if she knew I knew."

"Did Austin help run the place?"

"No. That was part of the agreement—no church influence."

"What would the phone-bill listing be for a call up there?"

"I don't know. Globe, maybe. Miami? Superior? You take a road out of Superior. It's almost another hour on a back road into the White Bone Mountains."

Wht.Bn.Mtn.! Kiernan smiled, recalling Vanderhooven's phone bill. "Now, tell me, would Beth be likely to call Austin collect from up there?"

"I can't think why."

"Someone did. If not Beth, who?"

"I don't . . ." Elias Necri smiled. "Of course. Joe Zekk. If you hadn't said collect, I might not have thought of Zekk." There was a note of disgust in his voice as he pronounced the name.

"Who is Joe Zekk?"

"Some deadbeat friend of Austin's. A dropout from the seminary. He was always after Austin for something."

"Influence?"

"No, that was too subtle for him. He was after money. Austin had family connections and ways to get money when he needed it. Austin told me that." One side of his nose pulled up as he spoke, and there was anger, too, in his voice.

"I don't know for sure what Zekk was up to," he continued. "But he did push Austin to contact his father for him. And Austin told me that meant money. By the way, 'deadbeat' was Austin's term, not mine."

Kiernan waited, hoping Necri would let slip why Zekk's manipulative behavior, or Vanderhooven's acquiescence to it, had gotten his own back up. Was it rage at seeing someone playing your own game, performing your routine, and doing it better? Kiernan knew that reaction only too well from her years of gymnastics. She could still feel her anger as she watched a first-prize trophy being handed to a rival.

Did that explain Necri's anger—he and Zekk were after the same prize? She leaned forward. "Austin Vanderhooven didn't admit much to you, but he did talk about money. Don't you find that odd, Elias?"

Necri shrank back almost imperceptibly.

"Could it be because that was what you asked him about?"

For the first time he seemed unsure of his next move.

"Is·that what you needed from Austin? Money?"

Necri looked up, clearly unsure now.

"Joe Zekk had gotten money from Austin's father. Why shouldn't you, right? You need it more than some *deadbeat* in the mountains, right? You're a doctor, not a financier."

He sighed. "I should have gotten a financial manager. My aunt keeps telling me that. And as soon as I get on my feet I will, believe me. I just need a shot in the arm to pull me through this period. Austin thought he could help me out."

"How?"

"Well, he said that I could be the doctor at the retreat in the mountains—"

"Hohokam Lodge, where Beth is?"

"No, that place is pretty run-down, as I said. He was going to put up a new building. There's enough land for that. The problem is the water. In this state the first guy who used the water got the rights. The head of a village near there controls them. He lets the church use as much water as they want, has for years. But he's too stubborn to transfer the rights legally, not till he dies. Austin saw the old man's will and the transfer was in it. No problem about that. But Austin was waffling about breaking ground with just an oral agreement."

"So he might not have built that retreat for years, then."

"The old man liked him. He would have worked out something."

"But for the time being that hardly solves your financial problems, does it? You needed Austin to contact his father now, right?"

Necri nodded.

"And did he?"

"He couldn't get him. His father was in Hawaii. Austin must have forgotten that."

"He got through to him for Joe Zekk."

"He was trying. Maybe the old man wasn't in Hawaii when Zekk needed him."

"And all those calls he made to you this week?"

Necri swallowed. His voice was barely audible as he said, "Returning mine."

No wonder the doctor is upset about his friend's death, Kiernan thought. "Did you expect, Elias, that if you falsified the death certificate, Austin's father would reward you?"

Necri didn't raise his head. He didn't answer. He didn't have to.

12

IN THE HOWARD JOHNSON'S across the street from Elias Necri's offices, Kiernan sat in a phone booth—one of the old-fashioned ones with the black dial phone and the brown corner shelf beneath it, with a seat and an accordion door—and tore open two packages of Alka-Seltzer. She dropped the tablets in water, half-aware that she was counting the seconds till they dissolved, just as she'd seen patients on morphine silently tick off the minutes till their next shot. In those medical-school days, the patients' faith in chemicals had been topped only by that of the students. Wearing their white medical jackets, called Doctor by their anxious patients, they had watched in fear and awe as the real doctors prescribed a shot or pill from their cabinet of miracles. As interns, many had trusted caffeine and nicotine to keep them awake for the first twenty-four hours of their thirty-six-hour shifts, and amphetamines for the last twelve. It wasn't till Kiernan took her residency in forensic pathology that she began to categorize nicotine as a poison. And it was then, too, that one of the interns died of an accidental overdose. He had been one of her first autopsies.

Five years of autopsies had erased her illusions about drugs. Then two years in Nepal, India, Thailand, and Burma had changed her view of Western medicine altogether.

But not of aspirin.

She downed the Alka-Seltzers, dialed Stu Wiggins, and left a message on his machine that Dowd had not notified the sheriff.

Diesel fumes filled the air in the bus depot. The heat steamed up from the macadam. When would the damned bus pull out? Bishop Dowd wondered. As if things weren't bad enough, now he had to get rid of the Sheltons and get to lunch halfway across town with Sylvia Necri, all in forty-five minutes. What the hell did Sylvia want?

He pushed the thought of Sylvia Necri out of his mind. In less than a minute he felt his eyes closing. If he had slept more than ten

minutes at a time during the last two nights his nerves wouldn't
have been so raw, vague thoughts wouldn't have floated unbeck-
oned through his head. He would have been able to steel himself
against that smoky, sweet smell of diesel, of adventure, the smell
that had marked the beginnings of family vacations at the ocean, of
adolescent weekends with cousins in New York, Saturday afternoons in the bleachers in Ebbets Field, and Saturday nights picking
up girls at Coney Island.

He shook his head; there was no time for that now. He had to
keep his wits. But his mind wandered. He saw himself climbing
aboard the Greyhound cruiser and heading east, sitting by the
window, listening to the crackle of wax paper from the seats behind him, inhaling the spicy aroma of fried chicken, the garlicky
smell of roast-beef sandwiches. He could feel the scratchy wool of a
sweater wadded between the window and his neck as he let his eyes
close and the rumble of the bus lured him to sleep. The dark safety
of the bus, broken by pinpoints of light here and there. Then the
bus would jolt, and he would shift in his seat, open his eyes, and
suddenly outside would be the gray of dawn. And he would look
out not at the endless miles of sand and dirt that had been his
prison all these years, not at that dry landscape that sucked the life
out of a man, but at green: lush green grass, pale green dogwood,
dark green pine trees, trees with canopies of green leaves so thick
they nearly blocked out the sky, leafy azalea bushes just ready to
bloom, miles and miles of rolling green hills. The desert would be
behind him. Austin Vanderhooven would be behind him. Philip
Vanderhooven would be behind him. Sylvia Necri would be in his
past. Bishop Raymond Dowd, the sun-seared shell he had become,
would be gone.

Forcing his eyes open, Dowd looked at Jesse Shelton, his wife,
his child, the family's three cloth suitcases, two cardboard boxes,
and a carry-on satchel with a frayed plaid blanket sticking out. Did
they have any sense of the promise of escape here? Or were they
too young, too much the Chevy pickup generation, to know the
possibilities the bus depot offered?

Dowd shook off his reverie. Thirty-five minutes till he was to
meet Necri. She'd want something for Elias. But what? It was
going to mean trouble. More trouble.

The loudspeaker crackled. "El Paso, Odessa, Abilene, Fort

Worth, Dallas, and points east." Oh to get on the bus and be gone. But his eyes returned to the Sheltons.

The Shelton clan. How many Sheltons had there been when he'd climbed off the bus here, when he had signed on in Phoenix? Maybe twenty. Twenty men, women, and children, a couple in the state hospitals, one in a nursing home he wouldn't have left his eight iron in overnight.

Of course, it hadn't been official. Nothing like that. Old Bishop Welborn hadn't driven him out to the old Mission San Leo and said, "The Shelton clan goes with the church. Get them out of our hair." Maybe Welborn had forgotten about the Shelton incident, more than twenty years earlier. Like those fools in San Francisco sitting on their earthquake fault, as if the big one would never come, maybe he had been lulled by the years that had passed quietly, scandal free, since then. To Welborn and the rest of them out here it was ancient history. None of them could see how easily it still could explode and spray scandal over the archdiocese. Lucky for them Dowd had had more sense. Street smarts they'd call it back East now. Whatever. As soon as he heard about the incident, he checked the links to the present, and made it his business to chop them off.

Looking at Jesse and Anita Shelton, he found himself smiling. The last links. He had gotten rid of the others, spread them out across the country, two here, a family there, far from Phoenix, far from each other.

"I guess it's time we got on now." Jesse Shelton eyed the Greyhound with a clear mixture of excitement and apprehension. But in his wife's eyes there was only trust.

"Bishop Dowd," she said, "you've done so much for us. We just have no way to thank you. All the times you helped us out when we needed food or a place to stay. I don't know how we would have managed without you. The jobs you got Jesse, even after he'd been let go before. No one's ever done for us like you have. We're going to miss you something fierce. You know that. Little Billy"— she looked down at the toddler who was staring at the buses with a fascination that seemed to have been lifted whole from Dowd's youth—"he'll miss you most of all. It's kind of scary, going all the way to Tampa, Florida. But if you say it's the best thing, we sure know it is."

"Tampa, Tampa, Tampa." Billy sounded like a miniature cheer-leader. He reached up for Dowd's hand. "You come on bus."

Dowd squeezed the small hand, swallowed hard, and forced himself to let it go, for the last time. He had to pull himself together. He could have sent them to L.A. They would have been better off there. Or to Houston—he could have wangled a good job there for Jesse. But L.A. and Houston were too close, too cheap a bus fare back to Phoenix. "You'll like it in Tampa. There are big trees, green like the tropics. The jobs are steady. Monsignor Bristow thinks he can get Jesse into an apprentice program. It'll be a new start for you." Bristow had owed him one. Not this big a one, but a little pressure had turned the trick.

In a minute they would climb onto their bus and the last of the Shelton clan would be out of Phoenix. And even if someone traced back the history of Mission San Leo and its property, there would be no Sheltons around to give the family's story, no one to make the connection to the Church.

When they had stowed their boxes and suitcases in the bus's belly and climbed into the bus, Dowd felt an emptiness in his stomach. In one of those rare flashes of certainty, he knew this move would be disastrous.

Dowd waved as the bus pulled out.

Once he had wondered if he really had a soul. Now he knew he did, but he had just sold it.

13

STU WIGGINS was home when the return call came. He picked up the receiver on the first ring. "Afternoon." He'd learned the hard way not to offer his name.

"Stu?" It was Jesse Dixon from the sheriff's office.

"Yeah. What'd you find?"

"Nothing. What you figured, eh, man?"

Stu nodded but offered no reply—he'd gained a few bruises learning that lesson, too. He didn't ask Jesse if he was sure there was no record of Vanderhooven's death. If he'd had to ask, he wouldn't have trusted Dixon with the inquiry. For the same reason he neither reminded him about secrecy nor mentioned the debt he had incurred. Before he replaced the receiver he said, "Thanks."

He sat a moment staring out the front window of the cottage that served as his office and home. If the sheriff's office in question had been in Maricopa County, he would have picked up the phone and called. He wasn't planning to talk long, but he didn't want this call to show up on his bill. He pushed himself up and ambled out to the faded red Mustang and drove the few blocks downtown to Heritage Square. Between the convention center and the concert hall was, for Wiggin's money, the best public phone in the area.

He dialed the main number for the sheriff's department. When the dispatcher answered he said, "Check the Haley's Funeral Home on Alma School Road, on the way to Chandler. There's a priest, Father Austin Vanderhooven, in their freezer. He was murdered at Mission San Leo on Tuesday."

14

THE SELF-HELP CENTER looked as if it had once been a grocery, the type the chains drove out of business. It had been painted school-wall green—painted, but clearly not prepped beforehand. Kiernan made her way through the waiting room to the women's center.

The bright yellow walls of the Women's Center were a welcome surprise, and instead of stale smoke, this room smelled of Play-doh and crayons. But a look at the dark-haired woman shifting nervously on a plastic chair across the room brought Kiernan back to the reality of the place. There was a hematoma on the woman's cheek and an incisor missing from her upper jaw. Fear, desperation, and physical abuse had beaten the youth out of her.

On the floor, a child coughed. Kiernan looked down. The boy shrank back under the chair. Beside him, a girl with hair almost as dark as her mother's sat staring suspiciously at a rocking horse in the far corner.

Kiernan's head throbbed as she looked at them. How many children like them had she seen in her medical school days working in the ER? Children with cigarette burns, with bruises from electrical cords, children who looked at teddy bears and rocking horses and saw only something to trick them.

A woman in a pale denim shirtdress strode in. She had a boyishly athletic look to her: a sturdy, winsome face, a thatch of sandy hair, and a splattering of freckles so dark that even her desert tan didn't mask them. Holding out an envelope to the dark-haired woman, she said, "Mrs. Allen, I've arranged an appointment with Dr. Herrera at three forty-five. He's about a mile down the street. You can catch the bus outside."

Mrs. Allen stood slowly, nodding. She took the envelope but continued to hold it away from her. The sandy-haired woman put a hand on her arm. In a soft voice she said, "It'll be okay now. You can do this. You're taking charge now, right? I'll keep your things in my office till you get back. Call me if you have any trouble; we'll be leaving at six sharp. Okay?"

Slowly the dark-haired woman pocketed the envelope. Her "Thank you" was almost too soft to be heard, but there was a solidity to it, as if in taking the envelope she had accepted an infusion of the freckled woman's strength. An unusual skill, Kiernan thought, one most doctors would give an added year of internship to possess.

Mrs. Allen picked up the boy. The little girl clasped her free hand fiercely. Kiernan held the door open.

When they left she turned to the sandy-haired woman. "Are you Beth Landau?"

"Yes," she said. Her gaze was still on the departing family, worry apparent in the set of her eyes.

"I'm Kiernan O'Shaughnessy. I need to talk to you."

"Yes?"

"It's about Austin Vanderhooven."

Her eyes hardened. "Shit! What is this? I'm sorry he's dead. Really sorry. But it's his own fault. And I've got my own responsibilities." She turned and strode down the hall.

"Hey." Kiernan ran after her, catching her outside her office. "Look, the man is dead."

"And his father's already been here to accuse me."

"His father came here?" Kiernan asked, taken aback. "Why?"

"To tell me I'd driven Austin to hang himself!" Beth's freckled face was drawn tight; her hand shook as she braced herself against the doorframe.

Kiernan's shoulders tightened. What was Philip Vanderhooven doing running around accusing people and making the investigation that much harder? She took a deep breath and said, "No wonder you're angry, Beth. He had no business doing that. I'm a private investigator and there are a couple of things I think you have a right to know about Austin's death. Can we go inside?"

Beth flicked a chip of yellow paint from the doorframe. "An investigator? Who's paying you? The Vanderhoovens or the Church?"

"*And* I'm doing this because I want to see that Austin gets a fair shake."

The color rose in Beth's face. "Austin Vanderhooven always got a fair shake, more than a fair shake. Austin's dead. You're not doing anything for him. What you're getting your money for is protecting the delicate Vanderhooven reputation, and, of course, protecting the Church from its bête noire, scandal. I don't give a damn about either one."

"Nor do I, believe me." Kiernan smiled. "But there's a good chance Austin did not hang himself, that he was killed. Murdered. I do care about that."

Beth Landau's face paled; her freckles seemed darker in contrast. "Okay," she said, "come into my office."

Kiernan followed her into a shabby yellow room and settled on a black plastic sofa. High on the wall a vent rattled, but no cold air came out. The small office was windowless and smelled of air freshener masking some dull, thick odor that Kiernan didn't want to identify. Beth perched on the other end of the sofa. Despite the warmth of the room she was shivering.

"So, investigator, how *did* Austin die?"

"This is not going to be an easy thing to hear. Mr. Vanderhooven had no business barging in on you and then not giving you the whole truth." Watching for Beth Landau's reaction, she told her the condition in which Bishop Dowd had found the body. "You can see the sexual implications, and why I have to ask you about your relationship with Austin."

Beth dug her fingers into her denim-covered thighs. She inhaled deeply, eyes closed, as if pulling together all her control. "Like I told his father, if he had any sexual activities at all, they weren't with me. And what you're telling me about him . . ." Her eyes flicked shut again and she seemed to shrink back into the sofa. "I just can't believe Austin would do anything so . . . so *seedy.*"

"Beth, I don't think he did. That's why I'm working on this case. That's why I have to ask you to be totally frank with me." It was a moment before Beth offered the slightest of nods. "Okay, you dated him in high school, right? And in college. Even after he entered the seminary you still wrote to him. And then you followed him to Phoenix."

Beth's eyes snapped open. "Followed him! Who told you that? Philip? Or was it Grace? According to her, I led Austin kicking and screaming to a bed of perversions. According to Grace, I created the poor so her son would have a police record."

Kiernan laughed. "And the bearer's-bond caper? I suppose that was your fault, too."

"Of course," Beth said, her voice only slightly calmer. "So what if we were both sixteen, and I'd never heard of a bearer's bond. In Grace's eyes, it was I who masterminded the escape to Mexico, I who chose a public bus from Tijuana with no shocks and metal seats that left our butts black-and-blue for weeks, I who found the Casa de la Playa, a 'hotel' that had more insects than a junior-high science project."

Kiernan leaned into the corner of the old sofa and pulled an ankle up on her knee. In the alley out back a truck rattled by; the vibrations reverberated through the stiff plastic on the sofa. "Still, that trip must have been great fun for a pair of sixteen-year-olds. I'm sure the hotel room didn't look as bad then as it does in retrospect. Nothing does when you're a teenager. When I think of the places I stayed in college . . ." She shook her head.

Beth's eyes softened. She shivered again but seemed not to notice. The shock was taking its toll on her. As Beth spoke Kiernan sensed that she was talking mostly to herself. "That room couldn't have been more than eight by eight. There was sand and dirt all over the floor, and so much on the bed that it crackled every time we made a move. And the glasses—afterwards I saw a kid washing them out in water that was brown. But I suppose either the alcohol or being sixteen protected us." She leaned back against the arm of the sofa. "It's hard to beat that for romance and adventure, when you're sixteen. There we were, on the lam, lying together in a real hotel bed." She laughed. "First thing we had a fight. I can't remember what it was about. When we made up we celebrated by drinking a Mexican liqueur called Culiacán. Culiacán became our peace offering after that—every time we fought and made up. We thought we were such hot stuff then, with our loot, and our hotel and our own bottle. After we drank it we made love, and I had to keep my eyes open the whole time so I didn't throw up." She laughed again, but with a hollowness this time. "And then Philip found us. Naked. No house rules about announcing guests at Casa de la Playa. Thank God it was Philip and not Grace. Once he realized the bearer's bonds were intact he wasn't too concerned that I wasn't."

Kiernan waited for her to go on. When she didn't, Kiernan said, "Fifteen years is a long time to be lovers."

Beth jerked upright, the spell broken. "Fifteen years! Haven't you heard what I told you? There's been nothing between Austin and me since he chose the seminary. What do you take me for?"

"But Beth, you followed him to Phoenix."

"Followed him! Look, I didn't follow him. If anything he followed me. I was here months before he ever thought of Phoenix. And don't start thinking I was front-trailing him like a dog. There was no way I could have guessed he'd be sent out here. He was in seminary back East. His godfather's brother is an archbishop. Austin got him to pull strings to get him out here."

"To be with you?"

"How do I know?" Her right hand was braced against the back of the sofa; she looked ready to push off, stand up, and stalk out.

Careful not to meet her gaze, not to challenge her, Kiernan said, "It's very possible I've been given false information. People lie to investigators all the time, Beth. *I* didn't know Philip Vanderhooven would come here. And believe me, I am not pleased he did. But there's more to the question of your relationship with Austin. I found a pair of red lace bikini pants."

Beth dug her fingers into the back of the sofa. "Anybody can buy bikini pants."

"These had been worn."

"So?"

"They are yours. From fifteen years ago? From the Mexican trip?"

She hesitated, then nodded.

"How did they get in his dresser drawer?"

"I don't know." Another truck rattled by. The plastic quivered under Beth's fingers, but she seemed not to notice.

"Those pants are a real damning piece of evidence, Beth. How do you think they could have gotten there?"

"Maybe Austin took them. He was the one who bought them. I never cared about them."

"When would he have been in a position to take them?"

"Look, I don't know," Beth snapped. "It could have been any time. I didn't wear them. They aren't pants you wear for comfort."

Kiernan sat silent, watching Beth consider her own danger. Beth ran her forefinger back and forth across the black plastic. Her eyes were half-closed, her lips pressed hard together. In the waiting room the phone rang again. This time Kiernan could hear the murmur of the receptionist's voice. Then Beth opened her eyes and swallowed. When she spoke, there was no sign of emotion in her voice. "I'm going to tell you about Austin because it's in my self-interest. And you can believe what I say or not."

Kiernan nodded.

"I don't know why Austin came to Phoenix. It's not that I haven't given the question thought. Here I am, head of the women's center. I'm supposed to have my life together." She gave a forced laugh. "Austin wasn't sleeping with me. We hadn't been to bed since college, since the night he told me he was going into the seminary. He took me to dinner, then to a hotel, made love. Austin was always good in bed. I didn't realize how good until it was over between us and I started dating other guys. But that night it was as if it was the last chance he'd ever get, which of course it was. I just didn't know it then. Afterwards we sat up, leaning back against the headboard. I remember it was a padded headboard like they had in the fifties. And Austin told me he was going into the seminary."

"Tantamount to announcing his engagement to someone else," Kiernan said.

"Worse. Another woman, well, you may not like it, but there's plenty of precedent, plenty of friends who've gone through that and are only too happy to console you. But the Church! It's not like there's someone better; he just doesn't want you!"

Beth's face had relaxed. In that face Kiernan thought she could see the bewilderment of the college girl Austin Vanderhooven had discarded.

"I'm not going to pretend it wasn't awful. Maybe I should have known. Probably. But I didn't. We'd gone together for years. It took me most of the next year to get myself in reasonable shape to deal with, well, anything."

"But you still wrote to him?"

"He wrote to me. I didn't answer, not for a long time. Then I convinced myself that answering his letters would be the adult thing to do, that it would prove to me I had gotten over him."

"And then you moved to Phoenix," Kiernan prompted.

"I got the chance to establish the battered-women's program here. It's one of the best in the state."

"And Austin showed up?"

"Without warning. He called me from across town, invited me to tour the church. 'Tour the mission' was his phrase. I thought it was going to be a historic monument. Have you seen it? It's a joke —Saint seven-eleven!" There was no hint of innocence in her face now.

Kiernan nodded. "And then?"

"Nothing more like that, but the next thing I know Austin's offering to help out here. And suddenly Jack, who runs the place, is telling me it would be a coup to have Austin on the board of the women's center." She shook her head in disgust.

"And it would have been, wouldn't it, Beth? A Roman Catholic priest endorsing a center that must support birth control, abortion, divorce?"

"Sure, but Austin wasn't ready to do that. One thing Austin was good at was covering his ass. Even in Mexico I was the only one lying outside the sheets."

Kiernan laughed. Beth looked up, startled, and then she smiled. On the wall behind her was an ill-colored poster touting the four essential nutritional groups: violet eggplants, light yellow eggs, orange strawberries, gray bread, and a couple of pale salmon circles that might have been intended to represent lemons or oranges or even apples. But on the faded yellow wall, the poster looked appropriate. "So Austin didn't actually offer to be on the board?"

"No, not Austin. He hinted. And"—her fingers dug into the sofa back—"he did do something else for us. But here's the point, he created a reason to be in contact. I saw him once or twice a month, sometimes more. Sometimes alone. He gave me a key to the rectory so I could get in if he was delayed. I never had to use it. He was always there waiting. But he never touched me . . ." The black plastic cracked. Beth forced a laugh. "The only time his flesh came in contact with mine was when he helped me on with a coat, something he would have done for any lady in the parish. He never said anything suggestive, per se." Carefully, she placed both hands in her lap and stared down at them. Despite her tan, a burst of tiny white lines was visible around her tense eyes. "And the question is Why?"

Kiernan sat motionless, anxious not to break the mood.

"This is what I think. I've given it a lot of thought. I've been furious that the man wouldn't get out of my life. I've been disgusted that I couldn't either get rid of him physically or at least free myself emotionally. I think he was using me to test himself. Just like these guys who beat their wives; they need to have someone to blame for their inadequacies. Austin used me to prove over and over again that he was pure, worthy. I don't know what he was making up for—impure thoughts, lascivious desires. It was as if he was telling himself that even if he had given in to them, there was a line he wouldn't cross—me. Giving up sex was a big sacrifice for him. For Austin the time that he spent making love was the one time he wasn't looking over his shoulder."

The air conditioner crackled and a gust of cold air skimmed Kiernan's shoulders, sending a shiver across her back. Beth's theory, she thought, could describe a guilt-ridden man who'd been in the habit of hanging himself for pleasure. "What do you mean?"

Beth leaned back against the sofa arm; her finger strummed meditatively on her skirt, and the look on her freckled face was that of a professor about to deliver a pet theory. "Austin was the most competitive man I knew," she began. "But in bed he was the best. He knew it. And for once he could relax and not worry about outstripping the competition."

"Was there competition? Were you dating other guys?"

She shook her head. "No, any competition was only in Austin's head. With him I never had the sense he was competing with other men; it was as if he had already outstripped them and the contest was on a deeper, more personal level. Competing against an ideal he had created."

The air conditioner turned off. In the silence Kiernan could hear the murmur of voices in the waiting room. A new client? Before Beth could react to that, she asked, "What else?"

"Austin was so cerebral. I used to picture the inside of his head as a medieval tower room in which a pair of emaciated scholars carried on a fierce but oh-so-controlled dialogue. The time was twilight, winter. The fire had gone out but they hadn't noticed. I told Austin about that room once. He accused me of dredging it up from ethnic memory. Of course, we Jews do have a history of dialogue. It's an important part of our tradition. But for us there's a joy in it. In Austin's icy tower room there was no emotion at all. No, that's not true; there was fear."

"Fear of what?"

Beth's eyes filled. She swallowed. "I don't know. I tried to ask Austin that, but he would never let me get near enough." She swallowed again and squeezed her eyes against the tears. "Sorry. The whole thing's been such a shock. But this conclusion of mine, it's not as if I reached it ages ago and presented him with it whole. It's only been in the last year that it's been clear. And we weren't having long talks against the padded headboards anymore." She looked directly at Kiernan. "It wasn't in my interest to keep poking at his psyche, you see." Her eyes remained steady, but her gaze diffused so that instead of being the bridge to Kiernan it had become a wall between them.

"What do you *think* Austin was so afraid of?"

She shrugged. "I don't know. Damnation?"

In the waiting room a child screamed. A stab of pain ran through Kiernan's head. She had forgotten about the pain. Despite her role as an investigator, she was probably the only person with whom Beth Landau had been able to discuss Vanderhooven. It didn't surprise her when Beth went on: "If you'd asked Austin, he would have told you his commitment was to truth, truth within the Catholic tradition. What he would have meant, of course, was what he chose to view as truth. Austin was a master at shaping reality to suit himself. And his inability to really feel for someone else he saw not as a failing but as a necessity for a man whose calling is to move from the body to the spirit."

"But he did let you have Hohokam Lodge."

Beth stiffened.

Kiernan wasn't surprised at her reaction—the sudden jerk back to reality—just at the topic that had triggered it. "That wasn't a question. I have the information, Beth. And it explains why you couldn't rid yourself of him. By the same token, if he controlled the lodge, it gives you a motive for keeping him alive. It also brings up the possibility of your clients' husbands—angry, violent men who want their wives back, who want their control back."

"I can't talk about my clients," she said, all business now.

"If one of the husbands discovered that Austin knew where his wife was, he could have gone to Mission San Leo. He could have been planning just to pressure Austin, not to kill him. Killing him could have been an accident."

Beth stood up. "I said I cannot talk about my clients. Even in the abstract."

She was on the verge of losing Beth, she knew it. She thought of that hollow Latin book of Vanderhooven's, hesitated, then went ahead and asked, "Did Austin keep any of your clients' records?"

Beth's face flushed. "How many times do I have to tell you—nothing about my clients."

Kiernan stood. "Beth, think about it, if one of these guys killed Austin, do you want your client, and her children, living with him?"

"Just get out!" She grabbed Kiernan's purse and thrust it at her.

Kiernan felt her body tense. Instinctively she steeled herself to avoid reacting. She extricated her card and laid it on the desk. "Think about it. I am very discreet. No one would ever know the women's center was connected."

Beth flung the card in the wastebasket. "You're damned right no one will know. Because I am not saying anything about my clients to anyone, no matter how discreet. And if that means Austin's murder goes unsolved, well, so be it."

Kiernan hesitated. Beth had trusted her, she knew, and now Beth felt betrayed. Anything she could say, any gesture she might make would only aggravate the situation.

As Kiernan walked down the hall toward the waiting room, she reminded herself that investigators weren't supposed to worry about bruised feelings. And they weren't supposed to let their own be hurt. She thought of what Sam Chase had said, that Austin Vanderhooven was not unlike her. Just what had Sam meant?

15

AT FOUR IN THE AFTERNOON Phoenix felt like a barbecue, or more accurately, a steamer. Pre-monsoon weather. Desert humidity. The heat from the sidewalks steamed up, the bright sunlight bounced off glass and chrome. Car windows were rolled up tight to guard the capsule of cool air inside. Kiernan thought of the icy tower, of Austin Vanderhooven's desperate single-mindedness. It had taken Beth years to get an understanding of Vanderhooven's mind-set, but for Kiernan it was no problem. The ability to put all else second, a distant second, she understood too well. For her it had been not so much a skill as a need. She had to exonerate Moira, to force Father Grogan to bring Moira back from the patch of dirt to which he had consigned her, to make him bury her in the churchyard, in the hallowed ground where suicides were not allowed. To grab back the way of life that was gone.

That icy tower of Austin Vanderhooven's described her home then. The single-family row house common to so many soot-gray Eastern towns. Small dark rooms, overcrowded with heavy cherry furniture—cluttered rooms, where every step had to be planned, where voices were lowered to keep from disturbing her father or mother in the kitchen or living room ten feet away. After Moira's death her parents had barely gone through the motions of family life. They were nothing more than the survivors of a suicide—Walt and Mary O'Shaughnessy, the parents of beautiful Moira, who killed herself. They had failed before the world, before their God, before themselves. If they had not been Irish Catholics, they would gladly have followed Moira. If they had not been Catholics in a Catholic neighborhood, the stigma of Moira's death would not have destroyed them.

Kiernan gave her head a shake. It felt as if her brain had broken loose and was clanging against her skull. Aspirin, she needed more aspirin. She climbed into the Jeep, wincing as the heat of the seat cut through her jeans. She started the engine and let it idle, then gratefully turned the air-conditioning on high and headed back to Howard Johnson's.

It was fine to understand Vanderhooven's mind-set, but that didn't bring her closer to knowing why he, who could have been the all-American boy, shared her obsessive single-mindedness. And what about him had led to his murder?

"Stu, I need a woman to get on the women's center van with Beth Landau tonight. The assignment could take a couple days. She may have to be 'on' all the time. There's a small chance of danger." Kiernan sat in the old-fashioned phone booth in the Howard Johnson's. Her booth, she was beginning to consider it. The brown plastic shelf was ample for her wallet but too near the phone to hold her fizzing glass of Alka-Seltzer. That she set on the floor.

"Patsy Luca?"

"Can she do it? She's pretty young, isn't she?"

"She won't get up suspicion."

"Hmm."

"Don't worry so much. I've got a friend who does the legal work down there; I know how they choose who they take to the mountains. I'll give Patsy a little coaching. Patsy'll handle the rest."

"Are you sure—"

"You don't have much time, Kerry. And I don't have anybody else to suggest."

Kiernan downed the rest of the Alka-Seltzer, willing it to work fast. Her head throbbed as she leaned over to put the glass back on the floor. "Okay. Give me her address."

"No need. I'll call her."

Kiernan hesitated. "I need to talk to her too."

"You mean you need to check her out." Wiggins laughed, but there was an edge to his voice that the laughter didn't quite cover.

"Okay, personal failing. Give me one, I've had a hard day. I've called Dowd three times today and he's never called back. Philip Vanderhooven was out questioning Beth Landau. You know, Stu, I'm getting a real uneasy feeling about this case."

16

BISHOP RAYMOND DOWD sat on the pale leather couch in Sylvia Necri's living room, waiting. The woman was taking her time with her "art work." But he couldn't rush her, the expert forger.

Forger! Forgery, maybe murder, how had all this happened? How had he gotten himself so entangled with this woman he didn't even like and certainly didn't trust? He still could barely believe he had called Huerta, his parishioner in the sheriff's office, and gotten the blank death certificate and an interment form, which Sylvia was forging right now. Surely there had been some way short of this to protect the retreat center. He tried to think, but his mind was too foggy. What was taking her so long? He glanced at his watch—4:17. Still plenty of time to get the forms back to Huerta. Dammit, he was an errand boy here! And now with this forgery scheme he was putting his life, his career, in Sylvia Necri's hands. What would happen if the forms weren't right, if someone found out? What if . . . but he couldn't hold together the strands of possibilities.

He shifted his bulk on the sofa, shifted his gaze to the framed photo on the wall. The figures were blurry; his eyes were too tired to focus. But he'd seen the photo often enough to know it showed Sylvia Necri's class of architects at Taliesen West, the bunch of them there with Frank Lloyd Wright himself. Dowd had been to Taliesen. He'd seen pictures of the hard chairs, hard benches, that were Wright's idea of "form follows function." Well, Sylvia Necri hadn't become famous like a lot of the others, but she'd sure learned to choose hard furniture—for instance, this sofa.

How had he gotten involved in all this? A bishop of the Church. Was he willing to break his vows for the power the retreat would bring? He looked desperately out the window. He wasn't going to lie to himself—sure he wanted the power. Sure he'd been disappointed that he hadn't seen the big-time possibilities young Vanderhooven had and that it was Vanderhooven who'd almost cashed in on them. And—he wasn't going to deny it, not to himself—the fact that the kid's death gave him back control of the retreat was okay by him.

But it wasn't just the power. No. No matter who would think that. And there would be plenty—business types, lawyers—who would never see beyond that. It was for the Church. The Church in Arizona had to have that retreat. Without it the Church would calcify. Already the clergy were dividing into the petrified forest of hardliners and the brushfire liberals, who demanded the ordination of married women. Among the laity, the basis of Church, many were giving up in disgust or despair—they were just plain tired of waiting for the Church to adjust to the twentieth century. Vatican Two—they'd seen those reforms tossed aside. Maybe if Dowd became archbishop . . . But he'd made his choice. He'd thrown in his lot with the retreat and there was no turning back. The retreat would bring liberal Catholics from across the country, the world. With their money and their press they would resurrect the Arizona Church for the people.

He'd given his life to the Church. The Church was his life. Men carried on about their wives, their children; they didn't know what commitment meant. He would not let his Church be maimed. No matter what sacrifices that involved.

Dowd inhaled deeply and pulled himself up straighter on the hard sofa. What kind of woman had cushions so damned rocklike in her own living room? No wonder she was an old maid.

He checked his watch again—4:19. He stood up. Once he got these forms back to Huerta he could go home and sleep. His hands were shaky; he could barely see straight. He needed the sleep.

"Here you go."

Dowd looked up, startled. He hadn't heard Sylvia Necri walk in. He stood and took the papers from her without looking at them.

"Bishop! You've got the death certificate and the interment permit there. Don't get them mixed up."

He glanced at the top form and nodded.

"If I do say so myself," Sylvia Necri did say, her voice surprisingly soft, "I did a helluva job on both of them. And, Bishop, if your man does his job right, once the interment permit is in place we—you, me, and the Church—are home free."

"And your new death certificate? That saves your nephew's hide, right?"

"Not just Elias. It clears the Church; it clears you. And if there's any blame it'll fall right back on Vanderhooven's detective."

17

KIERNAN PULLED UP in front of the address Wiggins had given her for Patsy Luca, in a development in south Phoenix that backed up against the base of the jagged mountains. The houses here might have been mass produced, Kiernan thought, but their yards were certainly statements of individuality.

The yard to the right of Patsy Luca's sported a decorative white ironwork fence around a carpet of thick green grass. Here and there ceramic rabbits poked their noses warily up through the dewy mat. A giant cedar shaded a quarter of the yard; a Norfolk Island pine drooped over another.

On the other side, was a "westernized" lawn that looked like a quilt of pebbles and cacti and bricks. No drop of water wasted here.

Probably the only thing that kept the neighbors from each other's throat was their common disgust with the yard between them —Patsy's place. Kiernan climbed from the Jeep down into the hundred-and-ten-degree heat and made her way across the barren yard. No grass, no trees, no cacti, not even a weed was still alive. The dry scaly ground was cut with crevasses the size of earthquake faults. Kiernan rang the bell, and waited on the unshaded stoop.

The sun pierced her thick hair and seared her scalp. Her throat felt like parchment. She rang again. Still no answer. Where was the woman? Irritably Kiernan looked at her watch. She was cutting it close anyway, without spending her time baking out here. She could have handled this on the phone and spared herself forty-five minutes of fuming in the rush-hour traffic; she could have trusted Stu Wiggins's endorsement of Patsy Luca. He hadn't led her astray before. But if Patsy Luca couldn't even get to the door . . .

The intercom gurgled. "Who's there?"

Kiernan pushed the buzzer, simultaneously trying to wet her tongue enough to speak. "Kiernan O'Shaughnessy. You *were* expecting me, weren't you?"

"I'm measuring out powder. Come on around back." The intercom clicked off.

Couldn't she shake the baking powder off her hands and walk the few steps to the front door? Kiernan trudged across the unshaded path past the double garage. Her feet sweated in the hot running shoes. She slipped on the edge of a crevasse in the side yard, caught herself, and—grumbling—headed to the back door.

She was just about to knock when a voice called, "Out here, Kiernan!"

Kiernan spun to see a blond head poking out of the shack in the back of the yard. The woman standing in the shed doorway was about five six, in her mid-twenties, with bleached blond hair finger-combed back and caught under a yellow headband, pale hazel eyes, and a surprisingly sallow tan for a Phoenician. From a distance her head looked like a small yellow beach ball plopped on top of a sleeveless Harley Davidson T-shirt and tight cut-off cargo pants.

Close up, Kiernan noted that Patsy Luca hardly looked like the weary, desperate, beaten woman needed to pierce Beth Landau's defenses at the battered women's refuge. With one muscular arm braced on the doorframe and the other on a hip, Patsy confirmed Wiggins's appraisal that she could take care of herself. "Come on in out of the heat," Patsy said, in an easy Western drawl not unlike Stu Wiggins's.

Kiernan stepped through the doorway and stared. A brace of pistols lay atop a stack of boxes on the west wall. A shotgun was propped against the boxes, and an engraved rifle lay on a towel on top. Target pistols, a .22, a .38, and a .45 automatic were in open boxes on a wooden chest, and ahead, on the workbench, was a turret press with a dusty black scale, a half-filled box of bullets, and a group of empty brass cartridges. Poking into the top of the turret press was a clear plastic colander filled with gray powder. The whole place smelled of dust and linseed oil. "My God! This is an armory!"

Patsy smiled uncomfortably. "That's what Stu said. He keeps telling me no one needs more than one pistol and one rifle. But of course that's Stu, and that's bullshit. What do you carry?"

"Quick wits."

"Hmm." Her face betrayed little, Kiernan could see the effort that that blank expression cost. Despite her wholesome appearance, there was determination in the set of the jaw and the pressure lines beside the mouth. Her lips were pursed in disdain—disdain for the gunless.

Kiernan shrugged. "What I sell is my medical background. I can take care of myself. Once or twice I've had to protect clients. But that's not what they pay me for. If they did, I'd find another line of work." She watched Patsy's face, but her expression gave no hint of her reaction. She was good, Kiernan had to admit. Not likeable, but good. Unfortunately, both qualities were necessary for this job.

Patsy leaned back against the workbench. "Well, I don't plan to be a patsy"—a smile flashed on her face and was gone—"for anyone." She ran a hand along a rifle barrel. "This is a varmint rifle, a specialized piece of work. It hefts heavy. But its trajectory is flat. Hit a prairie dog at three hundred yards. The guys who carry 'em have 'em because they just like to shoot. They don't miss often. Some of the city hunters like to use a thin jacket bullet." She laughed, scornfully. "Taxidermists hate to see them hauling their carcasses in. When those bullets hit, they splatter the innards like foam. Helluva mess trying to clean out the carcass."

Despite the air conditioner, rivulets of sweat ran down Kiernan's back. Her headache was back in force. Kiernan let a moment pass before saying, "If you want to play chicken with tales of gore, you're way outclassed. You want to hear about autopsies where you've got a body that's been lying out in the open, decomposing for months? You want to hear about the smells? Or the maggots?" She caught Patsy's eye. "Do I make my point?"

Patsy hesitated. "Okay, okay. Truce?" An instant later she smiled. Suddenly, the lines of suspicion seemed to melt and she looked like a giggly girl who would spend her Saturday afternoons handing her boyfriend wrenches and lug nuts while he fiddled with his Harley. She looked like the girl Kiernan needed to tackle Beth Landau—if she could play the role to match.

"Truce."

Turning back to the workbench, she said, "I'm in the middle of reloading cartridges. I don't like to leave here with the powder out and the shell casing in the turret press like this." She pulled up the handle of the six-inch-wide machine. "It'll only take a minute. See, the problem is that I got a good deal on a new rifle, a real good deal. The guy who makes them is a master, or at least he was. His eyes are going. It used to be that there was no space at all between the stock and the barrel. You couldn't have pulled a thread through there. Now, well . . . But for mine he was in top form. It's perfect. . . . Anyway, the thing is that the specs on the ammo load for the nearest factory-made gun just don't work as well for this one. I'll tell you what I think. Here, let me get the primer in the post." She fingered the small metal disk. "What I think is," she said, pouring gray powder into a small funnel at the top of the turret press, "is that the specs for the factory-made job call for a different weight of powder. They say sixty grains, but with sixty weight your trajectory's too tight." She pulled down the lever, then lifted it and removed a resized shell. "See, this way I can customize my ammo. Not only that, but it saves me over half the cost per shell—"

"You've got to be downtown by six. Let me explain the case while you work, okay?" Stu Wiggins had insisted Patsy was perfect for the job. She damn well wasn't perfect, but she'd have to do—*if* she could pull off the act.

"Yeah, sorry. I'm not usually so distracted. The rifle was my Christmas present to me. You can see how long I've been waiting. That's another problem with Dale Harmon. Time is nothing to him. And you don't dare fuss, because old and slow as he is, he's still got a waiting list years long. There are guys praying Dale lives long enough to get to them. See, he—"

"The *case*," Kiernan prodded.

"Stu told me about it. You need me to play a battered wife, right? Get on the bus with the rest of them, get into the safe house, and breach their files, right?"

"And be in town by six P.M. It means playing your part nonstop for a day or more. You've got to be a housewife, someone with no resources, someone ashamed of herself and her husband, ashamed of what she put up with. Someone who's used every bit of strength she has to drag herself out and get help." Her gaze rested on Patsy's biceps, muscles that could fling a menacing husband into the next yard. "There can't be any cracks in your performance. No one can have any suspicion. Do you think you can do it?"

Patsy lifted the last reloaded bullet out of the turret press, plunked it in the box with the others, and turned to face Kiernan. No one feature of her face had changed, and yet her expression had hardened. "The role calls for a fearful wife, not a gun nut. That's what you're saying, right?"

"Right."

Patsy closed her eyes and took a deep breath of the dusty air. She caught Kiernan's eye. "Yes, I can do it. I will do it. But let me tell you, it's not just the delicate little flowers who get their butts beat and their ribs broken. I know. Married at sixteen, divorced finally at twenty-one. Five years too late. I was never in one of those shelters. I didn't have kids; that was the one smart move I made in those years. But it got so that I believed my husband when he told me it was all my fault. I was on a first-name basis with the receptionist in emergency. It got so if I could make it I'd drive to Chandler or Scottsdale to get to a different hospital. But after a while they knew me at every hospital in the valley." She held her gaze. The tension lines beside her mouth dug deep. She looked older, as if the shadows of the past had settled beneath her cheekbones and under her eyes. Glancing at the bullets beside the turret press, she said, "No one's ever going to smack me around like that again." She took a breath. "Stu said you thought one of the husbands of the women at the center might have had it in for your priest. Well, if you want someone to find the bastard, you've got the right woman."

Kiernan put a hand on Patsy's arm. "I don't doubt you can do that. It's obvious you know the situation better than I do. But I want you to understand that this is my case. There's no free rein here. Your job is to get information, period." She could feel Patsy's arm tense under her fingers.

"These guys, these bullies—"

"Maybe you're too close to this."

"I'm close all right, but I'm in control."

"It's got to be *my* control. Can you deal with that? Think about it."

Slowly, Patsy nodded. "Inside the house I've got a wall full of trophies. They're from target matches, standard meets, skeet shoots. You won't find my ex-husband's balls over the mantel."

Kiernan released Patsy's arm. "Okay. I need everything you can get about the lodge, about Beth Landau, about her relationship with Austin Vanderhooven, and about what happens to her or for her now that he's dead. Try to get her to open up to you. Vanderhooven was planning to build a retreat near her place. See what you can get out of her on that. And her files, Patsy. There's something in those files she's hiding. She didn't balk at telling me about Vanderhooven, mind and body, but when I mentioned her files, she snapped shut. Can you get into the files?"

For the first time Patsy smiled full face. She was almost pretty, Kiernan realized. Or as pretty as a woman streaked with gunpowder and sweat could be. "Yeah. I can do locks."

"And there's a guy named Joe Zekk, a friend of the priest, if you hear or see his name, pay attention. It's ten after five. With traffic—"

Patsy laughed. "Don't worry about my making it on time. I drive just like you'd think I do."

"Don't get caught. By Beth Landau or the cops. Landau's in the center of this case. I've taken my shot at her. Yours is the last one we'll get. If you blow this, the case is over."

"Stu, it's Kiernan."

"Kerry, just the woman I've been waiting on. You get along good with Patsy?"

"I'll withhold judgment."

Wiggins's breath hit the receiver. "Trust me."

"I *am* trusting you."

"Good. Now, you ready for this? I've got this buddy at the phone company. He owes me a bundle. Well, he owes me a lot less than he did last night, maybe nothing at all now—"

"Stu?"

"Well, you know that long-distance number, the one that Austin Vanderhooven took collect calls from?"

"Joe Zekk's number."

"Well, my buddy got ahold of Zekk's billing record. Bad part is it just covers this week. Something to do with the computers or the filing system, or something. But the interesting part is that Zekk had a long-distance call."

"And your buddy traced that?"

"You're with me."

"To?"

"Philip Vanderhooven's hotel in Maui."

18

AT TWELVE MINUTES AFTER FIVE, Bishop Dowd pulled the Buick up to the curb by Sun Fun Pool and Patio Shop. The cold hollow feeling in his stomach had gotten worse. His hands were shaky. He had to pull himself together. He began reciting: "Through this holy unction and His most tender mercy, may the Lord pardon thee whatever faults thou hast—" He stopped abruptly, shocked to find himself murmuring the old Last Rites. Still, he was in better control. By the time he rolled down the window Tom Huerta was there, looking as uncomfortable as Dowd had ever seen the man.

"I've only got a fifteen-minute break, Bishop Dowd. This isn't the time I normally take it. I had to get a guy to cover for me. I've got three minutes to get back."

Motioning Huerta closer, Dowd pulled two sheets from the manila envelope. "Here you go, Tom. This top one's the interment permit. It's got yesterday's date on it."

Huerta nodded uncomfortably.

"You know what to do with it, right?" Dowd prodded.

Huerta nodded again. He closed his eyes and took a deep breath. "I could lose my job over this. Or worse."

Dowd's face flushed. "Look, Huerta, do you want the archdiocese to keep doing business with your brother or not?"

Huerta took a step back, as if slapped by the bishop's reaction.

Get hold of yourself, Dowd told himself. He closed his fingers around the steering wheel. "Now, Tom," he said more calmly, "I know you're putting yourself out. I won't forget it. And the men I'll be dealing with won't forget you either." He patted Huerta's arm. "There's nothing to worry about, Tom. You have a legitimate reason to be in the sheriff's office. No one's going to question that. So all you have to do is keep this operation to yourself. And nothing can happen. These forms are perfect."

"Nothing can happen! I answer the phones, Bishop Dowd. I already took a call from some guy, some *anonymous* guy, saying the sheriff should take a look in Haley's Funeral Home. Saying

Father Vanderhooven's body was in there. Saying he was murdered."

Dowd gasped. "What did you say you'd do?"

"I didn't say anything. Didn't have to. The guy hung up."

"What did you *do*?"

"Nothing." Sweat ran down Huerta's cheeks.

Bishop Dowd pressed his hands against his thighs to stop the
shaking. "Good. Good. Now, Tom, of course you realize Father
Vanderhooven was not murdered. We're not dealing with anything
like that. If there was a murderer loose, I would be—"

Huerta held up a hand. "Look, Bishop Dowd, I don't want to
hear any more. I'm just sorry I got myself involved in this at all. I
did it because a bishop of the Church asked me. I guess I should
have known better, but I assumed being a bishop meant something." Dowd started to speak, but Huerta held up his hand again.
"I'm in this too far to back out. I'll handle these forms. I know
what to do with them. But don't think the problem of that call is
gone. Every call that comes in to the office is taped. And if the guy
who called makes a fuss, the sheriff'll check the tapes and he'll find
the call. And he'll find me."

Dowd's hands shook but he kept his voice steady. "Unless you
can get the tape and erase it, eh, Tom?"

Huerta glared at Dowd. He shook his head, grabbed the manila
envelope, and strode away.

19

AT JUST SIX P.M. Patsy Luca walked into the waiting room at the Self-Help Center. Already she hated this assignment. This was not what she had become a detective to do. Forcing down the urge to square her shoulders and stride through the clumps of limp-looking men and women waiting for the soup line, or for vouchers for whatever miserable, paint-peeling, bug-infested, drug-filled dive they would spend the night in, she walked slowly to the women's-center door. In her white pants and flowered blouse she looked no different from anyone else in the center. She hated the pants, she hated the blouse; they were gifts from her mother. But most of all she hated being without a gun.

She pulled open the women's-center door and had to fight the urge to turn and run. The room stank of defeat, of hopelessness, of being trapped. In that instant she was fifteen again, standing in her mother's nine-by-twelve living room in Yuma, watching a soap on TV, listening to Jimmy, the baby, working up to a scream because his diaper was full, smelling the crap in the diaper, smelling the defeat that filled the house. The fear that had welled up in her then filled her now. She forced herself to step forward. "I'm Patsy Luca," she said to the sandy-haired woman by the desk. "I got here as soon as I could. I'm just so relieved that you're going to take me away from . . . from everything." She could feel her face flushing from humiliation.

"I'm Beth Landau. You talked to me on the phone. But Patsy, we didn't decide where you'd be staying. The place we're going is full."

Patsy couldn't believe it. The panic in her voice was real as she said, "No! I've got to go! I've got to get out of here."

"If you don't have money, I can get you a voucher for a room in one of the hotels that cooperate with us."

"No! I can't stay here in town. My husband, my *ex*-husband, will kill me."

"Patsy, he won't know where you are."

"Oh yes he will. He's got friends all over. And none of them work; they just hang out. And now they're hanging out looking for me. He'll kill me!"

Beth laid a hand on Patsy's arm. "Patsy—"

Patsy wanted to smack the side of her hand into the woman's wrist. She couldn't blow the whole job, not here, not before she even got on the bus. Her voice was shaking as she said, "He smashed three of my ribs the last time. He told me if I left him he'd find me and he'd break the rest of them, one by one. Don't you believe me? Do you want to see my scars?" She grabbed her blouse as if to pull it free. Her face was red, she could feel it.

Beth sighed. "Okay. I think you're probably worrying too much, but if you're that frightened, then we'll make room for you. But you'll have to sleep in the storeroom. I can roll a cot in there and—"

"Anyplace is fine. I'm just so relieved." Patsy was relieved, relieved to be going, relieved that she wouldn't have to talk her way out of showing her scars—her five-year-old scars.

Beth turned to the others. "Okay, let's go, then."

Two young women stood up and began to gather their belongings. In a carrier an infant slept. A toddler in an Olympic Crawling Team shirt lay on his back across two plastic chairs. A dark-haired boy and girl sat huddled by the legs of the chair. Facing the group, Beth Landau said, "I want to emphasize how important it is that we keep the location of the house where we're going secret. If its location gets out, the house will be useless. And more important, we could all be in danger. You understand?"

Patsy muttered, "Yes."

"You'll be gone for a few days. You won't be able to make any calls. Is there anyone you need to reach?"

"No."

"You sure?" The question was directed to Patsy. "There's no second chance."

Patsy nodded.

"Okay, then come on. We were just waiting for you."

Patsy squeezed her lips together and stared at the floor. By the time she looked up, the other women were out the back door.

She made a quick survey of the desk, but found no phone messages, no notes. There wasn't time to open drawers. Grabbing her satchel, she followed them, catching up with Beth by the van. "Listen," she said, "I really appreciate your waiting for me and all. If you need any help driving, I'm good behind the wheel. I've had to make a few fast getaways." Before Beth could respond, she climbed into the front seat.

After the first half mile through the tail end of rush-hour traffic, the kids in the back had settled down. The mothers were looking out the window or thinking—whatever, it was quiet.

"You said you don't have children, Mrs. Luca?" Beth asked.

"Yeah. I don't like kids."

Beth's eyes widened.

Patsy restrained a smile. It was the truth; it amused her to announce it, particularly to someone like this motherhood type. "What about you? You have kids?"

"No."

"Ah." Patsy nodded knowingly.

"But I like children."

"But you don't *have* any."

"Well, things don't always work out as you'd like. You know that."

The freeway was coming to an end. The van pulled off, over the last overpass, and quickly right onto the Mesa detour. The late-afternoon sun hung in the brown sky. In the distance loose-packed dirt swirled in the hot air.

"Dust storm," Patsy commented.

"It's moving north. We won't be anywhere near it."

"McDonald's!" one of the kids in the back called out. Patsy could see Beth's shoulders tense. She had told them there would be no stopping for food.

"So what happened that you don't have kids?" Patsy prodded. There was no answer. It was a pushy question. She *was* pushy. It made her good in this job. When Stu needed someone tracked through the bars in south Phoenix, she was one of the ones he called. But this subtle business wasn't her thing. Stu knew that. He never should have gotten her into this. Make her a better detective, more rounded, he'd said. She didn't want to be more rounded. Skip tracing through south Phoenix suited her fine. She had a good rep there. The word had gotten around. She'd seen to that. So why'd she have to be more fucking rounded? She hated this job. She needed the money, but not that bad. She could have just said no. She sighed. And let Stu Wiggins call her a wimp?

Turning to Beth Landau, she asked, "You married?"

"No."

The answer was abrupt; it suited Patsy's mood. She said, "You've *never* been married? But you must have lived with a guy, right?"

Beth cut into the center lane and passed the Pontiac that had been in front of them.

"So you lived with a guy, but you're not now, huh? What happened?"

"It didn't work out."

Ignoring the indication of finality, Patsy said, "How come? Another woman, huh?"

"No."

Patsy laughed. "They all say there's no one else. Then one night you're at your local having a beer and there he is with some blonde. And you don't need a crystal ball to tell you that they haven't just met, right?"

"It wasn't like that."

"Oh, a cult, huh? I had a friend whose old man got hooked up with a cult. He went off to the swami's and they didn't let him out for months, and then the guy was so wiped out from getting up at four every morning that he couldn't get it up anyway. Even if he'd had the urge, and he didn't. He was too spiritual." Patsy laughed. "Was what happened to your boyfriend like that?"

Beth laughed. "Yeah, a cult. Just like that except with his cult they go off and don't come back ever. And no women allowed."

Beth pulled the van into the right-hand lane. They passed a motel with a neon saguaro cactus, a boarded-up store, an abandoned car wash.

"Come on," Patsy said, "you can tell me about it. You listened to my problems. You took me in." She paused. "But maybe you don't think my listening is worth anything. I mean, I don't have any degree in social work from a college like you do."

Beth shrugged. "It's the old story. The guy was using me. It took me a long time to realize it, but the important thing is I did realize it, and the whole thing was over. And I'm a lot more aware with the guy I'm seeing now."

"What's this guy like?" Patsy cringed as she spoke. She hated boyfriend talk. It was almost as bad as listening to women carrying on about their kids. God, to have anybody think *she* was interested in this kind of stuff . . . But she wasn't going to get any more on the priest, that was for sure. She'd better at least find out about the new boyfriend.

Beth veered back into the left-hand lane. "The drive is going to take another hour. You might want to catch a nap."

From the back seat came the gummy smell of small children. One of the mothers was humming softly. Patsy gritted her teeth. She hated the smell, the sound, the van, everything about this assignment. But dammit, she was not going to come up empty on this trip. Even if she had to look like the biggest wimp in Maricopa County. She said, "Your boyfriend, what does he look like? I mean will he be up there at the place we're going?"

"I doubt it. He comes sometimes, but he's not going to bother you. Don't worry about that."

"But if I see a man up there, how will I know it's him and not someone else?"

Beth nodded. "Look, you don't need to worry. He's a nice guy. Besides, no one else knows where the house is. That's why I'm so fussy about keeping it a secret."

"But how will I know it's him?" Suddenly, the note of desperation wasn't phony.

"He's about six foot, dark hair, no beard or mustache. He'd be wearing cowboy boots, jeans, work shirt."

"That could be anyone." Patsy swallowed as loudly as she could. "I know you're trying to protect us, but my husband would kill me if he found me. And some of these other guys must be just as bad. If one of them followed us and broke in, how would we protect the kids?"

"Patsy, everyone's in the same boat you are—"

Patsy cringed.

"Trust me. The phone's locked. No one can call out. I've got protection. The place is on a hilltop; we can see for a mile in any direction."

"But—"

Beth caught her arm. After a quick glance at the women in the back she shook her head and said in a low voice, "The one man who used to be a problem . . . No one's going to be a problem."

So someone had bothered Beth, but it wasn't the dead priest. A dead man, a past threat Beth could have explained. Patsy sighed in relief, genuine relief. There would be a gun there. There would be a phone, with a lock that she could handle. And she would have something to report.

20

THE IDEA OF GOING BACK to her own motel and showering had crossed Kiernan's mind, but she shoved it on out. Philip Vanderhooven's motel in Phoenix was on her way, and for what she had to say to him, rumpled and sweaty was good enough.

She left the Jeep in a white zone at the curb and ran—fueled entirely by anger—along the walk to room 107. Steam rose off the macadam in the parking lot. Did this city never cool off, she wondered as she knocked on the Vanderhoovens' door.

No answer.

She knocked again, although she knew the effort was futile.

Furious, she checked the cocktail lounge and the restaurant, mirror-image rooms divided by a long stair-step waterfall. Each held plenty of potted palms, plenty of men in bolo ties and seersucker Bermuda shorts and women in white slacks or sundresses, but no Vanderhoovens. And they had left no word at the desk.

Kiernan walked slowly back, keeping to the covered walkway. The Jeep was sitting in the sun; no need to question how hot it would be inside. It was hard to say which was getting to her most strongly: the heat, the headache, or the fact that she had won barely one round in this game. She turned and banged hard on the Vanderhoovens' door.

To her surprise, she heard footsteps behind it, shuffling footsteps. Then it opened.

Grace Vanderhooven looked awful. It was obvious she had been sleeping. Her eyes were still half-closed; streaks of mascara made thin arcs down her cheeks.

"Kiernan O'Shaughnessy," Kiernan said. "The detective from last night?"

"Oh, um, yes." She took a step back.

Gratefully, Kiernan stepped into the cool. "Is your husband around?"

She looked slowly around the room. "I don't think so."

Kiernan shut the door. "Would he have left a note telling you where he was or when he'd be back?"

"A note? No."

"Have you looked?"

She shook her head stiffly. "No need. Philip wouldn't do that. He knows I'll wait." She gazed around the room more slowly, mechanically, as she had surveyed her son's room the previous night. Vaguely Kiernan wondered what had caused this habitual reaction in moments of stress. It was as if Grace were searching the blue brocade sofa, the mauve armchairs, the wet bar, the arrangements of irises and day lilies, for some sign of why she herself was there.

"Let's sit down." Kiernan took her arm, led her to the couch and sat next to her. She started to remove her hand, but Grace grabbed it with fingers so cold that Kiernan started. Grace's hand shook, and Kiernan expected to see tears welling in her eyes, but her expression hadn't changed. And Kiernan realized that the welling sorrow was her own—sorrow for this woman and the grief she hadn't yet faced. She left her hand in Grace's, thankful that, despite her lack of bedside manner, she could convey some comfort this way.

Grace's eyes moved slowly downward, as if the effort of holding her head up had become too great. Her pale blue silk robe reinforced the pallor of her skin. Whatever sedative she had taken, it was too much. And she was in no shape to be left alone.

Kiernan sighed, eyeing the wet bar across the room. She could use a scotch. It was the one thing that might improve this wretched evening, the one thing she couldn't have, not next to a woman who had swallowed who-knew-how-many downers.

But shielded by her half-drugged state, Grace Vanderhooven might find it easier to answer some questions now than she otherwise would. Starting with the least threatening issues, Kiernan said, "Mrs. Vanderhooven, do you remember five leather-bound books your son had in his bookcase?"

"Books?"

"Big leather books. The titles were in Latin."

"In the bookcase?"

"Right. The first four books were real. But the fifth book, Mrs. Vanderhooven, was hollowed out. It was a place to hide things."

Grace nodded. She had turned her head to face Kiernan, but there was no change in her eyes.

"Mrs. Vanderhooven, had you seen those books before last night? Were they family heirlooms?"

Slowly she shook her head.

"Had your son mentioned them to you?"

"No. There were a lot of things Austin didn't talk about. Very . . . private, that's the word he used, private. Always kept secrets, even as a little boy. I told him, 'Austin,' I said, 'it's like you think if you open your mouth, I'm going to stick my hand down your throat and yank out your soul.' "

"What did he say to that?"

Grace laughed a weak laugh. "Nothing. He was very *private*."

"Private with everyone, or just you?"

"Not with *her*." Her fingers tightened on Kiernan's hand.

"Her? His girlfriend?"

"Her."

"What about his other friends?"

Grace stared blankly.

"Did Austin tell his secrets to his other friends?"

"His friends!"

"Did he mention a friend here named Elias Necri? Dr. Necri?"

Grace snorted, issuing a sound that would have appalled the public Mrs. Vanderhooven. "Him! Austin talked about him. Elias, the doctor. Austin envied this Elias his freedom, his vacation trips, the parties, the women. He never said so—secretive!—but a mother knows. Austin missed that type of thing, but of course he'd never have admitted it." She swallowed but it was too late to dam up the emotion. A tear wavered at the corner of her eye. "Poor Austin. He died before he had a chance to know what he wanted. How could he die? How could he?"

Kiernan still held Grace's cold hand in her own. "Mrs. Vanderhooven," she said when Grace's tears had subsided, "is it possible that Austin might—"

The door banged open. Philip Vanderhooven strode in, pushing back a clump of damp blond hair. His eyelids were puffy, his eyes red and watery. The clenching of his jaw created thick pouches at the corners of his mouth. He was halfway across the room before he reacted to the women on the sofa. "Grace, do you realize what you look . . ." His voice softened. "If you're going to stay up, why don't you put some clothes on?"

"You want to talk to her, don't you?" she said, pulling her hand free of Kiernan's.

"Yes." Keeping his gaze on his wife, he waited. But Grace Vanderhooven made no move. Finally, Philip shrugged and said, "So, Miss O'Shaughnessy, what have you found out?"

"That Joe Zekk called you in Maui."

Vanderhooven's eyes widened. "Zekk? Austin's friend from the seminary? Why would he call me?"

"You tell me."

"He didn't."

"Fine!" she snapped.

"Miss O'Shaughnessy—"

Kiernan stood up. "I don't know what your game is here, but the biggest impediment to this investigation is you. You barge ahead and annoy Beth Landau so much that by the time I'm ready to interview her she's primed to snap at the simplest question."

"You're a professional, I'm sure you—"

"This isn't a proficiency test! You didn't recommend me to Bishop Dowd to see how many hurdles I could jump. Then there's the sheriff. As of noon there was no sign the sheriff had been notified."

"Bishop Dowd was handling that. He said, Miss O'Shaughnessy, that he would contact his parishioner at the sheriff's office this afternoon. I'm sure he did."

"Well, you have more faith than I do. Or maybe more contact with Dowd. I haven't been able to reach him all day. He was to give me some important photographs this morning."

"I'm sure," he began in the same tone he had used with his wife, "that the bishop—"

"Look, I agreed to try to find the facts of your son's death before Monday. I can't do that if I have to plow through the roadblocks you people are throwing up. Either you want your son's death investigated or you don't." She picked up her purse and slung the strap over her shoulder.

Vanderhooven spoke quietly. "What exactly have you discovered, Miss O'Shaughnessy?"

"Are you prepared to cooperate—"

"You have a contract."

"A contract with Bishop Dowd."

He turned and walked quickly to the bar but made no move to pour a drink. His cheeks were flushed—with anger? Sorrow? Both? Turning he said, "The stress is getting to us all. I had no intention of undercutting your investigation. It's not my policy to interfere with the person I recommend. Now let's decide exactly what we're talking about here."

Kiernan glanced down at Grace Vanderhooven. Her expression revealed nothing other than her medicated state. The desperate sadness of a few minutes ago had faded. Kiernan walked over to the bar and said, "There are the things I need to know if I'm to continue the investigation. First, the sheriff. If I don't have proof he was notified today, that's it."

Vanderhooven nodded.

"Second, Zekk. Why was he calling you? I want to know all about this man, and what his relationship with your son was."

Now Philip did make a drink, picking out a handful of ice cubes, unscrewing the bottle, and pouring the pale liquid well up the glass. Making no move to offer her a drink, he took a long swallow. "Miss O'Shaughnessy, I sympathize with your complaints. I will speak to the bishop. He will get in touch with you." His tone left no question. "As to Joe Zekk, he did call me there. He said he was concerned about Austin, that Austin had become increasingly withdrawn."

"Withdrawn? Specifically, what did Zekk say?" she asked, thinking of Vanderhooven's death, the kind a depressed person might come to.

Philip shook his head. "I don't know more. I wasn't about to pay some guy for his opinion about my son's behavior. Particularly, Joe Zekk."

"So you know Zekk."

Vanderhooven took another quick swallow of his drink. The ice cubes clacked back in a half-empty glass. "I only met the boy once, shortly after Austin entered the seminary. Grace and I were in New York. We took them both to dinner." Fingering the lip of his glass, he said, "Zekk was a complainer, a kid out to cut corners, the type of boy who giggles at smutty words. Hardly seminary material."

"Why would Austin keep in touch with someone like him?"
Vanderhooven shook his head.

"When Zekk called you he must have had an angle, some theory about why Austin was depressed, perhaps?"

"I didn't let him get that far. As soon as he mentioned spying I cut him off."

Kiernan watched as Philip took a long swallow of his drink. Hiding behind that glass, she thought. And what was he concealing about the Zekk exchange? Had he agreed to pay Zekk? Had he merely considered the offer briefly, but nonetheless felt compromised? Or had Zekk hit on suspicions he held himself but he couldn't face? "Mr. Vanderhooven, Zekk was making you a business proposition. What did he offer to find out?"

"I told you, I never gave him the chance."

"When you refused, didn't he dangle some information, some observation in front of you?"

Vanderhooven slammed down his glass. "He wouldn't have dared."

Behind them Grace started and then settled back on the couch. Philip busied himself reconstructing his drink. And Kiernan watched his abrupt movements, wondering just what Joe Zekk had suggested that so outraged him. When he turned back to her she said, "We need to know what Zekk knew, or suspected—"

"He *knew* nothing. Austin was not the type of man who would confide in Joe Zekk. Austin didn't confide in anyone. Never had. He would not begin with someone like Zekk."

Kiernan took a breath. Speaking even more calmly to balance Philip's mood, she said, "Can you give me directions to his place."

"It's somewhere up in the mountains past Globe. I don't know any more than that," Philip added in a softer voice, glancing at his sleeping wife. The tension in his face had not lessened, but the look of anger had given way to a general tautness. "What's the third thing you needed?"

"Access to Bishop Dowd, and the photographs he took of Austin's body."

Philip's eyes flashed. "In the church!"

Checking Grace out of the corner of her eye, Kiernan said, "Yes. Didn't the bishop tell you about the photos?"

He, too, glanced at his sleeping wife. "No. What the hell did he—?"

Lowering her voice, Kiernan said, "Those photographs show that Austin did not have the flexibility in his shoulders to get his hands into the position Dowd found them in. The photos are clear enough to make any sheriff think twice before saying Austin died by his own hand."

His fingers pressed white on the glass. "I will not have that type of picture of my son shown to anyone. Even if they in themselves prove Austin—"

Grace murmured.

Philip lowered his voice. "—didn't do it, once word of them got out everyone we know would be talking about them, speculating about them, and about Austin, and us. Look at my wife; she can't take much more of this. And certainly not that!"

"Mr. Vanderhooven, I know this is hard on you, both of you. I've had experience investigating things people want to keep hidden, and believe me, very little stays hidden forever. You will be better off seeing those photos, dealing with them now, rather than having them surface in six months, or six years. Or forever wondering if someday your wife will answer the phone and it will be someone who's got a set of prints."

"It's Bishop Dowd who has these pictures, not some common blackmailer. He will destroy them. You will forget they existed. Do you understand!" He banged the glass down again.

"Philip!" Grace murmured.

Vanderhooven ignored his wife. "Miss O'Shaughnessy, you will obey my instructions. Or you will be off the case."

Kiernan breathed deeply, trying to control her anger. "Your son was set up. Someone killed him, and you would let that person go free, let your son be branded as a suicide, or worse, because you're afraid to know the truth about him."

"Consider our arrangement over."

Kiernan took another slow breath. Austin Vanderhooven's memory would not be sacrificed to his parent's fear of humiliation. "I know how you feel, believe me. I know how you'll feel if you suppress the truth too long to vindicate your son." She shut her eyes momentarily, and when she continued her voice was colder. "Regardless of the personal arrangements you and Bishop Dowd may have, my contract is with him. Bishop Dowd hired me to find the truth, and that is what I will do."

21

IT WAS NEARLY SEVEN-THIRTY when Kiernan walked into her motel room, still fuming from her scene with Philip Vanderhooven. She understood Philip's desperate urge to bury the questions about Austin with him. She knew that was impossible, that Philip would realize it was impossible, and that that realization would come too late for Austin, and for this investigation.

A sensible person, a sensible businesswoman, would get off the case right now, she told herself. She could call Chase and have him negotiate a settlement, a damned good settlement. She could probably get the full twenty-five thou. Instead, what was she doing? Working on a case that her client would be pressured to drop, doing it for no more money than she'd get if she flew home now, and all because she couldn't stand to have Austin Vanderhooven branded as a suicide or a pervert.

And because she had to know the truth. And, she admitted, she wasn't about to be bullied off the case.

She dialed the number for the archdiocese, and when there was no answer there she dialed Dowd's residence. Gone for the evening, the housekeeper, a Mrs. Johnarndt, said. Yes, she would certainly tell him Miss O'Shaughnessy had called, again. She understood he could call her no matter how late. But she couldn't say how late he might be; she was, after all, only the housekeeper.

Dowd was probably sitting five feet from the phone! Kiernan resisted the urge to slam down the receiver. If the Catholics are right, I should get a couple of hours off Purgatory for this.

She looked toward the bathroom, the wonderfully synthetic luxury of the bathroom. She'd never have admitted it to Sam Chase, or even to Brad—it doesn't do to have your houseman laugh at you —but she loved all the accoutrements of motel bathrooms: the spotless tile, the endless supply of tissues, the little bottles of shampoo and conditioner. At home she never bothered with conditioner —her hair was too thick, too curly, too short—but in a motel she smeared it on every time she got in the shower. She lolled under the endless supply of hot water, letting the soap melt down to nothing. When there was a bottle of bubble bath, she dumped the whole thing into the tub at once and let the bubbles cascade over the sides. She used each towel only once, wadded it up and tossed it on the floor. And, in penance, she left the maid a tip worthy of a maharajah.

She picked up the phone and dialed Brad, picturing Ezra bounding toward the phone, tail smacking into whatever Brad had left on a table. She missed Ezra. It would be nice to have a canine head to scratch. She missed Brad, too. The phone rang. It would be almost dusk in San Diego. Were Brad and Ezra loping along the beach? Brad with his wiry, sun-bleached hair flying out in all directions, his San Diego Chargers T-shirt spanning the muscles he'd worked so hard to restore during his convalescence, and a grin of pleasure that transformed his unquestionably ugly face into one that drew smiles from every woman on the beach.

Brad Tchernak was hardly what she had had in mind when she advertised for a housekeeper. But he had arrived—not called, just arrived—with the best lasagna she'd tasted, an instant love for Ezra, and a need for a job with lots of small tasks to keep him busy while he figured out what was left in a life without the thing that had always been central to it. Kiernan knew that dilemma intimately. And Brad, she observed as the months passed, was handling it better than she had after she'd been fired from the coroner's office. For her the adjustment had been more philosophical. For Brad it meant redefining the focus of nearly every activity: learning to eat a meal without wondering if this combination of food would make him faster off the line of scrimmage, to run for pleasure rather than endurance, to think beyond the football season.

No answer. She replaced the receiver, stripped off her sweat-sodden clothes, grabbed a towel, and started for the shower . . .

Bud Warren would be an easy interview, just to verify Elias Necri's alibi. Either Necri had been up in the mountains dining with the oil-shale man or he hadn't. An easy loose end to tie up tonight. She dialed the number Necri had given her.

He answered on the first ring. "Warren here."

"Mr. Warren, I'm Kiernan O'Shaughnessy—"

"Necri's detective." Was that laughter in his voice? "You had dinner?"

"No."

"Neither have I. Pick your ethnicity and time, and ask me whatever you want."

The Warren interview was business, but the man sounded pleasant. Was this the cosmic compensation for Brad Tchernak's not answering the phone? "Mexican. Eight-thirty."

Kiernan hadn't asked for a description, but there was no mistaking Bud Warren when she walked into Enrique's. He was the lone male idling by the potted palm near the door. He was tall—he had spoken with the assurance that comes more easily to a tall man—and his dark brown hair was just beginning to show featherings of gray. He didn't have the star quality of Elias Necri—he was probably twenty years older—but there was a rugged appeal to him.

As they headed to the table, he patted her arm.

The small square dining room, with its dark wooden tables, hard wooden chairs, and tile-accented white stucco walls, looked as if it had come from a kit marked Mex. Rest. Three-generation families were gathered around tables, laughing and talking in Spanish. Their exuberance was echoed by the music that came from a radio near the kitchen. Warren's voice, deep but with a sharpness that cut through other sounds, was just loud enough. A vague overlay of Western drawl—superimposed on what, she couldn't tell—suggested he was a man who had spent years in the Southwest.

They ordered beer, and after the waiter had arrived with the bottles and glasses, Warren said, "So tell me, how'd you become a detective?"

"Got fired from my last job."

"Doing autopsies?"

"Right. I missed a key indicator in one of the postmortems. There was a lot of insurance money at stake."

"And they fired you? For one mistake? Couldn't you have fought it?"

She shrugged, trying hard to maintain a dispassionate air. "I probably should have. There were plenty of people ready to support me. I could have forced them to keep me on. But that incident hit a nerve." It had ended more than her career.

"And?"

"And I gave my furniture to the Good Will and bought a ticket for Bangkok. For the next two years I roamed around Asia, a week in Rangoon—you can't stay longer in Burma—a couple of months in Indonesia, nearly a year in India, Nepal, Sri Lanka, another week in Rangoon, and so on."

"What made you come back to this country?"

She smiled. "I woke up one morning in Madras; all my clothes were filthy. Suddenly I wanted a California laundromat and a life that had some focus. So I bought a ticket to San Diego."

"And then?"

"Hey, which one of us is the investigator here? You certainly ask a lot of questions, and you knew a lot about me to begin with."

Warren leaned back, his blue eyes twinkling. "I'll take that as a compliment. I guess the oil business isn't too different from the investigation trade. I've gotten in the habit of finding out what I can. And frankly, lady, you've got a more interesting story than most."

"But you didn't know that before. Or did you?"

"I hate to tarnish my image here, but the truth is that I didn't do a background check on you. Elias just needed to talk." His smile faded. "Poor guy, it's been a helluva week for him. I'll tell you, the state Elias is in now, I wouldn't want him making a diagnosis on me. He was worried about his practice before all this. . . . But you want to know about Tuesday night when Austin died, right? Elias was with me from eight-thirty till nearly one in the morning."

Recalling Elias's explanation of the meeting, she said, "That's a long time to spend with a potential investor who has nothing to invest."

Warren shook his head. "Elias! Did he tell you he was an investor?"

"What was he after?"

"A job. He thought I might need a doctor on call at the site. Figured that might help pull him through financially till the retreat center opened."

"Sounds like a pretty meager income. He must be desperate."

"He *is.*" Warren signaled the waiter. To Kiernan he said, "The chimichangas are straight from the ovens of the Aztec gods."

"Do they take long? I really am starved."

"We'll get chips and some guacamole in the meantime."

Kiernan took a drink of her beer and pondered Bud Warren. There was an air of confidence about the man; it might not go too deep, but she could see how it would comfort someone as unstable as Elias Necri. Would Warren lie to protect Elias? She doubted it. She downed another swallow of beer and said, "I understand you've got a shale-oil process."

"In a general sense." He leaned forward. "You know much about shale?"

"Not a whit."

"Well, then let me tell you. Now you stop me if I'm boring you." Warren's eager expression belied his words. "Shale's the wave of the future. We've got billions of tons of rock out there with oil just waiting to be boiled out. Most of it's north of here, but we found enough in Arizona desert for my purposes. Doesn't take a great mind to see that someday, and not too far away, the Arabs are going to turn off the tap. Or maybe their tap will run dry. But we have lots of land with lots of rock, and lots of oil in that rock."

"I thought the problem was the expense of getting the oil out."

Warren nodded so eagerly Kiernan wondered if he had misunderstood her question. The radio music came back on. At the table behind her a woman began to hum. "Sure, it seems like a problem now, with Arab being dirt cheap. When there's no Arab, no price will be too big. And the technology's getting cheaper all the time. How long are you going to be here? Maybe you can get out to my site and see the process firsthand. The semiworks are about two hours east of town."

"Near Hohokam Lodge?"

Warren looked surprised. "Right."

"I might be up that way."

Warren beamed. "Great! I'll give you the top-of-the-line prospective investor's tour." He leaned forward as if staking out a claim, dropped his elbows onto the placemat, and hung his hands over the middle of the table. "What we do is grind the rock, put it in a huge retort—a covered vat—and cook the oil vapors out of the shale. The kerogen boils down and the oil rises off with the rest of the vapors. Now that part is standard."

Kiernan nodded, wondering how close Warren's works were to

Hohokam Lodge, and whether Austin Vanderhooven's undesirable friend Joe Zekk was also nearby.

"But that's not my process," Warren continued. "See, the problem with the system is how to get the gases free of the dust. You can imagine how much dust there is mixed with the gases. The conventional way is to run the whole thing through a cyclone, swirl the gases around and get rid of some of the dust, and then pipe it into a hot baghouse."

The guacamole arrived. Warren didn't look down. Kiernan started to ask about Zekk, but Warren was too quick.

"But you can't use just any bag, you see that, right? The stuff's seven hundred degrees. You've got to go with a ceramic that will withstand that kind of heat—the type of thing they used on the space shuttle. But the problem is the dust clogs the bag—"

"Like a vacuum cleaner."

"Exactly," Warren said, delighted. "But we're not talking changing bags every month. Here it's every few minutes. If you have to stop and change and then wait for the original one to cool and shed the buildup, you've got a big bottleneck. You can see that, right?"

Kiernan nodded. If Warren's operation was near Zekk, he could provide a handy escape hole in an area where just getting a glass of water could be crucial.

"Now, what I've got is, to put it simply, a mechanism to shed the residue from the bags so quickly that instead of taking off one bag and putting on another you can close off the cyclone momentarily, dump the bag, open the cyclone and keep going. Whole process takes less than thirty seconds." Warren took a large, quick drink of his beer.

Before he could get a breath, she said, "You said your works was near Hohokam Lodge. Is it anywhere near Joe Zekk's place?"

"Not far. But Zekk doesn't have anything to do with my works. Now the thing about the process is that whoever gets it will have shale for ten bucks less per barrel."

"You?"

He shook his head. "Warren Works is too small. I'll tell you, I was lucky to end up with the site. You know shale was hot a few years back when there were still D.O.E. synfuel funds. Bunch of us formed a consortium. Then when the synfuel funds went, the rest of them wrote off their losses. Left me—"

"Holding the bag?"

Warren stared, then groaned. "Actually they left me with the whole works, which was just fine by me. Particularly considering that they were the ones with the money."

"So now you'll put your process out for bids?"

"Right. I'm in touch with most multinational corporations."

The waiter arrived, smiling, with plates of steaming crispy chimichangas. The spicy smell filled the air. Even Warren abandoned his tale for the moment.

"Getting to Zekk's place will be my excuse for stopping by the works. Can you tell me how to get to Zekk's?"

Mouth full he nodded, then said, "I'll give you my map. His place is a few miles before mine. There's a metal Z by the turnoff."

"Wonderful," Kiernan said. "A man who is this good on directions and on food should have no trouble selling his hot-bag process."

Warren laughed. "The demo's already operational. You'll love it." He laughed again. "Well, I'll love showing it to you. I *hope* you'll love it. It'll take a couple of years to showcase the process completely. The multis aren't interested in whether the system works the first time, or a month after that. What they're asking is Will it still be clearing bags in a year, in two years? That's where their savings come."

"So you've got to run your site for two or three years then?"

"Right. And I'll tell you it can be a headache. Not the process. The process is great. It's fascinating to watch. And the noise. It's like the end of the world, with the pumps pulling up water from the river, the rush of hundreds of gallons of slurry, the rattling of the conveyor belts, and the rocks crashing down in the hoppers, and the hiss when the water hits the bag box to cool it down. You'll love it, really."

Kiernan forked another bite of chimichanga. Holding it midair, she said, "Just how much water does the whole process use?"

Warren smiled. "Now that could have been a problem. But I was lucky. Sylvia Necri's the architect for the archdiocese's retreat. I'd be in a bind without her. The retreat's got an informal agreement for rights to the Rattlesnake River water. She's leased them to me for the next three years. That's plenty of time for me. And she knows damned well she'll never break ground before that. Not with the archdiocese involved."

"But the water . . . how much are we talking about?"

"It's not just the process itself that takes water, it's the workers taking showers, flushing the heads, it's watering down the dust so we don't choke: the whole business of living."

"So how much?"

"Half an acre-foot per day, more or less."

Kiernan whistled. "You said Sylvia Necri leased you the allotment from the retreat, the retreat that Austin Vanderhooven had been in charge of building, right?"

"Yeah?"

"How come this little retreat had all that water alloted? That's a lot of water for the desert."

Warren laughed. "Little retreat? This isn't like Austin's little prayer dome in the desert with the pink glass window."

"Prayer dome with a pink glass window?" she asked.

But Warren was not about to be stalled. "I don't know how big-city you are, lady, but in these parts we don't call a seventy-room building on the apex of a hill, with meeting rooms, chapel, and bar, little. That's not to mention the tennis courts, putting green, saunas, and the pièce de résistance—the Olympic-sized pool."

"My God, that sounds like a palace."

Warren laughed again. "Pretty much what it'll look like, a Spanish-style cathedral-palace. You should see Sylvia's sketches. It's no wonder Austin was able to get financing."

Kiernan put down her fork. "Wait. I need to assimilate this. I've been thinking of the retreat as something that would replace Hohokam Lodge, a place where two or three priests could go for the weekend."

"Well, think about the Shrivers and the Kennedys and Cuomo and whoever else holds the purse and power on the U.S. Catholic scene. You don't invite Teddy Kennedy and tell him to take a sponge bath. You don't ask the cardinals of the Church to golf on Astroturf. You don't—"

"I get your point. And the whole project is under the control of the priest at Mission San Leo, right?"

"Sure, and Austin was perfect. He had the connections to raise the kind of money a place like that would take, and he wasn't beholden to anyone in the archdiocese."

The waiter paused beside the table. Kiernan nodded at her nearly empty plate. Warren looked protectively at his nearly full one. "And now," Kiernan said when the waiter left, "who inherits control?"

"Bishop Dowd. The parish is under his supervision."

"Whew! How very rewarding for the bishop."

Warren stopped his fork midair. "Do I catch a note of snide?"

Kiernan laughed.

Warren put down the fork. "Professional reticence, eh? Okay then, let's talk about what you'd like to do now. Music? There's a great jazz—"

Kiernan hesitated, remembering her rule against dating men involved in a case. But rules shouldn't fence in their makers. There was something very attractive about this man who chose his game and played it all-out. Rules could be adjusted. Warren smiled, and those blue eyes of his, which had been so intense moments before, twinkled. Rules could . . . She took a breath, reminding herself why she had made the rule to begin with. "I'd love to, Bud. But I'm worn out, and I have to be sharp in the morning. Investigating is strenuous business."

He ran his fingers over her hand. "I would like to see you again."

She smiled. "Likewise. But talk to me next week, after this case is over. I don't dare mix business and pleasure anymore. I got burned once early on, and I'll tell you, it looks real bad to have to get up on the stand and testify that you found a key fact under the pillow of a guy who turned out to be one of the biggest money-launderers in the Caribbean."

22

NORMALLY BISHOP RAYMOND DOWD would have enjoyed his companion's unspoken speculation when the waiter called him to the phone. But this was hardly a day for enjoyment, what with not having had a decent night's sleep all week, racing back and forth between the sheriff's office and Sylvia Necri's apartment, avoiding the detective, and now this dinner with Bishop William Harrington, the man some had begun touting as successor to the archbishop. Harrington had barely settled into his seat before he started nosing around about Vanderhooven's death. Dowd's thoughts ricocheted off his skull. He hadn't dared to order a third drink, and he'd barely tasted his beef Wellington. He took the call in an alcove off the bar. "Bishop Dowd here."

"Dowd, what the hell got into you taking pictures of my son?"

Dowd stiffened. It took him a moment to think what Vanderhooven was talking about. When he did, he smiled. "You could call it foresight. Those pictures convinced the detective Austin couldn't have got himself into that position."

"You mean to tell me that my son is hanging there with his prick sticking out, and you run to get your thirty-five millimeter like some goddamned tourist?"

How much had Vanderhooven had to drink? He sounded as if he could slip out of control any moment. Wired and exhausted himself, Dowd could nonetheless spot the signs. An apology, even an explanation, would have calmed Vanderhooven down. Another time Dowd would have given both. Now he was too tired to placate Vanderhooven. "She asked about the knots. It was a good thing I had those prints."

"What's the matter with you, are you some kind of pervert, Dowd? What's going on in the Church here? Now look, Dowd, I want those photographs destroyed. I want them and the negatives here tonight. I'll destroy them myself."

The corners of Dowd's mouth twitched. "The detective, Mr.

Vanderhooven, she wants enlargements." He paused as long as he dared. "To see the knots better, she said."

"She's seen enough, dammit. Now get that film over here."

The smile took hold. "What shall I tell her then?"

"Think of something. Tell her the film was destroyed. Tell her anything."

"Doesn't matter, right? She won't believe it anyway." If he hadn't been through so much he would have controlled himself. But now there was no concealing the delight in his voice. Even Vanderhooven caught it.

"Dowd! Are you forgetting what's at stake here—pictures like that of a priest under your supervision? Pictures *you* took; if word of that got out, Dowd . . . You created this problem, you deal with it. You priests have plenty of practice convincing people. Think back to eating meat on Fridays. That was a mortal sin— straight road to Hell—for hundreds of years. Then all of a sudden it was fine. You guys pulled that off. Lying about the photos'll be a piece of cake."

Dowd winced. It was a sore point but not one he was going to defend now. "Mr. Vanderhooven, I share your concern about the film getting out. But as you mentioned, I am well aware of its potential. You can rest assured I'm taking good care of it."

Dowd could hear Vanderhooven's sharp intake of breath. "Dowd, maybe you think I won't use my connections in the arch-diocese—"

"You're right. I don't. Anyone you spoke to would want to know the content of the photos, and I would tell them. You'll just have to trust me."

When Philip Vanderhooven slammed down the phone, Bishop Raymond Dowd was still smiling.

23

KIERNAN HAD FORGOTTEN about her headache during dinner with Bud Warren. Now what exactly did that suggest? Whatever, the headache returned full force on the drive back.

She pulled the Jeep into the parking lot and jumped down, landing with a thud that reverberated throughout her head. "Dumb!" she muttered. She walked across the lot. Two more packages of Alka-Seltzer and a night's sleep—that would do it.

The insistent ringing of the phone came through the motel-room door. Jamming her key in the lock she opened the door and raced for the receiver. "Kiernan O'Shaughnessy here."

"Ah, Dr. O'Shaughnessy, this is Elias Necri. I hate to disturb you . . ."

"What can I do for you?"

"It's been a long day," Necri said, "and Austin's death, well, you can understand how I feel. We were close friends. It's so sudden, so, well, you know how it is."

She pictured his handsome face, the circles beneath his large, sad eyes. She sank onto the bed and waited for him to continue.

"After you left, I was thinking about Austin. I had patients, and that took my mind off him for a while, but whenever I was alone I kept coming back to the question of why he would kill himself, or be killed. And, well, Doctor, I realized that while we do want to present his affairs to the parish and the public at large, and even his family, in the best light, as his friend it is my duty to tell you everything I know, not to hold anything back. And besides," he said, his voice just noticeably lighter, "I'm sure you'd find out soon enough."

"Yes?" she prompted, ignoring his flattery. Pulling the receiver cord taut, she reached for the water glass on the desk.

"The thing is, well—I'm not making any accusations, you understand—but I just can't dismiss the question of Joe Zekk."

Me neither, Kiernan thought. In view of Philip Vanderhooven's refusal to discuss Zekk and his proposition, Necri's call could be a real boon. "Tell me about Joe Zekk. You said Austin called him a deadbeat."

"Austin didn't delude himself about Zekk. But he didn't break off the friendship, either." Necri sounded more relaxed, almost as if he was reciting a prepared speech. "They started seminary together. Zekk dropped out the next summer. That was years ago. But last year Zekk followed Austin here. He's not a Westerner. The mountains of Arizona aren't a place the average New Yorker elects to come."

"Austin chose Phoenix."

"There may have been professional reasons for that."

She reached for the water carafe. Too far. Hell, let the head throb! She sprawled forward on the bed. Speaking louder, over the pain, she said, "But something did draw Austin to Arizona. So maybe he talked up the area to Zekk, his friend."

"Perhaps," Necri said slowly. "And of course we can't always see what our friends see in their friends. But Joe Zekk, well, to be honest, he's not a guy I'd want to leave near an unlocked drug cabinet."

"You mean he's an addict?" That could open a whole new avenue of possibilities.

"No, no. Just a figure of speech."

"A crook?" she asked with less hope.

"Well, I don't know if I'd say a crook, but I wouldn't put money on his integrity either. That's the point: What was it that drew the two of them together? Zekk just wasn't the type Austin would seek out."

Fighting to conceal her frustration with the noncommittal Necri, she said, "So what's your conclusion?"

Necri sighed. "I don't know. I'm sorry. Now that I tell you this, it doesn't seem worth a call, does it?" He paused—giving her time to reassure him? Kiernan wondered. "Maybe," he went on, "it's just that Austin's death has unhinged me. You know if I hadn't seen his body hanging there . . . I don't know. But whatever Austin did see in Zekk, it was enough for him to pay Zekk two hundred dollars a month."

Amazed, Kiernan swung her legs over the side of the bed and sat up. Her head pounded in response. "Austin paid Zekk two hundred a month! Why?"

"I have no idea," Necri said.

"What do you mean you have no idea!" she shouted. "You've been thinking about this all day. You call me at ten P.M. Don't ask me to believe you have no idea about Zekk and the two hundred dollars!"

If he was affronted, he gave no indication. "Maybe I'm just too tired to come up with an explanation. In honesty, I was hoping you would."

Kiernan sighed. Clearly, Elias Necri was going to dribble out what facts or guesses he had at his own molasseslike pace. "How long had Vanderhooven been paying him?"

"Over a year. Maybe as long as Zekk lived out here."

"Could it have been a business arrangement?"

She could hear Necri's breath hitting the receiver. Then he said, "Not likely. Zekk's only business, if you can call it that, is marketing some pottery for the locals up there. Even if he sold boxloads to Austin, it wouldn't have come to two hundred dollars, not every single month."

"Okay, so the two hundred wasn't for the pottery. Then what?"

"I just don't have any idea. The best I can do is let you know about it and hope it somehow helps to clear Austin's name."

Kiernan sighed. "Okay. I'll give Zekk a go. Where can I find him?" she asked, hoping Necri might know of an in-town hangout of Zekk's.

"That I don't know. I don't know where he lives. Sorry."

His answer had come too quickly. If Elias Necri had been up to Bud Warren's place in the mountains, he'd passed Zekk's metal Z. He knew full well where Zekk lived. She had let him dribble out his bait long enough. Leaning back against the headboard, she said, "I guess this is a particularly hard time for you, Dr. Necri, this on top of your financial problems. And now there won't be any job at the retreat for you to escape to. With Austin dead, who knows what will happen to the retreat, right?"

His breath came heavy against the receiver.

She waited, expecting Necri to recover and attempt a diversionary move. When he didn't respond, she said, "So you've not only lost a friend, but your way out is gone, right?"

It was fully thirty seconds before he said, "I'll work things out. I'll just do it a different way."

"How? Not by working on call in the mountains, that's for sure."

Was that a gasp from him?

"What did you get in return for signing the death certificate?" She waited. Necri might have been a pro, but he was definitely out of his league in this game.

He hung up.

Kiernan rolled onto her stomach, and dialed Stu Wiggins's number. After the beep on his tape, she said, "First, Austin Vanderhooven's retreat is no little cottage in the mountains. It was to be more like a sandstone Taj Mahal. Lots of money, lots of power.

"Second, Elias Necri just called and tried to aim me at Joe Zekk. Does he want me to hassle Zekk, or just get out of town and leave our Dr. Necri alone? Think about it, and come by at nine in the morning. Oh, and Stu— Listen, there's someone at the door. I'll call you back."

She hung up the receiver; before she reached the door there was another knock.

"Who is it?" she called through the closed door.

"Sheriff's office. Open up."

She tensed. "Let me see some identification. Hold it up to the window." She pulled the drape. Parked by the window was a sheriff's department car. A man, thirty-ish, in tan uniform, held a shield against the window. She opened the door.

"Dr. Kiernan O'Shaughnessy?"

"That's right."

"I have a warrant for your arrest." He pulled out a card and began reading, "You have the right to remain . . ."

"Arrest! For what?"

Undaunted, he continued his Miranda recitation. When he finished, he pocketed the card and said, "Forgery and falsifying a public record."

"What public record?"

"Sheriff'll tell you that. He's waiting for you at the station. Bring what you need for the night."

"Wait. I have to make a phone call."

"You can make your call from there."

"At least let me take an Alka-Seltzer."

He shook his head. "The sheriff's waiting."

24

THE TRIP to Hohokam Lodge had taken well over two hours. They could have made it in an hour and a half if Patsy had been driving. Patsy's throat actually hurt from holding back; only once had she slipped and told Beth Landau to pass the goddamned—actually she hadn't said "goddamned"; she hadn't slipped that much— pickup that was going all of twenty miles an hour.

And the lodge! Patsy had pictured a lodge as a big stone country house where Rockefellers sprawled on leather couches under heads of moose and zebra, not a ratty, square wooden building with an oil heater in the fireplace and faded, stained sofas.

But she didn't get to see the living room for long. One minute all the "guests" were in there listening to Beth tell them they would find cereal in the kitchen in the morning and a list of work assignments posted on the refrigerator door, and the next minute they were zonked out in the tiny unheated cells that passed for bedrooms. No showers, no nothing. The whole place was dark and silent, as if someone had plopped the hood on a bird cage.

Patsy's cot almost filled all the space in the storeroom between the metal shelves and the windows. As soon as Patsy had seen the lodge, she'd known what her cot would be like: springs that poked out and squeaked every time she breathed; mattress rough as a dirt road after monsoon season, with a pissy smell. Still, she'd slept in worse places, plenty worse. For half an hour she investigated the contents of the metal shelves: generic-brand soap powder, paper plates, cartons of paper towels (white), cartons of toilet paper (single ply, white), a hundred-pound bag of rice, an equally big bag of potatoes, six packages of flour tortillas—what was with all this white? Was this some kind of social-work way to calm the guests? Or was it to save on food? No one was going to be asking for seconds here. Patsy reached into her purse, in the hope that she had thought to bring a chocolate bar. She hadn't. Disgusted, she sat on the cot and leaned back, squeakily, against the wall.

Were those footsteps in the hall? She held herself dead still.

Could it be the prowler Beth had told her about? Slowly, she got up. The springs squeaked. At the door she paused, listened. They were footsteps all right, but not the prowler's. Too soft to be a man's.

She eased open the door. There was no light in the hallway that separated the bedrooms from the living room. All the bedroom doors were closed. No light seeped from under any of them. It was dark, but she could just make out a figure heading toward the window at the far end of the hall. As Patsy watched, the shade was lifted and Beth Landau stood silhouetted by the moonlight. Patsy could see her peering out, moving her head very slowly, as if surveying the land outside.

Patsy stepped out. "What are you doing?"

Beth spun around. The moonlight showed the fear on her face.

"It's the prowler, isn't it? You were checking for the prowler."

"No. There's nothing to worry about." She put a hand on Patsy's arm.

Fighting the urge to shake it off, Patsy said, "Beth, *you're* worried." Reminding herself to stay in character, she patted Beth's hand. "Look, I'm awake. I'm strong. I can help you."

"It's okay."

"I know you think I can't take care of myself. Why else would I be here, right?" Beth's hand tensed on her arm. Patsy swallowed a smile of victory. "But I don't panic. I can help—if you're straight with me."

Beth pulled her hand free. "Look," she whispered, "it's no big deal, but I have had a prowler. He's never harmed anyone. He's never even come inside as far as I know. But it's just, well, I feel I ought to check."

"How often does he come?"

"Sometimes twice in a week, sometimes not for a couple of weeks."

Patsy walked to the front window and looked out at the hard ground that sloped down from the lodge, at the saguaro and ocotillo, at the bare, dry dirt. With all those stars and the moon, it was plenty light enough to spot a prowler out there. She leaned against the window frame, forcing Beth to stand in the moonlight facing her. Watching her reaction, Patsy asked, "Do you have any idea who he is?"

Beth ran her teeth over her lower lip.

"You do, don't you?"

Stiffly, Beth nodded. "I'm sure it's a friend of a friend, a guy in the neighborhood. He's not a danger to any of the guests here."

"What about to you?"

Beth shrugged, but her face remained tense. "He's not likely to hurt me, not physically. He's more of a nuisance than a threat."

"So why don't you call the sheriff when you see him?"

"Because I don't want to make things worse than they already are here. I've got women here who are poised right on the edge. All they need is to have the sheriff's men hanging around in the middle of the night. I can't do that to them."

"How long has this been going on?"

"Too long. I know that. It's just, well, the time is never right to deal with it."

Patsy wanted to shake her, to tell the dumb fool how to deal with this asshole. Instead, she swallowed hard and said, "What's this guy after?"

"I told you—"

"This place is five feet off the ground. From out there, you can't see anything unless someone's standing right by the window. No pervert's going to come back here week after week in hopes of seeing that. He's been inside, hasn't he?" When Beth didn't answer, Patsy grabbed her arm. She didn't shake her, not quite. "Hasn't he!"

"I don't know. Maybe. I couldn't prove anything. I thought something was gone. But it's not. Maybe it never was. I just have a feeling he's been in my office." She looked straight at Patsy. In the moonlight her face looked powder-white; even her freckles were pale. "But I could be wrong. Listen, you've got enough to worry about without—"

"Forget it," Patsy said, giving the arm a squeeze and releasing it. "It's good to think about somebody else's problems for a change. Look, if I can help you, it's going to make me feel a lot better about myself," she added, in the kind of social-work talk Beth would understand.

"Okay. If you see anything, knock on my door. It's the one at the end of the hall, nearest the office." She smiled. "And thanks, Patsy."

"Sure." Patsy walked back to her room, wondering how long she would have to wait to get into that office.

25

FEW THINGS aggravate a headache more, Kiernan thought, than being hauled into the sheriff's office in the middle of the night. What a great Alka-Seltzer commercial this would make: "Sheriff pounding on your head? Plop plop, fizz fizz."

The sheriff's deputy held open the gate in the pine counter. "Right this way, Miss—"

"Doctor," she snapped, without thinking. But the title had its effect.

"Right this way, *Doctor*," he said with slightly less assurance.

The county sheriff's department was lodged in a small weathered building with a covered walkway out front. It could have housed a sheriff when this area south of Phoenix was still Wild West. Everything about it was old, faded, and sere, as if the desert air had sucked it dry. It smelled of dust and ground-in grime and sour coffee.

Kiernan followed the deputy—tall, young, and apparently too dry of mouth to utter an unnecessary word—through the counter to the hallway that bisected the building. Above scuffed pine wainscoting the tan wall was dotted with clusters of thumbtack holes and rectangles of varying shades where notices had been hung over the years. Modern art, administrative style.

The deputy motioned Kiernan to the first door, into a room with a scarred wooden desk and two chairs. Silently, he indicated a chair for her, then reached into the drawer and came up with an ink pad and sheet with ten square boxes on it.

Kiernan recognized the booking form. "I'm not doing anything till I make my phone call, and until I talk to the sheriff," she said barely controlling her anger. This sheriff's department was not in Tempe, near her motel, but in the county of Mission San Leo. The deputy who had come for her had plunked her in the back of the patrol car, which smelled of ammonia and vomit. The window didn't open, and of course the car wasn't air-conditioned. The drive had taken half an hour. Four or five bumps had bounced her nearly to the ceiling; even small jolts had reverberated through her head. And the deputy had ignored every one of her questions.

"We'll do the booking first, Mi—, Doctor."

"I thought you said the sheriff was waiting for me."

"He is."

"Then please," she said through gritted teeth, "take me to him."

"Just as soon as we—"

"Now!"

"Just as soon—"

She leaned forward on the desk. "You book me, and you're talking a false-arrest charge. Not just the department but you personally, since you seem to be taking this upon yourself."

The deputy let a smile cross his tanned face. "You're from California, right, *Doctor*?"

She could see it in his small hazel eyes, that speed-trap mentality. "Right," she said, "but my boss isn't. He's a Phoenix lawyer."

The deputy ran his finger across the booking form. His smile did not fade.

This was one round she was not going to win this way. Taking a breath, she reconsidered. When she spoke her voice was calmer. "You know how much time you can waste going to court. Judges postpone. Lawyers can get one continuance after another. And that's before the trial starts. Every day that happens, you have to show up in court, on your own time. You know that. On a day when you could be in the mountains fishing, you'll be hanging around for a one o'clock court date." She didn't need to look twice to see that he'd had an experience like that. She said, "I used to work for the coroner's office. I know about that. But look, you and I are both just trying to save some time. You don't want to get hung up in court, and I don't want to spend time with booking and records and then hassle getting them cleared. The sheriff and I can handle this. Okay?"

"You worked for the coroner, huh?" he said, leaning back against the desk. "What'd you do?"

"Only one thing a doctor does there. And I'll tell you, in my line of work we didn't have a problem with recidivism." She laughed. It was a line that had worked before.

"Cut up stiffs, eh?" he said, smiling uncomfortably.

"Right." She put on another smile.

He shifted in his chair, started to speak, then changed his mind. He glanced toward the door, as if expecting someone to step in and make his decision for him. Then he drew his hand slowly back from the booking form. "Well," he said, "listen, I'll let Sheriff Grimm know you're here. He can decide . . ."

Sheriff *Grimm*? Not a good sign. She waited as the deputy hurried down the hall.

In less than a minute he was back. "Last door on the left," he said with obvious relief.

"Thanks." She stepped into the hall. Now that she was in control of the situation, the hallway looked less grimy, the wainscoting less scuffed.

The sheriff's door was open. His office was the size of the first room, furnished in the same style: one scarred wooden desk holding a blotter stained with rings from coffee cups or beer cans and smaller rings that could have been made by a shot glass. To the right of the desk was a metal bookcase, to the left a brace of file cabinets, and in front, one wooden chair. There was a smell to the room that was hard to name—a mixture of sweat, beer, dust, but mostly just the smell of staleness.

Kiernan looked at the man behind the desk and restrained a sigh. He could not have been more aptly named. Sheriff Grimm looked like a mummy: dark, dry, all sharp edges. He looked about fifty but might not be that old. The dry heat and wind, or the boredom of being a county sheriff, had carved lines around his eyes, beside his mouth, and vertically down his cheeks. His wiry dark hair was well mixed with gray. She glanced around the room, trying to get a hint of what he had expected from this job, but there was no picture of Grimm arm-in-arm with Bruce Babbit or Barry Goldwater, no framed citations or yellowed news stories lauding his triumphs. Whatever Grimm might have hoped the job would bring, it was clear from his expression and the weary slump of his shoulders, that he had settled for what he had got. It was also clear that in a hot, dull summer, she was a welcome diversion.

"Sit down, Dr. O'Shaughnessy. We're not often called upon to make charges like this. Very unusual." His lips parted again, showing long chalky teeth with spaces between them at the gumline. It was hard to tell whether he was smiling or baring his teeth.

"Sheriff, 'unusual' sounds like a doctor saying, 'This is a very interesting case.' The patient knows right off he's a goner." She sat down and leaned against the slat back of the chair. "What is the charge against me?"

"Surely you're prepared for it? You seem to have been quite well prepared to handle my deputy."

So that it was it. "If you mean am I prepared to insist on my rights, I am. You've dragged me out of my room in the middle of the night. And for all the answers your deputy gave, he might have been a deaf-mute. Now what is the charge?"

"Now, *Dr.* O'Shaughnessy, I know that my deputy did tell you the charge. "

"What he said was forgery and falsification of public records, and I know that can't be right. I've only been in Arizona two days and haven't been near a public office. Even if I wanted to, I haven't been in a position to forge so much as a mail-forwarding card."

Grimm nodded. "All the more amazing."

"Sheriff?"

"You're not licensed to practice medicine in this state. I'm right?"

"You are right. Now about the charge?"

Grimm's elbow rested on the desk. Moving only his forearm, he tapped the top sheet on a pile. "We've got a death certificate here. It's signed by you."

Kiernan's breath caught. Vanderhooven's death certificate! It had to be that. But Elias Necri had admitted to signing it. What was going on? "I did not sign any death certificate, and certainly did not forge anything."

Grimm nodded again, noncommittally. "According to Arizona revised statute thirteen dash two-oh-oh-two-A: 'A person commits forgery if, with intent to defraud, such person, one, falsely makes, completes, or alters a written instrument.' That's a felony, Dr. O'Shaughnessy."

Forcing back her rage, Kiernan said, "Be that as it may, Sheriff, I haven't seen Austin Vanderhooven's death certificate. It is Vanderhooven we're talking about?"

"It is."

"But I do know that Dr. Elias Necri signed that death certificate."

Grimm nodded once more, removed the top sheet from his pile, and passed Kiernan the next one. "This is a copy, of course."

She scanned the death certificate. The date was correct. The cause of death, heart failure. And the signature, her own! She moved the sheet closer. From the sharp curls of the *K* to the tail of the *Y,* it was *her* signature. She held it up to the light, looking for signs of erased pencil tracing. There were none. And no marks of hesitancy. It was *her* signature. What had she signed since she arrived? Nothing but the contract with Bishop Dowd, and that she had read. There was no way he could have switched sheets. She remembered all too well telling Dowd the penalty for falsifying a death certificate: a fine of $150,000, and four years in jail. Then it had been Elias Necri she had been thinking of, with Dowd as an accessory. She had given Dowd the figures simply to frighten him, although she was sure that the State of Arizona would not throw the book at one of their own bishops. But for an out-of-state detective there was no such assurance. A splashy case like this, with a sheriff who had bare walls to fill, with a district attorney on the make . . . It would call for a lot more than Stu Wiggins to get her off.

She took another breath. The heat of the closed room pressed on her skin. This whole thing had to be stopped before it came to trial, before the D.A. had an established interest, before Sheriff Grimm had invested more than an hour's time. She had to stop it here. "Sheriff," she said, sounding considerably calmer than she felt, "I can see why you were misled by this document. It's an excellent forgery. A work of art."

"Are you trying to tell me that you did not sign this form?"

"Exactly. Sheriff, I am a detective. I have a license to keep up. I also have a medical license. No way would I endanger them to come to Arizona and sign a death certificate for a man I never saw alive."

Grimm nodded, a mummy's nod.

Her armpits were sticky. "And, Sheriff, it says right here"—she pointed to the form—" 'Date of last medical observation.' How recently must an attending physician have seen the patient in order to sign the D.C.? A month, six weeks? There's nothing written in that space at all. This form would be invalid just on that basis alone. Only a fool would expect that to escape your notice."

Grimm nodded twice, then leaned back in his chair. "Very kind of you to say so, Dr. O'Shaughnessy. But a bit after the fact." The man even spoke like a mummy: no inflection, no emotion.

"Check Vanderhooven's body. I'm sure you *have* checked the body. You know damned well the man didn't die of heart failure without contributing causes."

"We can't say that, Dr. O'Shaughnessy."

"What do you mean, you can't say?"

"Body's gone."

"Gone!"

"Been cremated."

"But how?" she asked, amazed. "Don't you require an interment permit for disposal of remains?"

"We do."

"Who has to sign the interment permit?" she demanded.

Grimm's finger tapped the pile of papers. His face remained stiff, the upper lip retracted slightly, showing those chalky teeth. "The sheriff."

Kiernan leaned forward. "And you looked at that death certificate, with the name of an out-of-state doctor and nothing to indicate that doctor had ever seen the patient before . . . You saw a D.C. with the most common, most meaningless cause of death, heart failure . . . They all die of heart failure—the heart fails; they die. You saw all that and you signed the permit for them to cremate a Roman Catholic priest!"

He pressed his finger down on the papers. The knuckle went white. "Dr. O'Shaughnessy, we're not discussing—"

"But we are. Either you signed that form and you're trying to cover your ass—"

His fingers closed around the top sheet. "Are you accusing—"

"Damned right! Either you are too incompetent to sweep streets much less be sheriff, or there's another answer. The other possibility is that you did not sign that permit and whoever forged my name on the death certificate forged yours on the interment permit too."

Grimm didn't move. No nod, no nothing.

Her heart thumped against her ribs; her face was tight with rage. She took a breath to calm herself. "It'd be an easy thing to do, Sheriff: forge the form, stick it in your out box. How many forms do you sign in a week? More than enough so that you might forget a specific one. If for some reason you were going through your out box and came across that form and found your signature already on it, there would be no reason for you to go back and read it over. The probability is that you would never see the form at all. It would just be picked up, and one copy would go on to the mortician and the others to wherever they're filed."

He stared at her, yet appeared not to see her at all. The mummy stare. She leaned back against the slats of the chair, forcing herself to breathe more slowly. Sweat dribbled down her sides. From the front desk came the sound of a phone ringing. A low groaning sound came from the rear of the building. A prisoner? A dog outside? An echo of her own fear? Through the small high windows on either side of Grimm she could see no clouds, no stars, only darkness.

"Sheriff," she said, more evenly, "there is only one copy of my signature in Arizona, and that is on a contract I signed with Bishop Raymond Dowd of Mission San Leo."

"Bishop!" he exploded. "Well, lady, I can't speak for California, but here in Arizona bishops of the Church don't go around forging papers."

"Bishop Dowd has the only copy of my signature," she repeated, her voice controlled now.

"And a bishop of the Roman Catholic Church certainly could not steal into this office unnoticed and file away his forged form."

Kiernan restrained a sigh of frustration. "You're entirely right. Bishop Dowd couldn't have filed them. That, Sheriff, had to be done by one of your own people."

Grimm drew a long, angry breath. Kiernan waited. A minute passed, and another. She stood up. "I'm sure you'll be contacting me when you—"

"Sit down!"

She moved behind the chair and leaned on the back. "Sheriff. You can book me. You can hassle me. But my boss here is a lawyer in Phoenix. And when I call and tell him—"

"You'll get your call. Call your lawyer friend."

"I will. And you can bet that he'll be in contact with every local newscaster, and every reporter in the Valley of the Sun. They'll all be mentioning you. And they'll all be calling you incompetent.

And, Sheriff, I know for a fact that you were notified about Father Vanderhooven's body. You were told that it was in Haley's Funeral Home. Told that Vanderhooven had been murdered. The call was made today. Surely your incoming calls are taped."

Grimm's face turned red, his breathing was faster. "Lady, you have gone too damned far! You've just caught yourself in your own web. Now I'm going to check the tapes, every minute of every call we taped all day. And if I don't find this call you're talking about, I'm going to take extreme pleasure in adding obstruction of justice to the charges against you, and in making a complaint to the California licensing board."

"You'll find the call."

He yelled, "Harris! Get in here."

Kiernan turned as the door burst open. The deputy said, "Yes sir?"

"Put her in number one."

Harris reached for her arm.

"Hey," Kiernan insisted, "what about my phone call?"

For the first time Sheriff Grimm smiled. "I thought you said it was already on the tape."

26

TWO A.M., finally. Patsy Luca had been sitting on the storeroom cot for four hours. Two hundred forty minutes. Some humongous number of seconds. Three times she'd multiplied two forty by sixty and come up with three different answers. Math was one thing she wasn't going to win any award for. Meditation was another. Some weirdos would have come out of four hours of silence all refreshed and calm. Patsy Luca was hard-assed bored. Her back was stiff, her shoulders ached. The cot springs squeaked like a basement full of mice. The windowpane rattled in the night wind, and grains of dirt splattered against the glass. Nothing to cut the wind out there. She sat, nose to glass, hoping for a glimpse of Beth Landau's prowler. Even without her gun, she was ready for the pervert. Her biceps tingled at the prospect of him, face in the dirt, hands yanked up behind him. Had he really broken in, or was Beth just freaked? What was he after? She'd get the truth out of him. And the next time Stu Wiggins called her it wouldn't be just to *assist* another detective.

Patsy glared out into the empty desert night. The sky was dotted with bright stars. The moon looked like a big spotlight. But there was no prowler out there. Where the hell was he? Probably soggy with beer in front of some boob tube.

But now—finally—the time had come to make her move. She could feel her heart beating. The desert air had cooled, as if someone had switched off the burner. Shivering in her white pants and flowered blouse, she slung her backpack over one shoulder, eased open the door, and listened. The wind was playing the old house like a washboard. Every window rattled.

She peered into the hallway. It was black as a '47 Packard. Patsy half-smiled, remembering her triumph when she'd tracked down that stolen Packard to an alfalfa barn halfway to Tucson. That case had been a high-stakes job. She'd been, well, not scared, but worried about a couple of bouncers bouncing *her* against the sidewalk. Here the problem wasn't people she couldn't handle. Still, she couldn't let herself be caught, not before she got into the office. She couldn't come up empty.

Quickly she moved down the hallway, walking soundlessly as she neared Beth Landau's door. She looked through the archway into the living room; beneath the windows four lopsided patches of moonlight glowed on the floor. The window glass rattled against the moldings. Was it working up to a storm outside, or was she just turning chicken?

She crossed in front of the kitchen, moving carefully in the dark end of the room till she came to the office door.

The lock looked like no problem, but you could never tell. At least there was no dead bolt. It would have been a pushover if she could have used her Lock Aid Gun: Insert needle, pull trigger, and bam! Every pin in the lock goes snapping up and down. It could set those pins in a straight line on the first try.

And in a place like this, where everyone was on edge, it would wake up half the house.

Patsy pulled out her old tool case—"Pretty Nails," it said on the outside. It should have said "Pick and Rake." She grinned and slid the pick into the lock. Patsy was good at locks; she'd told Stu Wiggins that often enough. But it took all her concentration. She slipped the rake into the hole, feeling the pins as she pulled it back across them. Her eyes closed. Behind the office door, windows rattled.

The pins lined up. She pulled the knob toward her and turned it. Lifting up against the knob she opened the door slowly, eased herself in, and closed the door with care.

It could have been dusk inside the room, the moonlight was so bright. The walls were a light color, maybe green. A sofa with flowered cushions like the ones in the living room stood next to the door. Opposite it, under the window, was a big wooden desk. Its right side touched a tall file cabinet, and beyond that was a closet—hardly a great hideout, but better than nothing. The door slid open, revealing a raincoat and a pair of boots. It was, after all, monsoon season. Tomorrow it could be pouring. There could be flash floods out here, and the dry arroyos could be running full.

Patsy took out her penlight, pulled open the top file drawer, extricated the first seven files—A to G—took them into the closet, and closed the door partway. "Client files," she muttered. Pressing her teeth together she paged through the folders, skimming to keep the names from becoming real people, checking the men's names, writing them down. The files—all three drawers—referred to fifty-three males, none of them named Vanderhooven, Necri, Dowd, or McKinley.

An hour had passed by the time she pulled open the bottom drawer and found the first interesting thing, a liqueur bottle. Without a second thought she unscrewed the top and drank. Her eyes snapped open, and she had to smack her hand across her mouth to keep from coughing. What was this stuff? She held the offending bottle up to the light. It was eight-sided, about three inches wide; on the gold label was an adobe hacienda with a palm tree in front, and the name Culiacán. Culiacán? Patsy'd never heard of that. She could see why. No one in their right mind would drink the stuff. It tasted like powdered sugar and hot peppers.

She was tempted to jam it back into the drawer. Instead, she stuffed it into her pack. That was the problem with this type of case, working for someone else, there was no way to know what could be important.

Behind the divider in the bottom drawer was a manila envelope. In it was a deed, dated September 8, 1937. One John McKinley deeded thirty-six acres to the pastor of Mission San Leo. She made a note of the particulars and moved on to the desk. The bottom two drawers were filled with office supplies. *They* weren't important. The top drawer had pencils, paper clips, and in the back a packet of letters held with a rubber band. The return address varied, but the name was Vanderhooven. Now *that* was important. With a smile, she moved back into the closet.

She read the bundle of letters—love letters, letters that described the longings of the writer, of the priest-to-be, his speculations, his memories of licking Culiacán, that revolting stuff in the bottle, off the "furry little peaches" at the insides of Beth's thighs, his plans to bring an artist's brush, to stroke "the dark silky veil that hides my secret chamber." Patsy kept shaking her head. The letters read like something out of one of those *True Confessions* magazines her sister slavered over. So this was what they thought about in the priest houses! Stu would get a kick out of this.

She pushed herself up and jolted forward on numb legs. It was nearly four in the morning. Bracing her arm against the desk, she opened her tool case, extricated a small file, and trained her light on the phone lock.

Behind her the door opened! The light went on. Patsy jammed the file in her pocket and spun around.

Beth Landau stood in the doorway, holding a .38. It didn't take a detective to read the outrage on her face.

Patsy swallowed.

"You! My little friend in the car. So anxious to help me out checking the windows! So concerned about the prowler!"

Patsy swallowed again. How could she have let herself be caught! Caught with the names of all those husbands and boy-friends in her pack. There was no way she could ever remember more than a couple of them. The way things were going she could leave here real empty.

"You're the third person today who's been at me, Patsy. The others at least had legitimate reasons, but you . . ."

Patsy could feel her face flush. Not only was she going to leave here empty, but she was going to be responsible for exposing her connection to O'Shaughnessy. That was a lot worse than empty.

"I check and double-check everything so you can be safe here in the refuge. I drive around in town long enough to make sure no one's following, I keep the phone locked. Dammit, I give up most of my life for this place, and this is how you respond, by going through . . ." She stared over Patsy's shoulder. "By going through my files! Damn you! What were you looking for?"

Patsy's eyes filled. She squeezed her eyes shut. It was bad enough Stu was going to think she couldn't do a simple search; it was bad enough to blow the connection to the California detective. But dammit, Patsy Luca was not going to be seen crying! She squeezed her eyes harder. A tear rolled down her burning cheek. Oh, shit, shit, shit! Goddamn fuck!

Beth sighed.

Patsy opened her eyes to find Beth's eyes widened in sympathy. Patsy swallowed hard. "I feel so awful," she muttered. "You're right. You've been real good to me. And I've used you. But"—she swallowed again—"I had no choice. Oh, I know it's hard for you to believe that. But I've got all these bills to deal with. I had a job for a while, but my car got repossessed and I couldn't get there any more. My ex, they're his bills, but try telling that to a bill collector.

They know he won't pay. So they bully me. I won't live off the state. So when he offered me this job—"

"He? Your husband?"

Patsy shook her head. "Not Jack. Jack's too bone lazy to break into anything. There's nothing he could want to see enough to bother peeking in someone's window." She sighed. "But, Beth, you were right about this place being broken into." She watched Beth's eyes widen as she made the connection to her prowler. Maybe, Patsy thought, just maybe she wouldn't come up empty after all. If only Beth had told her the guy's name, this wouldn't be so hard. "But something happened, he didn't tell me what"—she shrugged —"I think he was too embarrassed. But he never found what he was looking for—"

"And he hired you?"

Head bowed, Patsy nodded.

"Goddamn him! That's just like him, the slimy bastard. Is he outside waiting for you, or were you going to walk to his place?"

Walk? Up here? To where? The prowler, the nameless prowler, must live around here. "Walk."

"Did he tell you it was thirty miles?"

Patsy shook her head. "He just said if I walked to the main road, and turned . . . But he made it sound like the main road was a mile away, not as far as it is."

"Well, if you'd known Joe Zekk as long as I have, you wouldn't be so surprised. Slimy bas—" She looked down at Patsy's pack. "So what is it Zekk told you to steal from here?"

Damn! Now she had his name, but she was still going to lose the list of husbands and boyfriends, all fifty-three of them. Unless . . . Patsy said, "He wanted me to steal your letters."

"I might have known. Slimy . . . slime." She reached toward the pack.

Patsy stooped, effectively blocking Beth's access to the pack. She needed to do something, or say something to knock Beth off balance. She felt in the pack, next to the bottle, and drew out the bundle of letters. Mimicking the look she had seen on her sister's face when she sat poring over her romance magazines, Patsy said, "I have to tell you, Beth, that I read these letters. Joe did tell me to. But, gee, this guy Austin, he can really describe it, huh? I mean the parts about his artist's brush, and the secret room, and how he

felt the sand on the sheets when he ground his knees down on the
sides of your . . . Gees. And—"

Beth grabbed the letters.

Patsy peered through her eyelashes to check Beth's reaction.
Beth looked embarrassed all right.

"This is what Joe Zekk told you to get?"

"Yeah."

Beth looked down at the letters, then at the backpack. "Slide
that pack over here. Let me see what you really got for him."

Patsy stared. Slowly she moved the pack. Dammit, what could
this guy Zekk have wanted more than those letters?

Keeping the gun aimed, Beth reached inside. She felt around and
came up with the bottle of Culiacán. "This! Did he send you for
this?"

Patsy hesitated, trying to read Beth's face. Then she shook her
head. "He sent me for the letters."

She reached back into Patsy's pack and pulled out the list. "The
husbands! Of course. He was going to use this to threaten me,
wasn't he?"

"I don't know. He didn't tell me. He just said to get it."

Beth tapped her teeth together. Then she sighed. "Okay. Get a
piece of paper out of the desk. There's a pen . . . but you know
where the pens are, don't you? I want a full confession, where you
met with Joe, when, what he was paying you, exactly what he said
to you, word for word."

Patsy thought. There was no way she could pull that off. She
considered trying for another tear. But dammit, there was a limit.
She straightened her shoulders. "Or what? You're not going to kill
me."

"Oh no, but I would be willing to maim you. Think about that.
We'll see if you're willing to tell me the truth tomorrow. In the
meantime"—she looked down at the nearly full bottle of Culiacán
—"you liked this so much, you can drink it. All of it!"

27

THE SHERIFF'S DEPARTMENT looked even seedier at dawn when a new deputy allowed Kiernan to make her phone call. Forty-five minutes later Stu Wiggins arrived. The deputy told them Sheriff Grimm had left an hour ago.

"I thought I was going to have to drag you out of there kicking and screaming," Stu said as they climbed into his old red Mustang.

"I thought you'd at least make mention of false arrest. You could have been picking me up after school for all the legal threatening you did in there."

Wiggins started the car. "Well, Kerry, now I know how it looked. But I also know Hobart Grimm. Hobart Grimm thinks just like he looks."

"He looks like a mummy."

Wiggins uttered a gurgle that might have passed for a laugh. "See, Kerry, I was trying to figure what was going on there. Here's what I came up with. You told Grimm about my call. Now if he checked his tapes and didn't find my call, you don't think he'd have let you snooze away the night in your cell, do you? He'd have had you back in his office within an hour, right?"

"But we know your call would have been on the tape. It's not like they'd have a tape they could erase. That would destroy the whole purpose of it."

"Okay, second option. Grimm found my call. He got ahold of the guy who took it, and he's checking into that. Then he'd have had you back in his office and been squeezing you for every bit of information you have."

"I threatened him with the newspapers. And there is the question of false arrest."

"Or he couldn't find the tape itself, and he knows he's likely to be up to his ears in shit. Now from our point of view it doesn't matter whether he found the tape or not. Either way, as soon as he can come across a reason to hold you, he'll drag you back in there and pump you till you're drier than the desert. We could take legal action, of course, but—"

"I don't have the time if I'm going to find Vanderhooven's murderer by Monday, right?"

"Right you are. So I figured we'd git while the gittin' was good. But Kerry, Grimm is still dangerous. It'd be a real smart move on your part to stay out of his way."

Stiffly, Kiernan nodded.

Wiggins rolled down his window and stuck his elbow through the opening. "So, how're you holding up after your night in stir?"

"Actually, not so bad as you might think. Furious as I was, I did sleep for five or six hours. It's one of the best things I learned in medical school—I can sleep anywhere, anytime. Even in India, when I had what the Indians call European stomach and the Europeans call Delhi belly, I could sleep. But, Stu, don't think I'm not pissed. If I had Bishop Raymond Dowd here right now, I'd liked to kick him so hard . . ."

Wiggins laughed. "Big-footed little lady! You figure it's Dowd behind the forged forms?"

"Dowd, and accomplices."

"How come?"

"If he has a signed death certificate and an interment permit, he can bury Vanderhooven."

"And avoid scandal!"

Kiernan rolled down her window and leaned back against the seat, letting the warm air ruffle her hair. "But I'm not quite comfortable with that conclusion, Stu. The problem is that Dowd could bury Vanderhooven, but it wouldn't solve his moral dilemma about burying a suicide in hallowed ground."

Wiggins shook his head. "Let me give you my educated guess on that one. From what I've been hearing about Dowd, he's not good under pressure. My guess is that he's not after the truth anymore, he's just looking for an excuse to salve his conscience so he can get Vanderhooven under the ground and out of his hair. So, suppose he takes to heart your theory that Vanderhooven couldn't have gotten his hands behind him like they were when he was tied up. Then there was no suicide! All Dowd needs to do is bury him and figure that'll end the questions about him."

"Then he doesn't need an investigation anymore."

"Right. When he hired you he wanted to know the whole truth. Now he's satisfied with the part that suits him." He gunned the engine as he pulled onto the Pima Freeway.

Kiernan nodded. "But he can't tell me that. So he's stuck with me. At least until Philip Vanderhooven starts pressuring him."

"What about Vanderhooven? Could he be the forger?"

"He's so worried about people finding out just how his son died that all he wants is the case closed and me fired. He's probably been on the phone to Dowd already."

"So, what now? You go back to San Diego and we file for breach of contract? It'll make one helluva case," Wiggins said.

"Oh no. Dowd, at least, ought to know about the stubbornness of the Irish. Even if Dowd and Vanderhooven's own parents don't want to know what really happened, I do. Whoever killed Vanderhooven is clever, ready to take chances, and real dangerous. And dammit, Stu, someone hit me on the head and tossed me into the bathroom. I'm not letting anyone get away with that." She stared out the dusty window. The pale greens and tans of the misty landscape shimmered in the early morning light. The air that rushed in through the front vents felt fresh and clean against her skin, but it did nothing to cool her temper. At not quite seven A.M. it was already rush hour. Lots of office workers worked seven-thirty to three, Stu had told her. And now every single one of them was on the freeway! "Stu, the truth is right now I'm mad enough to . . . Look, I've got to think about something else for a few minutes. To calm down. Otherwise—"

"Okay, there. How 'bout you think about breakfast, huh?"

"Perfect. I'm ravenous."

Wiggins veered onto the freeway exit. "You know, Kerry, if we were near my place, I could make my famous Wiggins Breakfast Tacos."

"You cook?" she asked, amazed. She hadn't seen Wiggins's house, but she realized she had created her own picture of it, and now she focused on that picture: an adobe rectangle; a dusty living room with old leather-strung chairs, a scarred wooden table that doubled as a desk, and worn leather tomes of the law covering one wall. Off to the right would be a small whitewashed bedroom with a washstand and a hard single bed, a room like the one she'd just come out of. The Wiggins house of her imagination had no bathroom, no dining room, and certainly no kitchen (though she did picture a doorway through which Wiggins went for beer). It was, she admitted, an abbreviated replica of the Spanish ranchos of the last century. And Stu Wiggins was its caballero.

"Kerry, you're looking at a damned fine cook here. Might be every bit as good as you."

Kiernan laughed. "If you can open a can you're that good. I don't have a houseman for nothing."

Wiggins slowed down at a sign announcing OLD ADOBE SHOP-PING CENTER and turned into the parking lot. A covered walkway similar to the one outside the sheriff's department fronted the row of stores—Micro Center, Half-Cost Baked Goods, Lamps and Shades, a Thai restaurant, and at the end, a place called Ben's Burgers. He pulled up in front of the burger shop. "Kerry, with the amount you chow down—"

"I didn't say I don't like to eat. My housekeeper played offensive line. He used to spend his days with guys who weighed over three hundred pounds and ate twelve egg omelets filled with half a hog. I went out to dinner with them—if you ever want to see a restaura-teur in heaven . . . I sat between a center and a left tackle and was still eating when both of them shoved back from the trough. I'm no pansy at the table, Stu."

"And you don't cook?"

She sighed. "You cooks are such snobs. You just can't accept that there are those of us who don't cook, and don't care."

"But Kerry, how do you—"

"See? You really can't accept it." She laughed half heartedly. "You're not going to let up on this, are you?"

"Probably should, but I'm a nosey old fellow, you know that. That's what you like about me."

"Okay, Stu. But I warn you, it deals with my sister's death and my adolescent reaction." Already she could hear the catch in her voice. "Ben's Burgers doesn't exactly sound like breakfast," she said. She knew she was stalling.

"They've got a breakfast burger with guacamole, egg, and better sausage than you deserve, on a roll your football friends would consider a meal." He opened the door and climbed down.

Inside, Ben's Burgers gave up any allegiance to the Western mo-tif. With its Formica-topped tables, it could have been a café anywhere in the country. An elderly couple sat by the windows. The woman pointed to the air-conditioning vent and reached for a sweater that hung over the back of her chair. Two solitary men at the counter were working on platters of something that smelled of onion and garlic. Stu and Kiernan settled at a table overlooking the Mustang. When they had ordered, Stu said, "Now tell me how a nice Catholic girl like you avoided the kitchen."

"Okay. You asked for it. You know about my sister, Moira," she said slowly, pressing her fingers against the glass salsa container. "Moira was beautiful—tall, with long curly red hair and eyes darker blue than mine. When we went downtown, men would stop in the street to stare. Moira had loads of boyfriends. Her biggest problem was which one to choose. She was bright, funny; when she laughed, everybody laughed. I take chances; I love to play the edge; I learned that from her. I don't know where she got it from, certainly not our parents. I used to fantasize that she and I were aliens hiding out in the most prosaic household in America. When she paid attention to me I adored her; when she didn't I hated her, like any little sister. I was twelve when she died. She was seventeen."

Kiernan pressed her fingers hard against the salsa jar. She took a breath and swallowed before she could continue. "It was the night of my father's cousin's wake. A wake is a time the Irish let go, or at least it was like that then. My parents knew they'd be drinking and they'd be out late. If it hadn't been for me, they would have taken Moira with them; she was old enough."

"Kerry, you can't be sure."

She shrugged and sat for a moment. "After they left . . ." She swallowed and began again, "After they left, Moira and I were in the kitchen. We were supposed to be making a Jell-O salad to take to the cousin's house the next day. Catholic ladies are big on Jell-O salads, Stu: red Jell-O with canned fruit, green Jell-O with pineapple chunks, orange Jell-O—" The salsa container shot out of her grasp and banged against the sugar. She grabbed it, pulled it back. "Moira said . . . she said I should make the Jell-O because it was bad enough she was stuck home with me when she could have gone out with Tommy Noonan. I said no. She insisted. And so on. Standard generic argument between sisters," she said, forcing a smile. "It ended up with me screaming, her screaming, and me throwing the open Jell-O package at her. The Jell-O was green, I remember that. I remember her standing there with the green crystals lying atop her red hair like something out of Disney, and on her face. And those green crystals floating down onto the brown-and-red linoleum. Moira was shaking her head and wiping her hand over her face to brush the Jell-O off, but that just streaked it. And she was yelling at me to clean the mess up. I yelled no. She started at me. She would have grabbed me by the shoulders and marched me to the mop closet. She wouldn't have hurt me." Kiernan swallowed hard, staring at the salsa container, trying to block the picture of Moira from her mind. "But I jumped back before she could get me. I screamed I was leaving and there was nothing she could do about it. It was eight at night. She said, 'Fine. Go ahead.' Of course that wasn't what I wanted. I tried to think what I could do to up the ante—to win." Her voice had become raspier. She coughed to open her throat. "Then I remembered the Sunset Hotel, where the hookers hung out. Moira had taken me past there the week before to show me real live hookers. It had been an adventure for me, our secret. Ma and Pop would have been scandalized. I yelled at her. I said I was going to the Sunset Hotel. I stomped out." She closed her eyes and swallowed, trying to get control of her voice.

"I hid in the old playhouse in the McCarthys' backyard. I wanted to follow her when she started searching for me, but I was afraid she'd get a bunch of her friends to help and they'd spot me. So I waited in the playhouse for almost two hours. Then I went home. By then, of course, she was out looking for me. She went to the Sunset Hotel looking for me. She died there."

"And you never told anyone?" Wiggins asked softly.

It was a moment before Kiernan could block out the picture of that brown clapboard hotel, and the red pulser lights from the police cars spraying over Moira's dead-white skin, the picture that had filled nightmares so long yet never lost its sting. "What?"

"You never told anyone that she went there to find you?"

"Stu, I told them all, my parents, Father Grogan, Mrs. McCarthy. They never believed me. They preferred to think that Moira was there meeting some man." She shook her head. "I spent the next six years battering my stomach muscles on the uneven bars."

"To forget?"

"And you can see how effective that tactic was." She laughed mirthlessly. "But it did keep me away from Jell-O. That was what I fixated on. I guess you pick some small, irrelevant thing. I picked Jell-O to connect with Moira's death. And I picked a sport that would keep me out of the kitchen when it was being made."

She could feel her face flushing. The picture of the kitchen—the green crystals floating down onto the brown-and-red linoleum—faded, and she was left feeling drained. And foolish. She unwrapped her fingers from the salsa container. "Sorry, Stu. It's been twenty-five years. A well-balanced person would be . . . better balanced. But then, very few people think forensic pathologists are normal."

Wiggins smiled. "Or detectives."

The waitress slid a platter in front of each of them. "Will that be all?" she asked.

Wiggins nodded.

They ate in silence for a while.

A fourth of the way through the huge burger, Kiernan said, "Stu, this really is good."

"I told you," he replied without enthusiasm.

Kiernan squeezed her eyelids together. She put down the burger. "Okay, I think we've had enough distraction. Now let's see where we're going with this case."

"If you can stay out of trouble long enough. From that blow on your head and the death certificate forgery we know someone really wants you out of here. If it's Dowd or Vanderhooven, they couldn't just pay you off. That'd reveal their hand. It'd be telling the world you know too much. And if it is Vanderhooven, Kerry, you be careful. He's got mean connections."

"I thought the Mafia went in for kneecapping, not forging interment permits and locking ladies in the john."

"Listen, don't be so smug. If the guy who hit you is one of Vanderhooven's associates, Vanderhooven could be reining him in, for the moment. At any time he could give him his head. And you could lose yours!"

"A mite melodramatic, but I take your point." She bit into the burger and chewed slowly. "What about you, Stu? What did you come up with?"

"I put out a lot of feelers that won't produce till tomorrow at the earliest. But I did have an interesting talk with my buddy the archdiocese lawyer about Austin Vanderhooven."

"You know, Stu, the picture of Vanderhooven I got from Beth Landau was not of the kind of man you'd want to confess your sins to."

"It seems the book on Vanderhooven was that he was real sharp, could talk theology with anyone, not that he agreed with anyone."

"How so?"

Wiggins put down his cup, leaned back in the chair, and rested the side of a boot on his knee. "Well, see, there are factions here like anywhere else. The conservatives call Vatican Two, Vatican Too Far. The progressives think a few old men are calling the shots in a show they don't know much about, what with bachelors, some of them virgins, telling married couples how to think about sex and love."

"And Vanderhooven?"

Stu laughed. "He ticked them off in both groups. Now a young guy like that with a California and New York education, you'd think he'd be a shoo-in for the liberal camp, right? At least on matters of sexual behavior. But there you'd be wrong. See, the liberals, they figure that unless a doctrine's based on one of the pope's infallible decisions, it's open for interpretation. Fallible decisions they figure were put together by a guy who was influenced by his times. They say you have to take those times into account and adjust the basic idea to suit life now. They figure there's a lot of unnecessary stuff that's keeping the people at a distance from the Church, a lot of it left over from hundreds of years ago. They don't want the people to pop in, pay their money, swallow their wafers and leave. They want the people to be involved. Of course, now, I'm not a Catholic, so what I'm saying is probably not how the red hats among the liberals would put it."

Kiernan smiled. "Probably not. What was it we said as kids? You'd get credit for mass if you'd had holy water on your forehead, marks on your knees from the kneeler, and the wafer stuck to the roof of your mouth. It rhymed then."

Wiggins finished his coffee. "Now the conservatives believe doctrine is doctrine is doctrine. And they say if a priest questions the Church's teachings there is always the danger of Scandal, with a capital S."

Kiernan squinted in puzzlement.

"Forgotten a mite of your R.C. lore, eh, Ms. O'Shaughnessy?"

"Most of it."

"Well, according to my source, the issue of Scandal is front of the herd. The conservative view is that Scandal is caused when theologians question sensitive issues *in public*. Okay for the priests to ponder and dither as long as they don't mention it. But discuss those questions, admit your indecision, and you get Scandal. And Scandal could mislead the lay folk, encourage them to make their own decisions, uninformed decisions, because a lot of this stuff turns on pretty obscure points. It could set the lay folk on the road to sin."

"But if *theologians* can't even discuss the issues in public, what's the point of having theologians? They might as well just have xeroxes."

Wiggins smiled. "Well, we can see which group you'd fall into. You're spouting the liberal line, Kerry."

"So which group was Vanderhooven's?"

"Neither one. Vanderhooven was troubled by some of the teachings, but his answer to that was to dig deeper in the Church books, to pray more, to fast, that kind of thing. He wasn't a guy to be out on the picket line. No liberal."

"But he let the women's center use Hohokam Lodge."

"Exactly. The conservatives couldn't stomach something like that. With any other parish priest they would have been raising Cain. But Vanderhooven had too much money and too many family connections in the Church hierarchy back East to be vulnerable on an issue like that."

Kiernan ran her tongue around the edge of the hamburger bun scooping up the overflow of guacamole. "You know, that doesn't altogether surprise me. Beth Landau said he pulled strings to get himself out here where she was. She said she had the feeling that he was using her to test himself."

"A female hair shirt? You believe that?"

"I had the sense that she was being pretty straight. And I do believe that Vanderhooven was still attracted to her. He contacted her about the women's center, he offered her Hohokam Lodge."

"Kerry—"

"Stu, the guy was trying to have his cake and eat it, with her. He didn't try to find an interpretation of the rules that said it was okay for him to be involved with her, nor did he give any indication he was deciding between his woman and his Church. He was just playing the edges of Rome's rules. 'Icy tower' was Landau's description of his mind, 'like a monk in an icy tower.'"

"A monk who got himself killed."

She stuffed the last of the burger into her mouth and nodded. "What could Vanderhooven have been up to that made someone go to all the trouble and take the chances he did to kill him?"

Wiggins sighed. "My first guess would have been the race for advancement. There's been a fair amount of jockeying for position to grab the archbishop's miter once he dies. To an outsider that doesn't sound like something you'd kill for, but hell, guys kill for half a dollar. But like I told you, our man Dowd hasn't been bothering to politic on this. And Austin Vanderhooven wasn't backing anyone. The only thing Vanderhooven was involved with was planning the retreat center."

"The retreat center for the rich and influential. Bud Warren told me about that. Sort of a Taj Mahal in the desert. With enough money and influence to make killing a small price to pay. How is it a little church like Mission San Leo came to be in charge of this?"

"Seems one of faithful gave them some land in the mountains thirty, forty years ago."

"They don't rush into these retreats, eh?"

"This is mosey country. But I don't think the land's all that much. It's out in the desert—dry. Not right on a river, which means it's not likely to get washed out in a flash flood, but it's also not likely to have much water—"

Kiernan held up a hand. "Not true. According to Bud Warren, the retreat planners—he said Sylvia Necri—control the rights to something like half an acre-foot a day."

Wiggins whistled. Conversation at the counter stopped momentarily, then resumed. "Well now, with that it could be quite a place. You know the whole Colorado River allotment to nine states is only sixteen million acre-feet per year. And that, Kerry, is based on a wet period in history. There are so many cities and farms pulling from the river that by the time it gets to the Mexican border it's so salty the Mexicans won't take the water without our desalinating it. The city of Phoenix, the city of Los Angeles, and any others with the money to do it, are buying up rural land just for the water rights. You look at the Owens Valley. Used to be a green fertile place. Los Angeles bought it and sucked the water right out from under it. Now it's desert."

"How come?"

"The rule is the first user gets the rights. And they can sell those rights and ship the water to L.A. so the Angelenos can wash their cars and water their lawns."

Kiernan nodded, recalling that Stu had represented a couple of losers in water battles recently. "Stu, I know water's a big problem here in the desert. But the retreat builders already have use of the water they need. They're promised it in perpetuity. So that's not an issue. They've got the land. They've had it for years. What is it that's changed?"

"What's changed, Kerry, is that all those years no one had much financial know-how or connections. Then Vanderhooven came along."

"Okay, so the land had been sitting around and Dowd had been pondering maybe someday building a retreat out there. Then Vanderhooven came along and took charge. Did he form a committee?"

Wiggins shook his head. "Vanderhooven wasn't the committee type. What he did do was contact some of the money men and lay the groundwork."

"Which money men?"

Wiggins shook his head. "Now, that I don't know. Cold be legit. Could be his father's associates. Could be a mix."

A middle-aged man in Bermuda shorts settled at the counter. Kiernan said, "What about Vanderhooven's friend Joe Zekk? Where does he fit in? Elias Necri said Vanderhooven labeled Zekk a deadbeat. Elias thinks Zekk was getting money from Philip Vanderhooven and he's pretty pissed that he's not. As for Philip, he denies even hearing Zekk out."

"You believe that?"

"I'm withholding judgment. Which is more than Bud Warren was doing last night. To hear him—"

"Now, Kerry, Bud Warren is not as pure as the driven snow."

Kiernan tensed. She could hear the defensive tone in her voice as she asked, "How-many-days-old snow is he?"

Wiggins leaned back in his chair. "Not like a gutter pile back there in New York City, if that's what you're thinking. Bud's an okay guy. But he is a speculator. He's always got something going. So far nothing's worked out, but Bud's always managed to come out smelling okay. He's always gotten backing. Money men don't veer off when they lay eyes on him. But he's not one of them, and he's learned to watch what he says."

"What he said was that Dowd stood to gain power over a retreat that would attract Catholic money and influence nationwide. And what Elias Necri said was that Zekk got Austin to contact his father for him. Austin himself was paying Zekk two hundred dollars a month, and he'd set him up in a house in the mountains."

"Ah hah! Well, then let me give you a spot of news."

Kiernan raised an eyebrow.

"That house is above a hamlet called Rattlesnake, on the Rattlesnake River. It's not all that far from the retreat site and Hohokam Lodge. And Kerry, it's right on the way to Sylvia Necri's construction site. If Sylvia knows where it is, you can bet Elias does. And that there's something up there he doesn't want you to uncover."

28

KIERNAN'S FIRST THOUGHT after Wiggins dropped her at her motel was to launch into a series of *Viparita Chakrasana:* backbend to handstand to forward bend, one after another. But she was already too wired, and backbends would only make her more so. Forward bends would calm her down, but they could sap what energy she had. She compromised on a long, easy headstand, letting the blood flow gently downward, feeling her scattered thoughts come into focus.

But the headstand didn't dislodge the cold ache of loneliness, the angry twelve-year-old's stab of abandonment she always felt when she'd talked about Moira.

Despite the time she'd spent at breakfast, it was not yet eight o'clock. Really too early to call home. Grinning, she lowered her legs to the floor, stood up, and dialed. The phone rang eight times before Brad Tchernak's thick voice said, "Yeah?"

"Hard night?" Kiernan asked.

"Huh? Oh, Kiernan. It's barely dawn, you know."

"Be glad Arizona doesn't have Daylight Savings Time or I might have called an hour earlier."

"I'm glad we didn't have an earthquake, too. But I wasn't planning to get up with the sun to celebrate it." The rustle of cloth rubbing over the phone, followed by a groan, suggested Brad was getting up. "I suppose you want to speak to *him.*"

Kiernan nodded. She always felt ridiculous doing this. It was like childhood prayer, when she'd mouthed words to a Being she pretended was listening. "Put him on." Now she pretended big, brown eyes were widening in anticipation.

"Okay, go," Brad said.

Feeling even more ridiculous, Kiernan glanced around, half expecting to see faces at the window peering in on her foolishness. "Ezra," she crooned into the receiver. "Ezzzzraaa. How's the guy? Have you been a good dog?" She pictured his long feathered tail wagging wildly. Was that panting she heard? "Good boy, Ezra."

Ezra gave a high-pitched yelp.

Kiernan laughed, picturing the big Labrador/wolfhound wriggling like a beagle. "Ah, Ezra."

Ezra gave the phone an unmistakable slurp.

"Gees!" Brad said. "If I had known this was going to be such a sappy job—"

"Come on, where else could you get a flat by the beach and still be in the sack at eight A.M.? Would you like to guess where I've spent the night?"

"Is this going to be something I'd be happier not knowing?"

Ignoring that, she said, "Jail."

Tchernak groaned. In his "servant" voice, he intoned, "So humiliating! How am I going to face the other guys below stairs. Their employers are sunning in Tahiti or gambling in Monte Carlo; mine's in jail!" He laughed.

"I suppose you're wringing your hands in despair—on an apron. No, of course not. You can't reach one. You're still in bed." She could almost see his dark brown eyes squinting against the intrusion of morning, his wiry hair poking out above his ears, the pelt on his tanned chest peeking above the unzipped extra-long sleeping bag he used for a blanket.

"Kiernan, I always wear an apron to bed, just in case. I aim to please, at any hour."

"And you do."

"So," he said, his voice softening, "when are you coming home?"

"The sheriff, the bishop, and the father of the deceased would like me to leave now."

"So that means you won't, right?"

"Not yet. I can't abandon a case midway. I have a dog and a housekeeper to support."

"Well, give me fair warning so I can shovel the beer cans out of your flat." He paused. "Seriously, call me tonight, huh?"

She smiled. "I can take care of myself, you know."

"Yeah, I know. But Ezra misses you. When we go for our runs on the beach, he's so anxious to turn around and start home he can barely keep up with me. When we get near the house he races to your door, with his ears perked up and his tail wagging so hard it almost knocks him over. He searches through your flat inch by inch; then, finally, he gives one long moan and drops down to the floor."

"He's not off his food, is he?" Kiernan asked, worried.

Brad laughed. "Well, no. There are limits to mourning. But he does miss you. And, frankly, so do I. So call me, huh?"

"Okay," she said softly.

At nine A.M. it was already too hot to climb into the high desert. It was too hot to climb into the Jeep. Kiernan put the plastic water bottle behind the seat and steeled herself against the searing heat that would penetrate her jeans as soon as she touched the seat. Jeans and a long-sleeved T-shirt were too warm, but the unknown desert was no place to go bare-limbed.

By the time she'd come to the first stoplight, between the Aqua Fria Shopping Center (salmon and teal) and the Lost Dutchman Mall (ragged mountain façade), the backs of her shirt and jeans were soaked. A mile later, when she pulled onto the Superstition Freeway, they were icy. The freeway ended a few miles on and she detoured onto Apache Boulevard. No longer were there shopping centers. Rather, dust-worn clusters of autoparts shops, plumbing suppliers, and gun stores stood between grassless fields and brown dry land that looked as if it should hold bleached bones but instead sported a spindly ironwood tree here, a group of squat cholla there.

The road began to ascend. The sun burned through the windshield onto her jeans. Beside the road there was some foliage now —pale green thin-leaved trees and insubstantial shrubs.

She wished she knew the names of the plants, how they were related, how the Pimas and before them the Hohokam, who were said to have lived here centuries before the Spanish invasion, made use of the plants.

She laughed. Years ago botany had fascinated her briefly, as had astronomy and mathematics. Those interests had always led back to medicine, to forensic pathology. The lure of the stars had never measured up to her passion to know about the body, to find out what made it live and what specifically caused it to cease living. To learn enough to find out what really killed Moira.

Her shoulders tightened and she was aware of the pressure above her eyes. She shook her head sharply, surprised that she could still feel the dismay she had felt when she finally accepted the fact that forensic pathology was no absolute. Forensic pathology would not reveal the truth. She had been with the coroner's office three years before she was forced to accept that. During those years she had seen court cases where experts staked their reputations on opposing theses. Doctors can be mistaken, she had told herself. Doctors can even be bought. The truth lay in the body, in the vials, in the tests. The truth was there, but some of those "experts" simply had not seen it. Some weren't sharp enough to spot it, some were too lazy to keep up with the research, some had preconceived notions to which they tried to fit their findings, some . . . She had built walls of excuses, desperately refusing to face the fallibility of the dream that had sustained her, the dream of explaining why Moira had died. As the ground beneath become more unstable, she'd patched and plastered those walls thicker and thicker, putting her faith in each new test, in every increasingly sophisticated machine, till the dream became like a solid adobe house sitting atop an earthquake fault. That house might have held forever if the killer quake hadn't hit.

That call—the quake—had come six years ago, at shortly after two in the morning: a high-speed head-on collision between two pickup trucks. Three dead.

The driver of the Datsun pickup was a thirty-seven-year-old man from San Francisco. In the Plymouth were two teenagers from town, a boy and a girl, who had been driving. The boy was in his first year at junior college. The girl had gone off to a New Age boarding school for two years and been back in town the last two years. In September she would have started college. Kiernan had seen them in town, had met their families, knew some of their friends, knew of their "wild" reputations. When she'd looked at their bodies she'd felt almost relief to find their faces unrecognizable.

The autopsies had taken hours. Because organs had been ripped open, some of the contents of stomachs and intestines had splashed into the abdominal cavities, mixed in with lung and heart tissue. The smell had been nearly overwhelming. She had cleaned away the splashings, keeping them separate from the fluids still inside the organs, and bagged samples of both for the lab. She'd held severed flesh against bones, checking the fit, assuring herself that this flesh belonged to this body. She'd searched through the man-gled bodies for signs of alcohol, drugs, aneurysm, heart disease, pressure behind the eyes, pressure in the Eustachian tubes.

She had taken the boy first. As she'd suspected, he was the least difficult. Then she did the man, a long, tedious procedure. There were signs of alcohol in his stomach, but owing to the condition of the body, it was impossible to guess how much was in his system.

Finally, there was the girl, Kimberly Everett. The force of the crash had snapped her neck. The engine had smashed back into the cab, sending the steering column through her right shoulder and crushing the arm to a red pulp.

Kiernan had drunk a cup of coffee outside in the fresh air, cleared her mind from the last postmortem, then gone back in. She scrubbed and began her description of the body: "Decedent is a well-nourished Caucasian female, eighteen years old . . ." There had been no abnormal occlusion of the arteries, no old petechial hemorrhages on what she could find of the epicardium. The liver, gallbladder, spleen, pancreas, gastrointestinal tract, adrenals, kidneys, and bladder showed no sign of disease or insult prior to the fatal injuries. She did find the lung tissue discolored, the odor of alcohol coming from the stomach, and signs of both pregnancy and gonorrhea.

Suddenly it all got to her. For the first time in an autopsy she ripped off her gloves, raced from the room, and leaned against the wall outside, shaking. She had seen bodies more mutilated, more decayed, handled smells much worse. But as she had looked down at the exposed corpse, she had a clear vision of what would become of Kimberly Everett's memory.

For the first time Kiernan considered omitting her findings from an autopsy report. Kimberly Everett had been driving, but neither her pregnancy nor her gonorrhea had caused the crash. Nonetheless, they would create a sensation when the insurance companies battled to assign guilt. In a court hearing these findings would overshadow the issue of alcohol. Kimberly Everett, like Moira, would be labeled a girl who had it coming.

Standing there, leaning against the wall, she told herself this case was not like Moira's, where competent forensic work might have shown evidence of LSD, a little-known substance in those days, or of some other little-known drug that could have led to her death. A decent autopsy might have moved the police to investigate Moira's death, instead of assuming, along with everyone else, that Moira had been turning tricks in the Sunset Hotel, had been distraught, and had thrown herself out the hotel window, as a girl of her character deserved to do. She told herself that in this case it would be all right to leave the findings about the pregnancy and gonorrhea unmentioned.

But she didn't. She couldn't. She went in, turned the microphone back on, and finished the autopsy, moving from the organs of the pelvis and the thorax outward to the legs, the arms, the shoulders, neck, and head.

Later the newspapers would say she had been too anxious to get it over with, that she should have taken more time. At the hearing, county supervisors would say that she should have spaced the autopsies better. They would say she could have done Kimberly Everett's body the next day; the early stages of decomposition would have been setting in, but they wouldn't have compromised her findings too much.

She told herself the same things for the next two years. But at the time she had simply finished the Everett autopsy, gone home, had three stiff drinks, and slept for twelve hours.

It wasn't till months latter—during which time the Everett family swore that their daughter indulged in neither sex nor alcohol, and the insurance companies hedged, and every facet of Kimberly Everett's life was hashed over in print and by word of mouth—that one of the insurance investigators turned up a neurologist who swore that the girl had had no feeling in her right hand. The nerves at the point where her neck had broken had been damaged in an accident three years earlier, during the time she had been away at school. Nerve damage, he had explained, was individual. A patient can lose control but still have feeling, or vice versa. In this case, there was some control, but no feeling. In other words, the neurologist had explained to the reporters, instead of moving with precision in response to the danger, Kimberly's hand had reacted clumsily. By then she was dead. She had, the neurologist concluded, no business driving. Certainly none drinking and driving.

The scars from Kimberly's earlier surgery were small, but a competent forensic pathologist should have spotted them, the insurance companies said as they altered their settlements. Faced with the threat of lawsuit, the county supervisors concurred. Pathologists from surrounding counties disagreed. In view of the greatly compromised condition of the body, and particularly of the arm and neck, overlooking the scar tissue was a mistake anyone could have made, they insisted. The families of the victims called for Kiernan's resignation. Her supporters urged her to fight.

But there was nothing to fight for. She had been wrong. Because of her error the scandal she had so desperately wanted to avoid had had time to blossom and flourish. The thought of Kimberly Everett filled her with grief. Over and over, she pictured the life that Kimberly would never have, the child she'd never bear. It was a grief she'd been too young to feel for Moira. And seeing the agony of the Everetts pictured on the local newscast, alluded to in the paper, bemoaned in the supermarket, she felt anguish for them, and for her own parents, who had been too intimidated by the notoriety of Moira's death, too shocked, too humiliated, to grieve at all.

But even more devastating than that was the undeniable fact that the science of forensic pathology had failed. If it had been merely her own failure, she might have handled it. She could have researched more, worked harder and longer; she could have given up friends, given up her lover, spent her free hours with medical journals, police journals, forensic journals, pharmaceutical journals, gone over every facet of every postmortem twice. She could have clambered on till she grasped the truth.

But forensic pathology, she learned, was just another tool. Her life had been a joke. Even if she had spotted the scar tissue and discovered the nerve damage in question, there was no way she could have known how greatly it had affected Kimberly's hand, whether it caused her death or not. If a competent forensic pathologist had found evidence of LSD in Moira's body, who could have said that LSD had *made* Moira jump? No drug residue would have explained whether Moira had braved the Sunset Hotel to find her sister, or had abandoned that search, met a friend with the drug, and later wandered into the hotel whose name stuck in her jangled mind. Sophisticated scientific analysis would have changed nothing. It had always been impossible to pronounce with certainty: Moira O'Shaughnessy was not a tramp. Or Kiernan O'Shaughnessy was not guilty.

Immobilized by despair, Kiernan did nothing; she didn't go to work; she didn't wash clothes; she didn't shop for food. She stopped answering the phone or opening the door to the friends who brought food.

The board of supervisors fired her.

When the dismissal notice came, she felt a surge of relief, as if all the energy she had been suppressing for the past months had erupted. She called Goodwill to pick up her furniture, gave away her car, and bought a ticket for Bangkok.

It wasn't till after her return from Asia, when her father died, that she came across a box of Moira's possessions. In it was a bank book with more money than Moira had had reason to possess, and a small notebook with the names of twenty-two men. On a separate paper Moira had written "Red" and a phone number. Red was the pimp.

Kiernan had sat, staring at the battered box, till her back ached, mourning her sister anew. She saw the Sunset Hotel as it had been on the day Moira had taken her by. What had gone on in Moira's mind that day, and all the other days she must have been there? What had Moira thought, what had she felt, feared, or savored before she stood in the window of room 609 and fell forward? Clearly she, Kiernan, had never really known her adored sister, her fellow "alien" on Rohan Street. Suddenly Kiernan had laughed at the ludicrousness of it all, laughed hysterically, her body shaking violently with each new wave. She'd laughed until her throat burned and her ribs ached and tears poured down her cheeks. One afternoon of detective work had told her more than all those years of forensic pathology. And still there were things she would never know.

29

KIERNAN SHOOK HER HEAD SHARPLY, forcing her attention back to the Arizona road. She was already well into the mountains. How long had she been enveloped in the illusion of her memories? She laughed mirthlessly. She was, after all, a champion of illusion, having clung for all those years to her sophomoric ideas of forensic pathology and its truth. No wonder Sam Chase had seen a similarity between her and Austin Vanderhooven—a likeness flattering to neither one.

She looked out at the dry red dirt beside the two-lane hardtop. It felt like monsoon season up here. For the desert, the air was muggy. The rains would be coming, hard and sudden, everyone said. But now the land looked as if it hadn't been wet since the turn of the century. Gaping cracks separated one section of dead desert grass from another. Only the cacti survived, huddled small and pale next to the earth, as if to escape the searing sun. No cars passed coming in from the mountains. No houses suggested life. Not even an animal was in sight. The White Bone Mountains had been aptly named.

Joe Zekk, what kind of man was he? Had he been thankful for this place to live, for whatever connection he had to the projected retreat? Or had he spent his hot lonely days brooding over his exile in the barren sands till he was eager to take revenge in as vicious a manner as possible?

The road crested the mountain and headed onto a plateau. She came to the metal Z, turned right, leaving the main road, and headed slowly down. The carpet of pale green snakeweed and palo verde gave way to creosote bushes and clusters of chollas; the teddy-bear chollas and the staghorn she recognized, but some of the others she could only assume belonged to that group of low cacti.

The narrow road cut back sharply, winding down the surprisingly steep hillside. There was barely room for a creosote bush beside the road before the hillside fell away. She squinted against the glare of the sunlight bouncing off the Jeep's hood, then turned the steering wheel hard right till the wheels squeaked against the axles. The descent became gentler, the cutbacks wider and less frequent. The creosote and cacti became sparser, till the sandy soil was virtually unscarred by vegetation. The barrenness was frightening, like a life sentence of solitary confinement.

She made a hard left at a cutback. Before her, on a narrow mesa that jutted out over a green strip of valley below, was a castle.

At second glance she could see that the house had neither the size nor most of the other features one expects of a true castle. It was the setting that gave it its dramatic impact. The mesa was only about two hundred yards long, less than fifty yards wide. The house perched on a corner of the mesa as if about to float up into the turquoise sky. Mottled stones of caramel and gray and pink sparkled in its sandstone walls, echoing the rocky rise on the far side of the valley behind it. Despite the starkness of the desert background, the small castle looked like something out of a romantic Hudson Valley School painting. The west side sloped up sharply to a tower, at the base of which was a round room with long narrow windows. From that room Zekk would be able to survey the hillside above and the narrow green valley below. If this house had been built on a mesa jutting out from Camelback Mountain in Scottsdale, it would have sold for a million, even small as it was. "Jewel box" was the term a realtor would use. Kiernan noted the way the house blended with its surroundings, and indeed, surprisingly, enhanced the vista. A jewel box in the tradition of Frank Lloyd Wright?

What marred the picture was a high circular adobe enclosure at the far end of the mesa, which had the look of servants' quarters, set as far from the main house as possible. Just beyond it, jutting out over the valley below, was what looked like a giant rocky forearm that ended in an upturned fist of red stone.

There was no vehicle in sight. No place to hide one. She pulled the Jeep up near the house and from habit turned it to face the road. She jumped down, suddenly aware of how stiff she had become in the two-hour drive. What was the altitude here? At one point a sign had said five thousand feet, but the road had descended sharply since then. Now she guessed she was no more than two thousand feet above Phoenix. The air still carried the faintly pungent odor of morning in the desert, but that creosoty scent must have wafted in from the plants closer to the main road. Here there was no creosote, in fact no landscaping at all to inhibit the flow of the dry reddish-tan ground up to the building; from there the eye was drawn up to the peak of the turret and the single incongruous element: a wrought-iron Z on the turret, which transformed the house into one of those miniature-golf castles that bellied up to the freeways around Phoenix.

The ring of the doorbell reverberated in the house. The door did not open. She waited, rang again, but still there was no response. To her right was the round room with the tall tinted windows. She circled it, checking each window for a crack in the tinting, but there was no spot through which she could peer in. A porch ran along the back side of the house. A few feet farther on was the edge of the cliff. She moved to the edge—no wall or fence and looked down at the valley a quarter of a mile below, almost straight down.

"Valley" was too tame a word for it. It was more like an earthquake crevasse, a mile or so long and no more than a five or six hundred yards wide at any point. At the bottom of the sheer red wall on the far side a river raced—the Rattlesnake. It fell suddenly from the narrow opening at the west end of the valley, sped along, and disappeared as abruptly when the walls of the valley closed at the east end. Kiernan looked up, past the round enclosure at the end of the mesa. That giant fist of red rock hung out over the west end of the valley.

From beside Joe Zekk's house a deeply rutted dirt road descended, weaving back and forth in ever-widening swings down the steep hillside to another dirt road that ran upstream beside the river, between two rows of wooden houses. There was no vegetation; the houses were gray; and the street was a dry desert brown. It looked like a ghost town.

On the near side of the switchback road, directly beneath Zekk's house, a dusty cemetery of perhaps fifty graves climbed the hillside. Beyond it was an explosion of green: layer upon layer of terraced fields like the ones Kiernan had seen in the Himalayan foothills. The hillside glowed, emerald-green, apple-green, bottle-green, as the narrow terraces—no more than two yards wide—climbed its sheer wall. It seemed to Kiernan a world completely separate from the dessicated village upstream.

She stared at the village. There were no cars, no signs of people either. Why the tilled and irrigated fields if no one lived there? If someone did live in the village, why had they irrigated just that much land and not the rest? Were they already planning for the day when the church retreat would swallow most of that rushing water?

Turning back to the house, she climbed two steps onto the porch and rang the bell, expecting no answer, getting none.

A whiff of breeze cooled her forehead, then vanished.

Partway along its north side, the mesa was attached to the higher cliff that led back to the main road. From the other three sides there was a sheer drop: on the east was the switchback road to the village; the south edge hung over the river; and the narrow west end, farthest from Zekk's, jutted out over the valley. The high adobe wall there effectively lopped off that end of the mesa and the fist of rock beyond it. Kiernan had been dazzled by Zekk's castle, but now, standing here, she realized that that tip of the mesa was the prize spot. Or it would have been if the wall hadn't blocked it off. She hurried toward it.

The sun beat off the adobe wall. She made her away around it to the far edge of the mesa. The rocky forearm was almost fifteen feet long. It hung precariously, like a diving board a quarter of a mile high, and seemed to contain within itself the coiled energy of millennia, as if the fist were ready to slam itself down into the valley exit and dam up the river forever. And most surprising was the lone, quite dead tree that had grown and died in front of that fist.

It was a moment before she noticed the circling hoards of blow-flies by the end of the mesa and looked down to see another dead tree fifteen feet below, and in its branches an animal carcass, too well scavenged to be recognizable.

She turned and hurried away, before the blowflies could find her and fly into her eyes, up her nose, into her mouth and ears, an experience she recalled only too well from on-site examinations of bodies left in the open. She ran along the wall to the gate, a solid wooden door as high as the wall. It was locked.

The tall smooth wall would make entry difficult—it would be hard to get a grip on its thick, rounded top. She opted for the door, backed up to get a running start, leapt to grab the top, and pulled herself over it.

The area inside the enclosure was smaller than she had assumed. A well-tended cactus garden hugged one segment of the wall, and a dome-shaped building, ten feet in diameter, fitted against another. The most amazing thing was the view, or rather the lack of it. Here, at the tip of the mesa, the spot that looked out over the beauty of the valley below, at the magnificent rocky fist hanging over it, the spot where one might have stood at dawn and watched the sudden lifting of the veils of night—here there was nothing to see but the wall.

She tried the door. Locked. Zekk might be a deadbeat, but he wasn't laid-back about security. The dome itself appeared to be windowless. It wasn't till she had circled to the far side, by the outer wall, that she spotted a triangular window of blue stained glass at the top. She hoisted herself onto the dome and peered in.

Underneath the window was what appeared to be a foam mat, a pillow, and sheets left in a wad at one end. She squirmed around and, balancing on her stomach, looked down through the low end of the blue window toward the far side of the room. She could make out the edge of a dresser or chest. No more. No rug, no books, no sign of electricity. She squirmed lower to get a better angle. On the floor she could make out the lower part of a crucifix.

"A monk's cell!" she muttered. The desert version of Austin Vanderhooven's icy tower room! Even blue glass, to make it look icy.

She slid down the side of the dome and reached for her Swiss army knife. Her fingers hit keys—Vanderhooven's house keys. Worth a try. Pulling them out, she stuck one in the lock, and the door opened.

Inside, the first thing that struck her was the heat. The dome looked like a small dark igloo, but the temperature was more suitable for a sauna. When her eyes adjusted, she looked around. The room held only what she had seen through the window—a chest, a crucifix, and a foam pad with the sheets pulled off. But what it told her was entirely different. The sheets had not been pulled off and left in a careless heap. They had been ripped off. Jagged tears broke the fabric in two places.

The chest was dusty, but for a circle the size of the crucifix's base. Kiernan lifted the lid of the chest. Books, six of them, large old leather-bound religious tomes, real books, no fakes like the one in Vanderhooven's bedroom. Clearly, they had been held open by their covers, shaken—to dislodge what?—and dropped. Now they lay one upon another, yellowed pages crumpled, several spines ripped.

And the crucifix had been broken in pieces. It took only a moment to spot the mark on the wall where it had been hurled. The top half had taken the brunt of the blow; the bottom half, which she had seen through the window, was almost intact. Looking at it, she thought of her own silver gymnast statuette, the one she'd so often hurled in frustration.

Had the dome been her own assailant's second stop after checking Vanderhooven's bedroom in Phoenix? Or the first stop? Whichever, the rage evident in his actions strongly suggested he didn't find what he was seeking here.

But if the thief looked here, that meant the treasure was something that could have fit under the mat or between the pages of a large book. This was like playing twenty questions. Was the item bigger than a bread box? Smaller than a standard book, flatter than . . . well, flat. A paper, a document.

A document that someone assumed Vanderhooven might leave out here. Why? Because he would think it would be safer here, unguarded, than in Phoenix with him? Safer than in Phoenix in his hollow book? Or was it because the document or paper had something to do with the retreat?

The room told her nothing more, except perhaps about the austerity of its former occupant. Even if the window opened, it would still be uncomfortably hot. She looked up, suddenly sure that Austin Vanderhooven's window would not open. She was not surprised to find no lever. She was surprised only to see that the stained-glass window, which had looked blue from the outside, looked pink, rose-colored, from in here.

She shut the door, hoisted herself back over the wall, and walked along the dry hot mesa to the Jeep.

She stood, listening. For someone used to the bustle of beach life, the silence was unnerving. She gave her head a shake, pulled out Vanderhooven's keys, and headed for Joe Zekk's back door. It opened on the second try.

With a final glance behind her, Kiernan walked inside, into the kitchen.

It took her a minute to realize that this place hadn't been bur-
gled too; it merely housed a slob. Dishes caked with brown topped
with green fuzz, dirty pots, pans, glasses, cups, a dust-encrusted
electric mixer, and enough beer cans for a Super Bowl party covered every counter and had spilled down onto the floor. The refrigerator contained nothing but beer cans, soda bottles, a stick of
butter, and a steak. The mild stench of beer, sugar, and decay hung
in the air.

A counter separated the kitchen from the living room, but there
was no possibility of peering through from one room to the other.
The pile of debris that filled the space beneath the hanging cabinets
was an architectural achievement. No dish had been centered on
the one beneath, but somehow the landfill of aluminum and plastic
maintained itself.

As she moved around it through the doorway, Kiernan found
herself walking carefully, as if each step could be the one to send
the pile cascading to the floor.

The living room, which constituted the west half of the house,
was shaped like a capital *D* lying on its side; its curved wall was all
windows. A sofa faced the windows. Only a few inches of a wooden
coffee table were visible under the litter of magazines, newspapers,
dirty dishes, beer cans, and little airline liquor bottles. Against the
wall were a television, a VCR, and three shelves of tapes.

Pornography tapes. All three shelves. A year's supply.

Austin Vanderhooven down there in the dome contemplating the
soul. Joe Zekk up here, contemplating the flesh. And Austin Vanderhooven had set this up. Or had he?

Not the best spot to ponder that. More to the point, all the tapes
were still in their boxes, so this place had not been searched. The
burglar had had the key that unlocked this house and both of
Vanderhooven's dwellings. Regardless of which he searched first,
the dome or the rectory, he'd have gone over this place when he
did the dome. Only one person wouldn't have. Joe Zekk.

So what had Joe Zekk been looking for and where in this pigsty
would he put it? She eyed the clutter. This really was a rubber-
gloves job. Where would Zekk—clearly not a systematic man, not
a disciplined one, and from the evidence of the bottles around, not
often a sober one—where would he put the document? Somewhere
immediately available. Not in a videotape box. He'd never remem-

ber which one. He would hide it in a one-of-a-kind place. The
freezer? She made her way back to the kitchen and pulled open the
door. The freezer was solid ice.

Behind pictures? The mirror in the hall? Taped on the bottom of
a drawer?

A quarter of an hour later she found it, lying beneath a pile of
wrinkled shirts in the dresser.

It was the last will and testament of one John McKinley of the
town of Rattlesnake. In it McKinley left to the pastor of Mission
San Leo thirty-six acres of land and first water rights from the
Rattlesnake River, those rights to supercede the claim of the vil-
lage of Rattlesnake. It was signed in large awkward script, *John
McKinley,* and witnessed by Aaron McKinley and Ephraim Mc-
Kinley. The date was September 13, 1937.

The will looked legal. It gave Austin Vanderhooven all he
needed for his retreat. Where had it been kept all these years? And
why had Austin Vanderhooven taken it out of there and put it
where Joe Zekk could find it?

She walked back into the living room. And where the hell was
Joe Zekk? Out peddling the Rattlesnake villagers' pots, as Bud
Warren had suggested? Some benefit those villagers got after giving
up their water!

The kitchen door rattled.

Kiernan stepped back inside the bedroom. She slid the will under the bed.

The kitchen door opened slowly. Footsteps, light, hesitant, came
from inside now.

Damn! Why couldn't Zekk have kept a gun in his shirt drawer?
The living-room carpet muffled the footsteps. She waited, letting
them reach the middle, then took a deep breath and said, "Put
your hands up! Lie flat out, face down!"

She peered through the doorway just in time to see a teenage boy
run for the door.

30

THE BOY raced out Zekk's kitchen door and around the house toward the switchback road to the village below. Kiernan grabbed McKinley's will and sprinted after him. She dropped the will in the Jeep and raced onto the downhill road, skidding in the loose dry earth. The boy was nearly a foot taller than she, with legs that seemed a yard longer. He hit the first switchback and shot down the next leg of the road, digging the sides of his boots into the steep banks. He was gaining.

Kiernan raced after him, tensing her ankles with each plant of a foot. The running shoes were useless here. The soil was too loose, with rocks the size of melons. She was guessing with each step, hoping the dirt she aimed her foot at was not concealing a sharp, uneven rock. She looked ahead, trying to judge the next ten yards, then glanced quickly over the edge of the road. The boy had cleared the next switchback. He was running all-out. Kiernan looked at the sheer hillside, frantically searching for a path down, a way to cut him off, but there was none. The hillside was too steep, with no trees to grab onto, but enough cacti to make a fall painful. At the edge of the road, the bigger rocks and boulders crowded against each other. She came up on the switchback, jumped for the banking, skidded, and fell to her hands and knees. She pushed up and ran on. Swirling dust struck her face, filled her nose, and dried her mouth. She tried to swallow, couldn't.

The boy was on the next leg below, going faster with each step. She ducked, grabbed a rock, and hurled it at him. Missed. She grabbed another. Hit! He clutched his shoulder, paused, his face rigid with anger. She bounced off the bank of the switchback, yelling, "Stop right there."

He pushed off, racing faster.

"Stop, I said. Next time it'll be your eye I hit."

He hesitated. He was right beneath her.

He had size but she had momentum. She leapt, landing hard on his back. She grabbed him around the shoulders and hung on as the force threw them over the side of the road. With her arms around his back, they rolled. The jagged rocks scraped her back, scraped *his* face. The cacti cut her hands. The puffs of earth shot dirt into her eyes. The boy let out a yelp. They smashed into a boulder, the boy chest first. The crash knocked the wind out of him.

She yanked his arms together behind him and demanded, "What were you doing up there?" Her voice was harsh and raw from the dust.

He made a gurgling sound.

"Answer me!"

He coughed. "Nothing," he squeaked out.

She pulled his arms tighter together. "This is your last chance."

A whimper came from his throat.

Kiernan yanked again. "Tell me!"

"Uhm." He spat. "Help him . . . haul stuff."

She pulled his arms up, sending his face into the dirt. "Don't lie to me. You were stealing, weren't you?"

He gasped, spat, gasped again.

"Now!"

"Okay . . . okay . . . let up!" he muttered. She eased up just enough for him to notice. He breathed in deeply.

"You were after the tapes, weren't you?" It was a fair guess.

"No!"

She pulled his arms tighter.

"No! Leggo! You're going to break my shoulder."

"The truth! You were after Zekk's tapes, weren't you?"

"His porn tapes? No. I don't need that."

"Sure."

"I don't!" He giggled. "I can see the real stuff."

She eased his arms slightly. "Where?"

Now he made an odd sound. It took her a moment to realize it was the laugh of an awkward, embarrassed adolescent. "The titty-shaped love nest up there." His face flushed. "You know, through the blue window." He giggled. "Like a blue movie."

"You've done that?"

"Yeah, sure," he said, his tone indicating less certainty than his words. "Me and my friend."

"Not much to do out here, huh?" Kiernan offered, letting him loose.

By tacit agreement the two of them sat, panting. "Nothing like that, not in Rattlesnake. Only three girls in town, and none of them are like her."

"Her? Who?"

"The one up there. She's real tan, and she's got a white X on her back—"

"From bathing-suit lines?"

"And she's tan all the way down to . . . Then she's got this great round white . . ." His face was even redder.

"Short hair?"

"Huh?" he demanded, redder yet.

Kiernan swallowed a laugh. "Her hair, was it sandy-colored and cut short?"

"Yeah. Hey, you don't know her, do you?"

Ignoring that, she demanded, "Who was she with?"

"Some guy. He was on the bottom." He turned away and gestured toward the house. "Zekk owes us. He cheats us all the time."

"How? He sells your pottery, right?"

His breath was becoming calmer. "He takes twenty pots and platters, big ones, to town. And he comes back with a hundred dollars. None of us go to the city, he knows that. We don't deal with strangers. He thinks we're just dumb hicks. But my cousin worked construction a while back and a guy there told him what pots sell for. Zekk's cheating us."

They sat staring at each other. "So what were you going to do about it?"

"Wait for him, make him admit it."

"And if he didn't? He's bigger than you, isn't he?" It was a guess.

"Yeah, maybe."

"He's got guns, doesn't he?" Another guess.

"Sure. But—"

"And you're what, fifteen? Don't tell me you're the one who speaks for your whole village."

"Somebody's got to. He's cheating us. Before Mac got sick he'd have taken care of it. He's too sick now. He's dying. Somebody's got to."

"Mac?"

"My granddad."

"John McKinley?"

"Yeah," he said, standing up. He started down the road, waiting till she fell in beside him. When the road switched back he kept on straight along a path toward the cemetery.

The cemetery was so steep the corpses might almost have been standing up; the thought made her laugh irrationally. The sun bounced off the dry hillside, the brittle tombstones; it burned her back. Sweat coated her body. It ran in dirty rivulets down the boy's arms. His shirt stuck to his back.

As they walked along she noticed the shabby tombstone of Matthew Shelton, 1901–1938. She looked at the tombstones in the row above: Sabrina Shelton, 1906–1938; Benjamin Shelton, 1917–1938. She shifted to see the next one; Hazel Shelton, 1909–1938.

"What happened in nineteen thirty-eight?" she asked.

"Flu."

She looked back at the weathered headstones and the bare dirt around them. "How come no one cares for these graves?"

"No relatives left."

A center path divided the cemetery into two sections. This shabby section had three rows of eight graves each, a top row of two. The other half had three rows with six each. Headstones had been carved from the red rock of the hillside. But that was the sole similarity between the two sides. The far section had been watered down, and the dirt had been raked. This one looked like a potter's field: nearly half the stones had been blown over; dirt clumped against them. All it needed was tumbleweed to complete the picture.

"Those graves over there, they're McKinleys, right? How come they're all cared for?"

The boy didn't answer.

"And how come so many of them survived the flu?"

"George!" A man called from below. "Get her down here."

She looked down. Whatever suspicions she had had about Rattlesnake being a ghost town disappeared. A crowd of roughly thirty people—women, children, men—stood on the path beneath the cemetery. Two men stood on porches of the wooden houses to the left. Many carried heavy-looking rifles. Every one of them stared at her, eyeing her masculine attire and her short hair. And every one of them looked angry.

31

KIERNAN SAT on a rawhide chair in a cottage that could have been taken from a Wild West movie set. Two men with rifles propped beside them kept watch on her. One guarded the front door. The other—Frank, by name, and clearly the leader—stood stolidly across the dark, ill-ventilated room by the bedroom door. Everything about him was thick—his belly pushed at his belt, his jeans spanned his thighs, the short sleeves of his shirt clung to his biceps. He looked like the ancestor of Brad Tchernak's perfect offensive lineman, the man no human could move. A man a not-quite-five-foot-one detective was not likely to push aside.

It was he who had hauled her down from the cemetery, leaving the boy in obvious disgrace. The villagers had watched silently, their faces pinched with anger, their eyes squinting in curiosity. They looked as if they had all been dropped from the same mold: tall, thick, long-haired people; men in jeans and flannel shirts, hefting heavy rifles like Patsy Luca's varmint rifle; women in cotton dresses. They had followed her along the steaming treeless street to the first house and stood silent as Frank shoved her inside.

What kind of place was this? Were the villagers members of some cult? Renegade Mormon polygamists with armed men ready to fight off any threat to their harems? Fundamentalists equally eager to shoot? Generations of families, hiding some shameful secret? One thing she knew was that they were McKinleys and Sheltons, and Austin Vanderhooven had been planning to visit one McKinley today. He had had "McKinley" written on his calendar. A second thing she recalled was Patsy Luca's description of the varmint rifle: an accurate high-velocity rifle, likely to blow its victim's insides to mush.

A low moan came from the bedroom now. Was that John McKinley, the dying village elder?

Moving her head as little as possible, she surveyed the room. The hot damp air smelled of smoke, stale sweat, stale onions, camphor—an odd combination. An old leather trunk stood beside the soot-coated fireplace. On the mantel were two graceless pottery bowls with a quartet of black vertical lines for design. Two worn rawhide chairs stood next to a stained oak table. The bare floorboards had been worn down in the center, and decades of dirt-covered boots had ground the red-brown earth into them. Faded, frayed curtains hung limp beside dirt-encrusted windows.

"I came to see John McKinley," Kiernan said.

Frank made no reply. His eyes were sunk back above leathery cheekbones; his thick shoulders sloped. He had the look of a tired, anxious man. His eyes wandered to the closed bedroom door just as another moan broke the silence.

"He's dying, isn't he?" she asked.

Frank's only response was the tightening of his fingers on the rifle. Behind him the door remained shut. The stale muggy air in the room seemed to carry the heat of his tension.

Kiernan weighed her options. Neither man had spoken; neither had touched her after the big one shoved her in here. They seemed to have no curiosity about why she was here, but neither did they show any urge to let her go. She could wait. With a small, quiet woman they might relax their guard. Watching for her moment, she might escape. But patience was hardly one of her virtues. She needed to get to John McKinley before he died; she needed to learn why a copy of his fifty-year-old will was in Joe Zekk's house. She stood and took a step toward the bedroom.

A moan broke the silence—louder this time. Frank shuddered.

Kiernan braced a foot on the arm of the chair. "How bad is he?" she said, eyeing the closed door.

Frank said nothing, but a flicker of fear was visible in his dull, brown eyes.

She guessed. "You're not sure, are you? But he's too sick to take chances with, right?" She couldn't read Frank's reaction, couldn't tell if she was playing him right. "I'm a doctor. I can help him."

Frank's eyes narrowed in disbelief.

"Had a doctor," the younger man said, disgust clear in his tone. Frank scowled at him.

"What did the doctor say?"

Frank's lips quivered but he didn't speak.

"The doctor, did he leave any medicine? Penicillin, tetracycline, streptomycin?" From the younger man's disdainful shrug she guessed that there was medicine, medicine that wasn't doing much. "With medication, even the right medicines, sometimes the doses need to be changed. Sometimes the patient reacts badly, the prescription has to be different. Show me what he's taking."

The younger man looked at the door, then back at his companion. A tremulous moan pierced the door. Both men started. Kiernan shivered.

"For Christ's sake," she said, "you can hear how much pain he's in. Don't you care?"

Without appearing to move his mouth, Frank said, "Morphine."

Kiernan sighed. That might mean something else, but chances were that a prescription of morphine left in this remote village with apparently no one trained to administer it was for a cancer patient, and one who didn't have much time. If they gave him too much, if they created addiction, it wouldn't be for long.

And that explained the somberness of those hostile villagers.

She said, "Morphine? Obviously, it's not making him comfortable. You know the dose can vary. The amount he needed yesterday may not do it today."

Not looking at Frank, the younger man said, "Not taking it."

"Not taking it? Why not? He's got cancer, right?"

For the first time Frank winced.

The younger man said, "Old Mac knows what morphine does. He was here when the town was booming. He saw the miners strung out on drink, a couple on stuff like morphine. Minds like mud, he said. He won't take it till the priest comes back."

"Father Vanderhooven."

He nodded.

"You expected him today, right?"

The younger man's eyes snapped open.

"Father Vanderhooven is dead." Before they could even gasp, she said, "He was murdered. Murdered before he could get here."

To the younger man she said, "Why was Father Vanderhooven coming?"

"Last rites."

She shook her head. "It was more than that. Mr. McKinley's name was on the priest's calendar. He planned to come here today. You expected him today, right? So, there was no need for Mac to wait in pain all week. He could receive Extreme Unction in any state; his mind wouldn't have to be clear. There must be more to it than that."

Frank shook his head sharply.

Pacing toward the bedroom, Kiernan said, "Had the priest come here often?"

With his free hand, Frank grabbed her shoulder and shoved her back in the chair.

Her head banged against the hard chair back. Swallowing her urge to yelp, she took a breath and waited till she could be sure her voice would be steady. "He's your father, right?"

Frank didn't answer. Kiernan kept her gaze on him, ignoring the younger man.

"Your father's in there dying. He's been in pain how long—a week, a month? All that so he could deal with the priest today. And now someone has killed the priest to keep him from seeing your father. And you don't have enough respect for your father to find out why?"

Beneath his leathery tan, Frank's craggy face reddened. He stepped toward Kiernan, lifted an arm, and backhanded it across her face.

Her head snapped left, the pain clanged through her skull, setting off the throbbing anew. She jammed her teeth together and waited for the pain to ease up. "Are you going to find out what your father is desperate to know or not?"

He took another step toward her.

Involuntarily, she stiffened.

"We don't deal with strangers. We don't go to town. We don't let strangers in here. We don't let them snoop around our graveyard. And we don't put up with this kind of shit." Holding the rifle in his left hand, he leaned back, drew his right arm back.

From the bedroom came another shrill tremulous moan. Frank spun toward the door. The old man moaned again, louder, his pain obvious in every note.

Kiernan stepped back. "He's really suffering. There's nothing for him to wait for now. With the morphine he won't care. It'll be like the pain is in someone else's body."

Frank made no move toward either Kiernan or the bedroom. His father wailed, the sound of hopeless desperation. Frank took a step toward the bedroom door, then stopped, as if he couldn't bring himself to go inside. His face was tense with fear and shame.

Kiernan had seen faces like that only a few times. And then she had seen only the dregs of shame as a husband or daughter confessed to her after the death. She had never been out to patients' homes, never seen the relatives when they still had Frank's decision to make. But she knew his reaction was not uncommon. She said, "You've never given him a shot, have you? Isn't there someone else here who can do that? A woman?"

"He won't have a strange woman. Wouldn't have no one but Ma. She's dead. Been dead ten years."

"Any man who's good with his hands?"

He shook his head.

Kiernan took a breath. She needed to get to John McKinley. But to administer a shot to a patient she'd never seen before? An invitation to a malpractice suit. She almost laughed; how deep the medical conditioning went. Frank McKinley was hardly going to file suit. "Get me the syringe. I'll do it."

"I said no strange women."

"How's his eyesight?"

Frank looked puzzled.

"Look, the people outside stared at my short hair like they couldn't decide which sex I belong to. He won't even have that question. He'll assume I'm a man. Frank, he will be grateful."

Frank's hand tightened on the rifle. He stared at Kiernan, then looked at the bedroom door. Finally, he said to the other man, "Get Evan and James over here." To Kiernan he said, "Sit."

The two men who arrived were smaller, darker, older than Frank. They filed silently into the bedroom with him, leaving the other man to guard Kiernan. Once the door was closed Kiernan could hear the sporadic murmur of words inside but could get no sense of what was being said. In ten minutes they emerged, again silently, and walked out the front door.

The old man moaned louder.

Before Kiernan could speak, the younger man said, "The shot. Did you give it to him?"

Frank shook his head.

Then what, Kiernan thought irritably, were you and your friends doing in there?

Frank took a step toward her. His whole body seemed to hang back, as if his foot alone were dragging the rest of him. "I'll do it now. You tell me how to do the shot."

He opened the bedroom door just as the old man wailed. Frank's eyes closed, then opened. Kiernan followed him into a small, bare room, darker, hotter, closer than the one they had left.

The old man was mostly bone. His gray skin hung from prominence to prominence, like the canvas of a sagging tent. His eyes were clouded with pain. Despite the nearly suffocating heat, he was shivering.

To Frank she said, "Start by filling the syringe. Take the needle, depress the plunger all the way, then pull it back slowly till it fills. When it's full, move the plunger forward very slowly till a drop of solution comes out. Then you know there are no air bubbles inside. Then the needle is ready. Okay?"

He nodded skeptically.

She moved to the old man's side and took his hand. Minutely, his moaning eased. Bending near him, she said, "The priest? Why are you waiting for him?"

He moaned louder.

She couldn't tell whether he understood the question. "The priest?" she repeated.

"Hey!" Frank snapped. "Be silent!"

She turned to him. He was fingering the syringe fearfully.

"Give it to me. I'll just fill it." Before he could protest, she took it, and depressed the plunger into the ampule of morphine. "Now you take one of his buttocks, and in your mind you divide it into four sections, like quarters of pie. Then you take the outer corner of the upper outside quarter—got that? That's where you're going to give the shot. You rub the spot on his buttocks, just like you were scuffing it up a bit. He won't react to the needle so much. Then push the needle in, just this far, and slowly, slowly depress the plunger."

He nodded.

"Now do it!"

The old man cried out. Frank's whole body shook.

Kiernan steeled herself against the pain. "Do it!"

The old man wailed. "The priest. The priest. Give back. Give . . ." The word faded into another wail.

Kiernan reached for the syringe. Frank shook her off. "I'll do it. You wait outside. Go!" he yelled with such force that the old man stopped moaning.

Kiernan hesitated, then turned and walked out.

When the younger man put out a hand to stop her, she said, "You heard him. He told me to leave. I'm leaving." She walked through the front door into the blinding sunlight. All the tension she hadn't dared acknowledge welled up. Her head throbbed, and her shoulders were so tight they squeezed her neck. She had to fight the urge to run up the hill.

The street was as empty as the first time she'd looked down at it from Zekk's—empty but for the younger man, who stood with one foot on the front steps of John McKinley's house, looking first at her, then peering nervously back inside. Suddenly he straightened his shoulders, shut the door, and ran toward her.

Had Frank called to him? Knowing it might be futile, she quickened her pace.

But he made no move to stop her. He fell in beside her, rifle in hand.

Kiernan resisted the urge to look back at the doorway. When Frank finished with his father's shot and started looking for her she would hear him yell. She gazed up the hill, searching for escape routes she didn't believe would be there. The early afternoon sun seared her face. The baking heat rose up from the dry dirt street. "Look," she said as they started up the switchback road, "I'm trying to help you and Mac. You understand that, don't you?"

He hesitated, then nodded.

"Then tell me why the priest was coming."

Again he hesitated, again he acceded. "Nobody but the old man knows why the priest was coming. Like Frank said, we don't like strangers. Those before us"—he nodded at the cemetery—"had bad times with strangers. Was a time when Rattlesnake was a boomtown. Stagecoaches stopped here in those days, leastways that's what they told us. And the miners from the copper mine— it's not a copper mine now, hasn't been for years. Warren's doing something with oil there now. You can hear the noise from it. Boom. Boom. Boom. Never stops. He's ruining the land there. Dust and noise. Enough to drive you crazy."

Bud's site was that close! But too far to do her any good now.

"Back then Rattlesnake was mostly bars and whorehouses. They came here because it was close, and it's the only place with flowing water for miles around."

Kiernan glanced back. Frank's door was still shut. "And then?"

"A priest came along and my great-granddad saw the light. He saw that Rattlesnake was a bed of sin. He had to fight hard, but he got the gin mills closed and the whores rid out of town, and he didn't let strangers back in. And no one has since."

She moved faster as they rounded the second switchback. "What about Joe Zekk?"

He shook his head. "No one but Father Vanderhooven."

"How come?"

Again he shook his head. But this time he added nothing.

There was no way to guess how long Frank McKinley would take giving that shot. She had heard of husbands standing, holding the needle for an hour, then suddenly shaking themselves, stepping forward, and plunging the needle into flesh. She had heard of some who, with the best of instructions, hit bone. She quickened her pace.

The younger man matched her step for step.

"Mac said, 'The priest. Give back.' What could Mac have been planning to give to the priest?" she asked. "Did he have anything of Father Vanderhooven's?"

"Don't know," he snapped.

She turned to him. His face was pulled tight, but she couldn't tell whether it was in fear or anger. "Did Father Vanderhooven have anything of his?"

"Mac wasn't a giver."

They turned on the next leg of the road. Four switchbacks to go. Kiernan looked down at the cemetery with its two sections. Moving faster, she said, "What happened in nineteen thirty-eight? What did all those people die of?"

"Flu," he said too quickly. "Flu. They all got sick, one after another."

"Did they have a doctor?"

"They died too quick." His breath was coming in pants.

She picked up the pace. Her own breath was short. "Did the priest come to bury them?"

"No. They died . . . too quick. Couldn't be left out . . . of the ground."

She took the next switchback. The Jeep was visible over the edge of the mesa. Gulping for breath, she said, "The McKinleys . . . died . . . all different years. Only a couple . . . died in . . . nineteen thirty-eight? All the Sheltons died then. How come?"

"God cursed them," he panted.

"They weren't Catholic?"

"Fake Catholics."

Kiernan recalled hearing of sects that had split from the Roman Catholic Church, sects whose members considered themselves the true guardians of the faith. Rounding a switchback—two to go— she said, "Are there Sheltons . . . in town now?"

With the rifle barrel, he pointed down to the graves. "All there."

"Not one of them . . . survived that flu?" She was nearly running. One more switchback to the top.

"Cursed."

She rounded the last switchback. The Jeep was twenty yards ahead.

The man braced his rifle and stopped.

She fingered her keys and slowed her pace. "What happened?"

A yell came from below. She looked back. The man with her turned and stared down too.

She ran for the Jeep and stuck the key in the lock. As she flung herself in she could hear another, louder yell from below. Still she couldn't make out the words. She turned the key and floored the gas pedal.

She was a hundred yards above the mesa when a shot shattered the rear window of the Jeep.

32

KIERNAN DIDN'T STOP till she reached the main road. Then she pulled over, closed her eyes and flopped forward over the steering wheel. Sweat rolled down her face and coated her back. Her heart thumped. She turned on the air conditioner and sighed as the air chilled her sweaty body. She pulled out the plastic bottle of water Wiggins had reminded her to carry in the Jeep, chugged greedily, and leaned back to think.

Surely, she decided, Joe Zekk must have been down in the village at some time. Even if he was aware of the trigger-happy habits of the villagers, it would be almost impossible for a man to live in virtual isolation right above there and not be curious enough to sneak down. And then surely he too must have had questions about the Sheltons in the cemetery.

She took another drink of water. There were so many questions. What *had* caused the Sheltons' deaths? Had the McKinleys killed them in a feud? In a religious battle? If so, where did Mission San Leo fit in? Had the priest there covered up for them because McKinley willed him the land for the retreat the previous year? And what did the old man want to give or take back? That land? Was that why Joe Zekk had hunted out the will? Or had Austin Vanderhooven brought the will out here to the dome, and Zekk had come across it after his death?

But the will itself was nothing. If McKinley wanted to supercede it he had only to write another. He had had plenty of time to do that all these years. And the land was still his. No one had to give it back. So what did he want?

And Austin Vanderhooven? He came to Phoenix, revitalized Dowd's retreat plans, he got backers, then ignored them. He planned a great retreat, and what he built was a ten-foot meditation dome. The man was a jumble of contradictions. Even his dome —was it for meditation or for screwing Beth Landau? And what in all of that had moved someone to kill him?

Suddenly, surprisingly, Kiernan found herself ravenously hungry. Sweat rolled down her forehead. Throwing aside caution, she took another drink of water, and another. "Damn you, Stu Wiggins," she muttered. "Why didn't you tell me to bring food, too? I'm not likely to find a McMiddle-of-the-desert."

Following the map Bud Warren had given her, she turned right onto the main road. Ahead the land was as flat as it had been in Phoenix, only thousands of feet higher up. The only vegetation was the low chollas and other cacti and the thin wisps of mesquite. No rodents skittered over the hardtop; no birds broke the beige of the sky. If the hardtop had not been there, the arid mesa would have looked the same as it had a hundred years ago when they named the area White Bone Mountains. She shivered and found herself scanning the horizon for bleached skeletons and wondering how many of them, over the years, had been human.

Ahead the sky was becoming browner. The air seemed thicker. She stepped on the gas.

The turnoff to the Warren Works came a mile and a half farther on. It was a well-rutted dirt road. Despite its four-wheel drive, the Jeep bounced in the deep potholes. She steadied the wheel and overrode the urge to step on the gas and try to skim the top. Instead, she braked, steering to the side of the road, almost on the embankment.

The road cut through a rocky promontory and descended sharply, down a hundred feet. An explosion shook the Jeep. Kiernan slammed on the brakes.

She was poised at the rim of a huge hole. The center was another couple of hundred feet down. The remains of the strip-mining the villager had mentioned. Five-foot rocks rolled down the loose side, bouncing wildly against one another at the bottom. Huge clouds of dust flew up, engulfing them, as more rocks careened down from the site of the explosion. Rock hit rock; the noise was like a battlefield. Like battalions of McKinleys.

Suddenly she found herself shaking so hard that the Jeep stalled. Despite the cool air in the car, her skin had a sick, clammy feeling. Closing her eyes she breathed deeply, and it calmed her. After a few minutes she opened her eyes, started the engine, and drove on, around the rim to a road that descended into a similar depression.

Although she had heard Bud Warren describe his oil-shale retort as the size of a five-story building, she wasn't prepared for the magnitude of the project. In the center of the site stood the retort, like a giant metal ampule, surrounded by a scaffolding of pipes and ladders and chimneys spewing brownish gas. Conveyor belts moved giant buckets of rock from the pile in the strip-mine depression to one shaking machine after another and carried the crushed rock to the top of the hundred-foot hopper and dumped it in. Dust was everywhere. The banging, smashing, and clattering of machines echoed and bounced around the side of the depression, melding into a painful wall of noise. The smell of ammonia and sulphur and dust made it hard to breathe. The scene was like a picture of Hell.

Steeling herself against the noise, she drove down the road to the edge of the works. The sign simply said WARREN PROCESS WORKS. A man in a gray jumpsuit knocked on her window. She asked for Bud Warren, and in less than a minute she spotted him walking out of the low building at the south corner of the site. Despite the heat, Warren wore jeans and a work shirt. He had the easy walk of a man at home here. The wind tossed his dark hair, and his clear blue eyes seemed to light up as he came toward her. Kiernan found herself smiling too.

"Kiernan," Warren shouted as she opened her window. "Great. I didn't dare hope you'd come up here so soon. I was afraid you might not really be interested." He grinned. "Sometimes, you know, people don't quite share my enthusiasm. But it is a fascinating process. Let me show you around."

"Can you give me food first? And a beer?"

His tanned forehead creased. "Did I invite you for lunch? No matter, we'll pretend I did. Will a sandwich do?"

"Perfect."

Warren walked around the Jeep and climbed in. "The office is at the far side. Take the road straight through." He looked at the shattered back window. "Are you okay? What happened?"

"Unfriendly McKinleys in Rattlesnake. I'll tell you about it after I eat."

"I'll have one of the guys tape some plastic over the window. That should hold you till you get back to town."

"Thanks." Kiernan rolled up the side window against the dust outside and headed around the conveyors that joined the giant machines—what were they called? "Are those the lock hoppers?"

Warren laughed. "No, they're the grizzlies."

"Grizzlies?"

"Rock crushers. We've got three different sizes of grizzlies—"

"Poppas, mommas, and babies?"

Kiernan could almost see Warren changing mental gears. It was a moment before he laughed. "Right, poppa over there takes the big bites. See?" He pointed toward a huge, rumbling machine. "Then he spits them out onto the conveyor belt to momma, and she chews it better, and spits . . ." Warren laughed. "Maybe regurgitation similes aren't the best way to make a good impression before lunch, huh?"

"Good save. It'll take a lot more than rock-crushing stories to dim my appetite."

"My kind of woman. Okay, here, veer around this building."

"The conveyors lead in there. But there are no windows? What's inside?"

Putting a hand on her arm, he said, "That, my dear, is the process. It's the baghouse!"

"Eyes only?"

"You got it. I can't afford to take a chance. Everything's wrapped up in that process. And when it sells, Kiernan, I'll take you to a lunch fit for a queen."

Following Warren's directions she drove around the baghouse to a one-story stucco building in the far corner of the site. It too was windowless, and the walls, she found on entering, were three feet thick. "Like a bomb shelter," she said.

"Noise'll kill you otherwise. I can't have the workers wandering off half the day to find a little peace. This doesn't muffle it entirely, but it's not too bad. Here"—he pulled a chair out from one of the two red Formica tables—"sit. Ham, roast beef, or pastrami?"

"Pastrami."

Warren's green metal desk and file cabinets filled one end of the room. The other housed a sink, a small refrigerator, and the table, which reminded her of a 1950s kitchenette. On the wall was a poster of the Denali National Park in Alaska.

Warren plucked two bags from the fridge, plopped them on the table, and went back for cans of beer. "Carta Blanca, okay? It's your only choice."

"Great." She took a bite of the sandwich. The pastrami was

good, the rye bread fresh, the mustard sharp. Nodding at it she said, "Do you have a hot line to the only kosher deli in Phoenix that delivers?"

Warren laughed. "I figure the guys are out here in the middle of nowhere, at least I can provide good food."

"I'd work for you." She took another bite.

"I'd like you to think it's because I'm such a nice guy, and I am, of course. But it's good business. Things like this room, the movies, the food, it keeps the guys out here. Otherwise they'd be driving into town every night, and in no time they'd have found other jobs. It gets pretty tedious out here."

"How do *you* handle it?"

Warren laughed. "Same as they would. I take every chance to get into town."

Warren took a bite of his own sandwich. In the silence she was more aware of the thumping outside, like a kid across the street playing the drum. Enough to cause suburban feuds. Enough to cause rural feuds. "Bud," she said, "all the guards and the precautions outside, it's not just because of spies, is it? The villagers in Rattlesnake complained about you. How much of a threat are they?"

Warren held his sandwich halfway to his mouth, staring. "They told you that much? You are good at your work. They don't let strangers down there. No one but Vanderhooven, and him not often."

"Well, you saw the Jeep window. They didn't exactly invite me to stay. But they did answer some questions—"

"What'd you ask them?"

"About the cemetery mostly."

"The old man, he still alive?"

"He was then, but he didn't sound good."

"Didn't you see him? I mean, you are a doctor, right? It'd be reasonable for you to see him."

She shrugged, then asked again, "Are the villagers threatening you?"

Bud put down his sandwich. "There's always some monkey wrench in the works with a project like this. Usually, it's the delivery schedule; whatever you need most doesn't get delivered. Or it's union hassles. But this time things were racing right along. No problems setting up meetings, no hassles getting deliveries. In the beginning I assumed that the village would be a source of labor. It would be good money for them. But I'll tell you, those guys in the village, they just don't want to work. They farm a little and they sit on their porches, or inside the houses, to be accurate. They can't even get it up to plant a tree to shade them."

"They said you were destroying the area."

Warren smacked a fist against the chair back. "Damn! I might as well have talked to the walls there. I told old man McKinley that I would take this hole here, this hole that White Bone Copper just walked away from, and I'd turn it back to what it was. I showed him my papers from Environmental Protection. You can't get a better record with them than I have. E.P. saw the plans for this place and they applauded me. I told McKinley, this place is going to look better than it has in thirty years. Did no good."

"Have they been vandalizing?"

"Stuff's been missing, small stuff. Could be them, could be someone else."

"Someone specific?"

"Well . . ."

"Zekk?"

Warren hesitated. "I don't have proof. But the stuff that goes is wheelbarrows, air conditioners, things he could stick in the back of his van and fence when he sells the pottery. But"—he shook his head—"I don't know. Zekk's around a lot, but maybe he's just bored."

"Why do you still let him on the site?"

"I hate to banish him. The guards keep an eye on him. Isolated like this, you get to know everyone, and you take what company you can get. And besides he's got a collection of porn tapes you wouldn't believe. Like an outlet. Hundreds. Keeps the guys here at night."

"So the occasional wheelbarrow is worth it?"

"You bet."

"And, presumably, Zekk isn't complaining about the noise like the villagers are. And even so, the villagers still share their water with you."

"Have no choice, Kiernan. I get my allotment from the church land. That's one good thing. I don't have to deal with the McKinleys at all."

"But the church gets its water from the McKinleys. They have an informal agreement, right? So they could turn off the tap any time if they wanted you out of here badly enough."

Warren shrugged. "I'd say that proves my point."

She finished her sandwich and took a long, slow drink of beer, thinking of Joe Zekk. Zekk, who had had McKinley's will. Zekk, who called Philip Vanderhooven in Maui. Who cheated the villagers and got $200 a month from Austin Vanderhooven. She put the can down. "Bud. What did Joe Zekk do before he came out here?"

"Bummed around. The guy's not a powerhouse. He'd be happy down there in the village if they had electricity. Well, and bars and women."

"Bummed around? In the U.S.? Overseas?"

"I think he worked tramp steamers."

"A sailor? Someone familiar with knots."

"Yeah. Why are you—? Oh, knots." He nodded.

Kiernan finished the beer. "You don't seem surprised."

He leaned his head forward over his arms. His dark hair hung. Tan dust still coated the top, and the occasional gray hair, kinkier than the dark ones, stood out. "I don't know," he said, looking up. "I can't picture Joe Zekk hanging Vanderhooven. The guy was his friend. And yet . . ."

"Yes?"

"Well, this probably doesn't mean anything."

"Yes?"

"I went up to the main road to meet Elias the night Austin was killed. Since I was up there, I stopped at Joe's to change movies. He wasn't home. And after Elias left, he still wasn't home."

33

THE KHAKI-COLORED SKY muddied the outlines of Joe Zekk's castle-house. It blurred into the dome at the end of the mesa and the rocky peninsula of land that overhung the valley.

The switchback road down to Rattlesnake was empty. The village itself looked the way it had when Kiernan had first seen it: deserted. There were McKinleys down there, of course, but they were not bursting out of their houses for another shot at the Jeep. Not yet. Still, she didn't kid herself that her arrival would go unnoticed.

A green panel truck stood by Joe Zekk's front door. She parked next to it, took a drink of water, pulled her shirt free where it had become stuck to her back, and headed to the house. The quicker she could deal with Zekk and get away from Rattlesnake, the better.

She knocked and waited. In California the change from blue to overcast sky signaled a decrease in temperature; here it meant merely a qualitative change, like stepping from a barbecue into a steamer. She was about to knock again when she heard slow, heavy footsteps approach.

Unlike the McKinleys below, the man who opened the door was no behemoth; he was just out of shape. He wasn't fat—yet. But there was an unhealthy roundness to him, to his cherub cheeks, his squishy arms, and the abdominal flesh that pushed against his teal polo shirt and blue deck pants. Looking at him, Kiernan realized that at some level she had been picturing a leftover hippie. But this man's short dark hair was swept stylishly back from his face and stood stiffly in place. His porcine face was remarkably pasty for a desert dweller, and the lines that crossed his forehead and ran down under the mounds of his cheeks gave him the appearance not of maturity but rather of a dissolute adolescent.

"Are you Joe Zekk?" she asked.

He nodded, eyeing her appraisingly.

"I'm investigating Austin's death. Can we talk inside?"

Zekk leaned back against the doorframe and continued his survey of her body. An adolescent smirk played at the corners of his mouth. She'd seen that look before, the look of the bully assuring himself he could handle this small woman. From experience she knew he'd need to be set straight, fast. "Zekk, Austin Vanderhooven has been killed, and you are in a very bad position. 'Deadbeat' is the kindest word I've heard to describe you. Somebody strung up your friend, and everyone involved in this case would be delighted to hear that that somebody was you."

Zekk's fleshy face stiffened. He glanced nervously at the room behind him, then at the bedroom.

Had he already discovered the McKinley will was gone? Or did he have a weapon she had missed in her earlier search? "You have a gun in there? Forget it. Half of Phoenix knows I was headed up here today."

Zekk took a step back.

Keeping an eye on him, Kiernan moved inside, grateful for the icy air, and made her way through the litter to the sofa. Dislodging a blue striped jacket, she sat. Joe Zekk flopped down on the far end of the sofa and landed on a pair of gray sweat pants and a brown slipper. He made no move to pull them out. She felt sure he no longer noticed the pervading stench of old soda, old food, old God-knows-what. He looked so much like a rebellious adolescent it was hard to remember he was over thirty.

Using the most parental tone she could muster, Kiernan said, "Let's start with the two hundred dollars a month Austin Vanderhooven was giving you—"

"What? Two hundred dollars?"

"Don't lie about something that's so easily traced. Now why was he paying you?"

She could almost see him mentally regrouping. Hardening her voice, she said, "Elias Necri reported the money, Philip Vanderhooven knows about it. What did you have on Austin?"

"It wasn't blackmail!" He sighed, glanced hopelessly at the bedroom door, and said, "Okay, I'll tell you about it, but let me get a drink first." He grabbed a brown-ringed old-fashioned glass from the table, shoved a pile of *Hustler* magazines to the floor, and excavated a one-serving bottle of rye. He emptied it into the glass and drank slowly, eyes half-closed in thought. "He paid me to be the caretaker; he wanted someone he could trust here."

Kiernan laughed. "No one has called you trustworthy."

Zekk shrugged, but the movement looked forced. The flesh at the corners of his mouth quivered.

She had hurt his feelings! The man really was an adolescent. "Okay, start from the beginning. You were in seminary with Austin."

He took another drink. Already the glass was nearly empty. He lifted his right ankle and set it on his knee. The teal bulge of his stomach protruded over the edge of his blue pants. "One of the big mistakes of my life, seminary. I don't know what I thought I'd find there, but it sure wasn't another year of catechism and a bunch of asshole rules and years of running errands for a flock of old duffers who think the world hasn't changed since the first encyclical. It didn't take me long to see what bullshit the whole business was."

"You left after the first year?"

"Yeah."

"What about Austin? How come he stayed?"

Zekk took a mouthful of rye and swished it noisily around his teeth. "It was different with Austin. He realized the bullshit, of course. Anyone'd do that. But the thing was, he just couldn't believe that was all there was. See, Austin wasn't like me. Now, I know what people think of me, what you think of me, what they thought of me in seminary. They figured I was lucky to have squeaked past the admissions board. But Austin, he was a star. He abandoned graduate school for the church. Star, scholar, it was written all over him. He was going places, and he was going to carry the good fathers with him. He was one of the ones who'd be sent for graduate courses to the North American College in Rome, maybe the Pontifical Gregorian University, maybe Academia Alfonsiana, who knows? Maybe he'd be the one to take charge of the Church's investments, which would have been a damned sight more appreciated than any theological insights he might have come up with." Zekk laughed, a whiny sound. "Besides, when Austin made his decision to enter seminary, he burned a *lot* of bridges. He couldn't give it up without looking a fool."

"What are you saying—Austin was committed, or just too embarrassed to quit?"

"Austin and me, we were on the same wavelength. We stayed up half the night more nights than not, talking, trying to make sense out of that ridiculous system. I finally got out. But Austin kept assuming that there was a nugget of truth buried under the doctrine." Zekk snorted. "See, Austin figured if he just worked hard enough, dug deep enough, he would find *the* secret."

Kiernan shivered. She knew that obsession only too well. "And did he?"

"It was ridiculous. He was one of the brightest guys I knew. He had advantages I would have killed for—whoops, wrong choice of word, huh?" He let out a high-pitched laugh.

Kiernan grimaced.

"The point I'm making," Zekk hurried on, "is that I knew him in the first year of seminary. I talked to him two weeks ago. And in all those years nothing had changed. He was still the same green kid looking for the same nugget of truth. Oh, he'd stripped off a lot of layers, he compartmentalized a lot of bullshit, like the pastor stuff. He really hated that. He couldn't get into these people whining about their problems with their second cars and their teenagers smoking dope or getting knocked up. He realized that he was wasting his time with that. I could have told him. I did, in fact, that first year. He just couldn't see it then. It took him all this time to realize it. That's why this house. First he figured if he could just get away and spend time talking to the one person he could trust. Hey, don't laugh."

"I'm not laughing. Go on."

Zekk downed the rest of his drink. "Yeah, well," he said tentatively, "Austin still had access to family money."

"No vow of poverty for him, huh?" Kiernan asked, anxious to nurture his nascent trust.

He leaned forward. "There are ways around them. Money wasn't an issue. And he got a good deal on building this place."

"From Sylvia Necri?"

"Yeah. He used to come out here every other week, on Monday and Tuesday, his days off. He'd want to talk sometimes about the *Humanae Vitae*, you know, the papal encyclical from nineteen sixty-eight. Or he was caught up in what is the difference between the assent of faith in the new canon law and the *obsequium religiosum* of the mind in regard to the authoritative teachings of the pope." Zekk shoved a pile of papers off the table, looked under them, then pushed another. They slid silently onto a pile of sweat gear on the floor. He eyed his empty glass accusingly. "Damn." To Kiernan he said, "You want a beer?"

"No."

He shrugged and leaned back against the sofa cushions, apparently unwilling to walk to the kitchen. After a moment he yanked another pile closer to him and rooted through it, coming up with another tiny bottle of rye. "Ah. Now this is better." He downed half and poured the rest. "Well, time may have stood still for Austin, but it hadn't for me. I'd stopped worrying about that garbage years ago. He must have figured that I'd be just like I was when I left seminary, as if I'd been stuck on a shelf all those years, just waiting for him to pull me off, wind me up, and have me cock an ear for him."

"When he realized you'd changed, did he ask you to leave?"

"Leave!" He flopped back possessively into the sofa corner. "Who else was he going to get to live out here in the middle of nowhere, with a pack of lunatics at the bottom of the gorge down there?"

"In Rattlesnake?"

"Yeah, who else would have the time to haul their pots around and see what tacky tourist shop would pass them off as Indian. You see their stuff? It's junk, not that that would keep it from selling. You wouldn't believe the crap tourists cart home." He laughed. "Sometimes I wonder what people in Minneapolis think of Arizona. They look at what their friends bring home: the lopsided pots and the sandbox-quality sand paintings; and they must figure the Valley of the Sun is desert-to-desert kitsch."

Kiernan laughed. Despite all that had been said about Joe Zekk, she was finding him not wholly unlikeable. "So why did you handle their pottery then?"

"Money. They need it. I need it. More to the point, that was part of the deal with Austin. He wanted them to have the income."

"To be dependent on him for it?"

Zekk shrugged. "Put whatever meaning you want on it."

"They say you cheat them."

Zekk jolted forward. "Cheat them! Hey, they're paying for first-class acting here. They should see my performance when I bring their stuff into a store. I earn my money."

The rest of Zekk's statements may have been questionable—certainly they merited more thought—but this one Kiernan took whole. From the looks of the pottery she had seen on John McKinley's mantelpiece, if Zekk moved any of it he was a master salesman. She shifted her weight, resting an elbow on the sofa back. The air cooled the underside of her arm. "Austin had something the old man down there had given him. The old man is hanging on, waiting to get it back."

Zekk laughed. "Lady, there's nothing down there anyone would want. Have you looked down there?" He didn't wait for a reply. "I haven't been down there in a year. Not since I caught one of them peeking in the windows and sent him headlong down that road of theirs."

"Maybe they got something since."

"No way. When it rains that road's a mud puddle. And they'd shoot at a stranger before he could bring them anything. It's not a place UPS delivers." He grinned and checked Kiernan's face for a corresponding reaction. When he saw it, he seemed genuinely pleased. "Austin went down every time he was here. And he never came back up with anything."

"Maybe McKinley gave him the item when you were away."

He shook his head. "I was always here when Austin was due. You see what a godforsaken place this is? I go days without seeing another human face. If it weren't for the process works up the road, I'd have lost my mind ages ago."

Kiernan nodded, feeling a stab of sympathy. Was this, she wondered, what mothers of chronically unwashed teenagers felt? "And, Joe, without the works, you'd have missed out on a good bit of trade." She glanced toward the cassettes on the bookcase next to the television.

"Hey, none of your bus—"

Kiernan sat forward. "It's all my business. Your best shot is with me. You're savvy enough to know that. You can refuse to tell me, of course, but if you don't have a real clear explanation of your income and your time, it might end up as the sheriff's business. How much?"

He hesitated. It was clear he was hiding something. The question

was, did that something concern the tapes, or was it another secret
he was guarding? The widening of his eyes indicated he'd made his
decision. "Three hundred a month."

"Three hundred, that's peanuts. You've got a captive audience
out here."

Zekk flushed. "Hey, I know that. They'd take one every night if
I'd let them. Hell, two or three a night. But you don't do business
that way. You've got to think of the future. I don't want the guys
getting bored in a couple months and pressuring Warren for something different. Not different movies, but buses to town or live
entertainment. Then I'd be cooked. So I dole out those tapes. Good
business."

Kiernan smiled. Joe Zekk the porno and pottery entrepreneur.

"Point is," he continued, "that when Austin came up here, I
hung around. His coming was a big event for me. Even after he
built his monastery."

"Monastery?"

"Yeah, well, that's what I called it. The dome outside. He used it
like a play monastery."

Kiernan's breath quickened. "Because that's what he really
wanted, right? To be in a monastery?"

Zekk dug his toe under a tan T-shirt on the floor and kicked it
into the middle of the room. "If he could have done it by his own
rules, yeah. He wasn't likely to put up with monastic bullshit anymore than he was doing with pastoral bullshit. So here he had his
very own monastery two days a week."

"Where he entertained his old girlfriend?"

Zekk's eyes shot open. He reached for the glass, knocked it over.
Half of the liquor sloshed out. "Well . . . hell, whatever he did
there was his business."

Could Zekk be refusing to rat on his friend? If so, the much-
maligned Zekk's loyalty to his friend was greater than anyone
else's. "Joe, I don't believe you didn't know what went on down
there. The place is two hundred yards away."

He interlaced his fingers and pressed his knuckles together, like
stunted hands in prayer. "Hey, I wasn't Austin's keeper. He hardly
bothered to talk to me when he got here. He just went down there.
If I knocked on his gate down there he got pissed. You'd think I
was going to contaminate the place. He never let me inside the

gate. Me, or anyone else. Whatever he was doing down there he really got into it. Eyes all sunk into his head. He got a call once here and I went to get him. He looked like something from the psych ward. Wouldn't take the call either." His hands were shaking.

"Who was it from?"

Zekk shrugged. "It was late. I have my own way of passing time." His hands relaxed and he began twiddling his thumbs. But the stiff deliberateness of the movement betrayed him.

"Joe, can you tell me where you were Tuesday night? I know you weren't here all evening, till late."

"Figure it out yourself."

Kiernan leaned forward. "Joe, I am trying to help you. You don't understand how much trouble you're in. And you know no one's going to help you but me."

Without actually moving he seemed to draw slightly closer.

Kiernan softened her voice. "You're admitting that you have no alibi for the night Austin was killed?"

He shrugged.

Pointedly looking at the shelves of tapes, she said, "You didn't have money when you got here. You've got thousands of dollars in video here. Where's your money coming from?"

"There's the pottery—" He sounded as if he was making up excuses for not doing his homework.

"What about Philip Vanderhooven? You called him in Maui. What are you selling him?"

"How'd you know—"

"What'd you offer him?"

His thumbs rotated faster, snapping at the web between thumb and forefinger. "Look, I told you Austin was getting screwy. I figured his father should know."

"You figured his father would pay you to keep tabs on him."

"Well, so? I've got to live."

"How much, Joe?"

He stared at his hands. "Another two hundred."

"Still not enough. Who else are you getting it from?"

"No one! I got the tapes discount."

Kiernan eyed the shelves of them. "Okay, so you bought them in bulk. Where'd you get the money for that?"

"Austin. Austin paid me five thousand in the beginning."

"Five thousand! For what?"

Joe grinned, clearly delighted at her surprise. His hands flopped on his lap. "Background," he said.

"On . . . ?" She smiled encouragingly.

"The villagers. Look, it's nothing sinister. He had a tricky situation with them."

"About nineteen thirty-eight, huh?"

"Yeah. How'd you . . . ? You'd think the sheriff was hounding them, or all those dead Sheltons were threatening to climb out of their graves and get revenge, the way they act. Hard as hell to get them to talk about the shoot-out."

She could feel her shoulders tightening in anticipation. "But they did tell you, right, Joe?"

He grinned and held up his glass proudly. "Me and my friend here."

She leaned forward. "Tell me."

He drank. "Can't really blame it on the Church. It's their own stupid fault, them down there, the McKinleys. They're Catholic. The Sheltons, they're the ones in the cemetery, they were some kind of fringe Catholic, but not the real thing. Now, I know I never got the real straight story from McKinley, but the gist of what I got and figured out was that something happened between John McKinley, the old man down there, and some Shelton, and they got to fighting. The whole thing turned into a feud, and then they pretty much formed two camps down there, small as the town is. There was a shoot-out, and the McKinleys won. And after that, mind you, after that the McKinleys started to rationalize and believe they killed off the Sheltons because they weren't legit, Catholicly speaking."

"The graveyard is full of Sheltons, but only a couple of McKinleys died that year. It doesn't sound like a very fair fight."

He laughed. "Didn't say it was. John McKinley was no fool. He got himself help."

"How?"

"He said he was smart."

"Who helped him?"

Zekk leaned back and let a smile stretch across his face. "Took me a long time to weasel that out of him. You know where John

McKinley got the money to buy the guns that killed all those Sheltons in the graveyard down there? I'll tell you. He got it from the Roman Catholic Church."

Kiernan whistled. Joe Zekk looked so delighted with himself that he was almost appealing.

Kiernan said, "And that's what Austin Vanderhooven paid you to find out."

"Yeah. And I loved it. Jesus, you should have seen Austin's face when I told him. I'd have done it for free just to see that look."

"Once Austin found out about the Church's role in the killings, what did he do about it?"

Zekk's grin spread across his face. "Not a damned thing."

34

IT WAS NEARLY 3:30 P.M. The drive from Joe Zekk's place up to the main road, then on a few miles east, past the turnoff to the Warren Works, and onto the deeply rutted dirt road to Hohokam Lodge had taken forty-five minutes so far. For Beth Landau, three quarters of an hour would make rather a pleasant anticipatory interlude on the way to a rendezvous, Kiernan thought. Just enough time to tickle herself with thoughts of Austin Vanderhooven slipping out of his cassock. Kiernan laughed. The man wouldn't have come to the mountains in full regalia. There in his dome he would have looked like any other reasonably well-built blond unzipping his jeans.

Kiernan left the air conditioning off and opened the window. The air was muggy, but the breeze made it almost bearable. Khaki-brown clouds covered the sun and blended into the horizon. She felt as if she were driving into the open end of a manila envelope. The wind sputtered streams of dirt across the hardtop, the dust smacked her face, but the thick spikes of cacti and the round squat cholla stood firm.

Austin Vanderhooven, the man was still an enigma. The obsessive monk she could understand. The man who couldn't give up his lover she could reconcile with that picture. She could even imagine Vanderhooven bringing Beth to his dome, combining his passions. And then there was the retreat. Vanderhooven the financial wunderkind, the fund-raiser, who planned what sounded like the biggest Catholic gathering-spot in the country. He would wield immense influence once it was built. How did Vanderhooven the monk fit with Vanderhooven the host? Why could she not merge the two aspects of him into one picture?

Momentarily the sun burst through the clouds and illumined an undisturbed peak that drew in sharply from a broad base to a tall obelisklike pinnacle. It echoed the lines of Joe Zekk's house. Or more accurately, Kiernan thought, Austin Vanderhooven had had the house designed to echo the lines of that peak. And that peak, of course, would be the site on which he planned to build the great retreat. It was half a mile behind Hohokam Lodge.

In contrast to that peak, Hohokam's mound seemed as squat as the chollas, as did the lodge itself. Behind it a little girl hung face down over a swing, moving lackadaisically back and forth despite the increasing wind. Kiernan noticed a young woman—was she the one in Beth's office yesterday? But no, that woman had had toddlers. This one carried an infant. Kiernan slowed the Jeep, looking for Patsy Luca. Patsy should have called Stu Wiggins last night. She hadn't. Stu hadn't hidden his concern. Patsy was reliable, he had assured Kiernan. Things happen, they had agreed. Still, a glimpse of Patsy would have been comforting.

She pulled up behind a van and got out. She climbed the three steps to the door. Before she could knock, it opened.

Beth Landau's freckled face tightened in anger. She kept her hand on the door. "You! What are you doing here? How did you find this place?"

Kiernan laughed. "I am an investigator."

"Well, go investig—"

"And I know about you and Austin's dome. I don't expect the contributors to the shelter would be pleased to hear about that."

"That's blackmail, isn't it?"

Kiernan laughed again. "Merely the threat of blackmail." Then she sighed. "You want Austin's killer caught. I want the same thing. Can we do it with a little less drama? I've had a hard day with the inhospitable McKinleys in Rattlesnake. And with Joe Zekk," she added, watching Beth's reaction. "I could use a sane conversation."

Beth stood fingering the collar of her Florida shirt. She had it tied at the waist, exposing a brown triangle of skin above denim shorts. Her arms and legs were deeply tanned, and the freckles across her cheeks looked like a spray of chocolate. She stepped back abruptly. "Come in, for now."

After Zekk's house, the main room of Hohokam Lodge, with its blanket-and-toy-strewn floor, looked merely homey, a comfortable place to end this long, hot, exhausting day. She flopped down on the end of a flowered couch. "Are all your guests outside?"

Beth sank onto the other end. "Not all of them. Look, I've let you in but this isn't a social visit."

Kiernan forced herself *not* to straighten up. "Fine," she said. "Let me start by telling you what I've discovered about Austin and the retreat and the shoot-out." She summarized Zekk's comments, barely finishing before Beth laughed.

"And there," Beth said, "you've got Austin Vanderhooven's character in a nutshell. He knew the holy Roman Catholic Church was behind a massacre—"

"I didn't say they orchestrated it."

"But they condoned it," Beth insisted. "Same thing. And Austin knew and chose not to do anything. And you know why? Because of his high-powered Catholic retreat and monastery out here. Every person in the state of Arizona could have been killed and Austin would have walked over their graves to break ground for his place."

For Kiernan, the exhaustion of the day vanished. She loved this part of an investigation, when things came together. "Beth, you said retreat *and* monastery. Was he planning to build a monastery out here, too? A monastery where he was in charge?" *That* made more sense with what she knew of Austin Vanderhooven.

"You got it, or part of it," Beth said. "Let me tell you how outlandish his plans were. He wanted to build a monastery with the retreat to support it. He figured he'd have to put up with the bigwigs only a few times a year. The rest of the time he could board himself up in the monastery and unearth the Truth. And yet"—she drew her legs up under her—"he wanted to hedge his bets, in case there really was no Truth." She leaned forward, digging her elbows into her thighs. "Listen, this is how out-of-touch Austin was. What he suggested was that we, the women's refuge, could stay here at Hohokam. He would build the retreat up on the hill back there, and the monastery on the far side. Then the refuge would be the monastery's charity. Can you believe that?" She uncrossed her legs and smacked her feet to the floor. "I mean, the man missed the point all around. How many times did I tell him that the key thing about a refuge is that its location is secret? A *secret,* and he's planning to build a retreat next door to lure hotshots from all over the country!"

"How did Austin respond when you told him that?"

Beth pulled her legs back up under her.

No wonder the couch is so threadbare, Kiernan thought. If Beth were any more indignant, we'd be sitting on bare springs.

"Austin reacted like he always did," Beth said. Her foot was already twitching toward its next move. "He shoved the argument aside. He said he'd work it out. Like he was God. He just couldn't let the facts get in his way. He told me it would be a good opportunity for me to meet men. He said he'd introduce me to ones likely to take an interest in me. Like I was some kind of on-campus whore!"

"And you said . . . ?"

"I told him he had the makings of a fucking, or more to the point a nonfucking, voyeur. But that was a mistake. Austin ate it up when I got angry and used 'unpriestly' words."

The windows rattled in the breeze. Kiernan shifted, turning toward Beth. She said, "Austin had financing for his retreat, right?"

"Oh yeah. Austin had connections, and one thing he never forgot was how to use them."

Beth's face was still pinched with anger, but her anger was focused on Vanderhooven now, Kiernan thought, not on herself. As she had the day before, Beth was spitting out something on which she had chewed till it made her sick. And there was no one she could tell but Kiernan. Kiernan said, "So it would have been no big deal for Austin to build a monastery too."

"He didn't seem to think so. Not that that's proof. But I can't see why it would be a problem. The retreat was to draw Catholic men, Kennedy types. As long as Austin wasn't planning to have the monastery encroach on the putting green or the sauna, or the bar, there'd be no problem."

"So then, the only problem was this, the women's refuge. Why didn't he just evict you?"

"Well, he did eventually. When they set a date to break ground, we go, if we don't find another place before that. Just as well—this place was a mistake. It's too hot, too isolated. We've had a prowler on and off, or maybe Peeping Tom is a better description. These women have made the hardest decision of their lives; they need, they *deserve,* a safe house that's safer than this."

Kiernan leaned forward. "You want out of here; your guests want out; the refuge was a roadblock in Austin's plans. Why did he keep the refuge here this long?"

Beth swiveled and smacked her feet to the floor. "I thought I made that clear to you. You know, you're just like Austin." She got up and paced toward the windows, hitting the floor with heavy staccato steps. At the window she turned and started back toward Kiernan. "I think I've gotten through to you. I think you really see something, and then I realize I might as well be explaining to this—" She reached down and grabbed a small, fuzzy panda off a chair. "You don't get it anymore than Austin did. He wanted the refuge here because *I'm* in charge of the refuge. He wanted the monastery to run it so he could have an excuse to come by here." Angrily she propped a foot on the sofa arm.

"Because you were still sleeping with him," Kiernan said. She held up a palm. "Don't waste time denying it. I know about his dome over by Zekk's. You may have slid by Zekk when you met Austin in there but not by the local teenagers. I've got a kid who can describe the strap marks on your back and the curve of your butt."

Beth flushed. Her toes curled against the frayed sofa arm and she laughed—hard, humorless waves of sound that left her increasingly breathless and gagging. "You know, Austin would have loved that. He would have spent nights fantasizing. And more nights flagellating himself for his fantasies. How many times do I have to tell you that there was nothing physical between Austin and me? Nothing! I made a mistake accepting his help. He wanted power over me, like a possession he'd lost control of. And he wanted to be sure that I had no power over him, that he could dismiss me at any moment."

"Oh, come on!"

"Sure it sounds ridiculous. But that's how Austin was, all or nothing. You only have power if you have no attachment, he said. He needed to prove to himself that he had no attachment to me."

Kiernan shook her head in disgust. "Beth! The teenager saw you in the dome!"

She laughed, more normally now. "Yeah, he did all right. Me. But not Austin. You know Austin's not the only man in the world. *I* didn't take a vow of celibacy when he chose the monastery."

Kiernan sighed, this time in disgust with herself.

Beth laughed harder. "Jumped to a conclusion, huh? Lots of pitfalls for you hotshot detectives."

Kiernan bit back a retort. In the back of the house a door banged. Women's and children's voices mingled. The refrigerator door slammed, then slammed again. A gust of wind rattled the windows, and dirt blew in under the front door. "Beth," Kiernan said, "you may have been sleeping with someone else. But to do it in Austin's dome, his private monastery, you can't tell me there isn't a little revenge involved in that."

Beth grinned. "Better believe it! From the moment I got the idea of using it, I loved it. I loved every moment of every hour there. I loved feeling a man's hard body on mine while I looked at Austin's altar. I loved the whole idea of using Austin's little prayer dome with the pink glass window like a cheap motel."

Austin's little prayer dome with the pink glass window, she'd heard those words before. To Beth she said, "It couldn't have been easy sneaking past Joe Zekk. Or was Joe Zekk in there with you?"

She glared down at Kiernan. "Zekk! That slime! I wouldn't be in the same room with that revolting creep."

"Were *you* paying him too?"

"Paying him! Hell, no. But Austin was, huh? I knew it!"

"What was he paying him for?"

"To spy on me. What else?" Beth began to pace again. In the kitchen, the refrigerator door slammed again, a pan clanged. At the windows Beth spun on the ball of her foot and started back. Her brow was wrinkled, her hands on her hips. She seemed oblivious to the clatter of the windows and the sounds from the kitchen. "Who do you think it was sneaking around here week after week, peeping in the windows? Once he even broke in. And last night, you know what the goddamn fucking slime did?"

"What?"

"He hired some floozy to pretend she needed my help." Beth smacked the sofa arm. "But I'll tell you one thing: She'll think twice before she tries something like that again."

Kiernan let out her breath, slowly. "Where is she?"

Beth's mouth dropped open. "You! It was you. I can't believe it. I thought only Joe Zekk would be slime enough to hire that woman—"

"Where is she!"

"I found her in my office in the middle of the night. I made damned sure she wouldn't be any more trouble. Follow me. She's all yours."

Beth stalked to the storeroom, took out a set of keys, and unlocked the deadbolt and the door.

There was barely room between the gray metal shelves for the flimsy cot. Lying on it, Patsy Luca looked like an illustration from a text on jaundice. No hint of tan remained on her sallow, sweaty skin. Her blond hair stuck to her scalp in gooey clumps. Her eyes appeared to be glued closed.

Kiernan put a hand on Patsy's arm. "My God, Patsy. What happened?"

Before she could answer, Beth said, "She seemed so interested in a bottle of liqueur of mine that I had her drink the whole thing. Very sweet it was, right, Patsy?"

Patsy groaned. "Damned eight-sided—"

"Eight-sided?" Kiernan exclaimed. "Was the bottle about three inches wide?"

Patsy groaned again, but this time added the smallest of affirmative nods.

"Did it look like this?" From her purse, she extracted a copy of the stain on Vanderhooven's blotter.

Patsy's eyes opened. "In the trash, there." She rolled over and plucked the bottle from a wicker basket.

Kiernan held it against the copy of the stain. "Perfect fit." To Beth she said, "Culiacán, the peace offering you and Austin had. When did you get this?"

"A year ago."

Patsy sat up, lowered her feet to the floor, and groaned once more. Wind smacked the window behind her. "I found more than that," she said, with the merest suggestion of a smile. "I found a stack of love letters. From Vanderhooven. Hot stuff, huh, Beth? Latest was four years ago, and things had cooled down a lot by then."

"But you kept them, Beth?" Kiernan asked. "His ardor cooled, but you kept his letters. That doesn't sound like disinterest."

"What business is it of . . . Oh, hell! I started to burn them probably twenty times. Once, I had the match lit. Look, I never said I had no emotional attachment to Austin. But it wasn't love anymore. I just needed to get to the point where I could read one of those letters and have it mean nothing."

"So you could prove you weren't attached to him?" Kiernan said. "And have the power?"

Beth started to retort, then appeared to think better of it. Slowly, Patsy pushed herself up and stood, balancing her shaky body against the cot. Then she walked slowly into the hall and leaned against the wall.

Kiernan sat down on the rumpled cot, vaguely listening to the window rattling in the sash, vaguely wondering if this was going to be one of the dust storms Stu Wiggins had warned her about, mostly pondering Austin Vanderhooven. A spray of dirt hit the window. She said, "Beth, Austin Vanderhooven sent you the Culiacán as a peace offering a year ago. That's when he told you about the monastery, right?"

Beth said nothing.

"Why would he give you a peace offering then?"

"Because Culiacán was always our peace offering!"

"Why would adding a monastery building to the retreat make any difference? Why would that merit a peace offering?" She caught Beth's eye. "What difference would that make to you? Your problem is with the construction of the buildings. Why should you care if he changed what they were to be used for?"

"I don't. I didn't care what he changed, because, as I told him, and as I told you, I am not going to be here. Even he finally got that."

Kiernan sat, tapping her forefinger against her knee. "Vanderhooven hadn't contacted the financial backers in a year. That doesn't sound like the competent retreat organizer you were describing. Backers need to be nurtured, particularly on a project like this where the rewards are merely tax write-offs and good will. A year's a long time for them to dangle. A year ago was when he made a peace offering to you. More like a farewell offering." She took a long deep breath. "He gave you a peace offering because he was telling you he would never see you again. He was planning a life of seclusion, right? There wasn't going to be any retreat, was there, Beth? No retreat, just a monastery."

35

Kiernan hurried down the steps from Hohokam Lodge. The wind sliced the hard dirt into her cheeks. She raised her hands to shield her eyes and ran for the Jeep.

"What is it you're supposed to do in sandstorms, Patsy?" Kiernan asked.

"Go back in the lodge."

Kiernan laughed. "It'd have to be a blizzard before Beth Landau would let us in there again." She started the engine, put on the dims, and headed slowly down the pockmarked trail. On the unprotected mesa the wind raced in, scooping up dirt, swirling it around, and slapping it against the windows. The predusk sky had darkened. She could barely see beyond the front of the Jeep. Dirt scraped against the side windows. It hit the windshield like myriads of tiny BBs and coated the glass. The plastic that covered the shattered back window fluttered but held firm. She turned the wipers on; they smeared the dirt. She hit the water spray; it cleared a small triangle under each wiper, but the blades covered them with dirt on the swing back.

"Keep the water on, Patsy." Kiernan steadied the wheel with both hands, bent low to see through the clearing, and headed down the dirt road. The Jeep hit a pothole and Patsy lost the spray button.

"You okay?" Kiernan asked Patsy.

"Yeah. Now that I've had a few aspirins I might pass for human."

The Jeep hit another hole. Patsy's hand stayed on the button. Kiernan braced her left foot against the floorboard, thankful for the first time that the Jeep was an automatic. The windows were closed, but dirt flew in through the minuscule cracks around them. Kiernan could feel it on her face. It clung gritty to her teeth. It was on her tongue, in her throat. She coughed, but her throat didn't clear.

"You want to know what I found, Kiernan?"

The Jeep ricocheted and landed halfway up the bank. Kiernan yanked the wheel left. The tires spun then caught. "I can't see the ground at all," she said.

"We can't stop here in the middle of this road. With the engine off the headlights won't last. And if anything comes along it'll plow into us."

"I know," Kiernan said. "Hang on."

"I can give you the names of seventeen of the husbands and boyfriends Beth had in her files." Patsy cleared her throat and began to chant to the tune of "Rock of Ages": "Travis Arlen, Jake Bierstrom, Will Furgood, Fred-Greep McCue—"

"What is this, detective sing-along?"

"Ben Hmm Meader, Jos Mendoz—"

"Hose Mendoze?"

"José Mendoza. Look I've got to do it this way."

"Okay."

"Travis Arlen," Patsy began again.

When she chanted "Darryl Washington," Kiernan said, "Well, there's nothing there."

"Nothing there! That damned tune and those names are going to circle around in my brain for the rest of my life!"

"Get a Walkman to wear tomorrow and a couple of new tapes and charge it to the case. Look there, I think that's the road ahead," Kiernan said. "Hey, I can see the road. I can *see* it. The storm's letting up!"

"Yeah. Most times dust storms don't last long. Problem is you can't be sure. Normal thing is they end in rain. I was afraid we'd be caught in a downpour. It's monsoon season. The rains are what can be dangerous here in the mountains. And there are flash floods. I was afraid of that. I just didn't want to tell you."

"Thanks," Kiernan said sarcastically. "This *is* a Jeep. I grew up driving in snow. And I spent one monsoon season in India."

"It gets really bad here," Patsy said, clearly unimpressed. "You know all those dry bridges in town, the ones that go over dry washes or riverbeds? Well, when there's a good rain, those rivers are like the Mississippi. Floods washed out the main bridge between Tempe and Phoenix one year. People die."

"Nice it's not us." Kiernan pulled onto the hardtop. The wheels grabbed and the Jeep leapt forward. And as suddenly the air cleared. It had become just a mildly foggy evening, clear enough to forego the dims for the headlights. Kiernan could feel the muscles of her shoulders releasing. She was aware of the pressure of her clenched molars. She swung her jaw side to side. "Is there any water in the bottle under the seat?"

"Yeah. Here."

Kiernan drank and passed the bottle back to Patsy. "Besides the 'Rock of Ages' men, Vanderhooven's letters, and the Culiacán, anything else?"

"The prowler; but you know about him. And the deed to the land."

"Deed? From John McKinley? McKinley left the land to the church in his will. But you say he deeded it over. Are you sure?"

"Oh, yeah. The deed was in the office closet. Since nineteen thirty-seven. Straight quitclaim. John McKinley deeded thirty-six acres of land to the pastor of Mission San Leo."

"That's all?"

"Yup. Just the land, no buildings. Nothing. But there probably weren't any buildings in nineteen thirty-seven."

Kiernan pulled around an ancient pickup truck. The road was completely clear now. The wind had died. And surprisingly, the sky was a royal blue, flecked with spotlight-bright stars. In the distance she could see headlights and farther on, in the valley, the pinpoints of streetlights. "John McKinley deeded the land to the church in nineteen thirty-seven. Then he willed it to them again. Just to be sure? The will was also written in nineteen thirty-seven. So what does that mean? Okay, so Austin Vanderhooven knew that the McKinleys had deeded the land to the church, but he didn't know why. He paid Joe Zekk five thousand dollars to go down there to find that out. He must have heard about the massacre, but he wanted to know exactly what happened, and how it affected the church."

"And what did Zekk find out?"

"That the Catholic Church didn't just support the McKinleys when they wiped out the Sheltons; they supplied the money for the guns. The Rattlesnake massacre was in nineteen thirty-eight. But the deed and the will were written in nineteen thirty-*seven*!"

Patsy whistled, then groaned. "Talk about blackmail! I guess you don't need to ask where Joe Zekk got the rest of his money, huh?"

"No. Not Zekk. That information was Austin Vanderhooven's cache. If he was smart enough to go after it, he was smart enough to make sure Joe Zekk didn't undercut him when he wanted to pressure Dowd himself with it." The road had dipped; a rise in the distance hid the lights of Phoenix. Beneath the brightness of the stars everything was black. As the headlights flashed on the ocotillo at the edge of the road; they looked as if they were waving prickly arms, holding up spiny thumbs for a ride. On the dashboard the pale yellow light from the odometer and the radio gave the Jeep the aura of safety and intimacy. She smiled at Patsy. "Zekk's selfish, immature, and unscrupulous. But at least until recently, he did consider himself Austin Vanderhooven's friend. Could be Vanderhooven was his only friend."

Patsy took another drink of water. "What about Vanderhooven?"

"Well, my suspicion is that Vanderhooven choose Zekk not because they'd been friends in seminary but because he knew that Zekk would do pretty much anything for a buck. What he didn't count on was that Zekk would do it for anyone else for another buck. So here's Zekk, an insecure, unlikeable guy, who really did think Vanderhooven, the star of his seminary class, chose him to be his confidant. Vanderhooven brings him out here and sets him up in what he considers the middle of nowhere. And then he ignores him. And Zekk responds by drinking too much and buying enough blue movies to keep the crew of a battleship happy and renting them out. Then he calls Vanderhooven's father in Maui and arranges to spy on Vanderhooven for him."

Headlights filled the rearview mirror. Kiernan looked at the speedometer. She was doing seventy-five.

"So, Kiernan, Joe Zekk was snooping around Beth's place for Vanderhooven's father?"

"Possibly. But my guess is that's what Vanderhooven himself paid him for."

"Maybe he sold whatever he found to both of them."

Kiernan laughed. "Of course, Patsy! But still, four hundred from them, three hundred from the films, and whatever he made hawking the McKinley's pottery, it's not enough to support his life-style." The lights from behind turned the mirror into a spotlight. Kiernan squeezed her right eye shut against the glare.

"Maybe he had money when he got here. What did he do before this?"

"Merchant sailor of sorts."

Patsy laughed. "I don't picture merchant sailors making a bee-line from the boat to the bank. Do you think of Zekk as a saver?"

Kiernan nodded. "Not unless you consider what he knew about Dowd a nest egg. Now there's an alliance made in heaven."

Patsy laughed.

The mirror went dark. Kiernan looked to her left as a vehicle flashed by so fast she could barely make out enough to classify it as a pickup. The Jeep crested a ridge, and suddenly all of Phoenix was spread out below, like a plate of tiny yellow lights with the shiny red and green dots of traffic signals splattered among them. The air was so clear that each individual light stood out. Beside her she could hear Patsy's breath catch. And above, against the blackness of the sky, the piercing bright stars seemed as near as the town.

She let a moment pass before turning her attention back to the question of the dead priest's friend. "Zekk figures Dowd has no more scruples than he has. Dowd can't afford to alienate Zekk because he knows too much. Maybe Zekk just blackmailed him. Or maybe, Patsy, he figured that here was one person who would want whatever dirt he could find on Austin Vanderhooven. One person who'd be dying to get even."

"But what was Dowd going to do with whatever he got from Zekk?" Patsy unsnapped the seat·belt and leaned back against the door, propping one boot precariously against the dash.

Kiernan eyed the boot warily, envisioning the heel flying into her cheek, but the camaraderie of nocturnal travel forbade comment. "Dowd could force Vanderhooven to go ahead with the retreat. It may not have made any difference to Beth if Austin Vanderhooven substituted a monastery for the great retreat, but it would be like night and day for Dowd. Dowd and Sylvia Necri had been planning the retreat for years. Stu Wiggins said Dowd'd given up trying to succeed the archbishop. He had all his marbles up here."

Patsy laughed. "And Vanderhooven kicked them aside."

Kiernan slowed to a stop. It was the first traffic light she had seen since morning. In contrast to the sudden stillness of the un-moving Jeep, her skin seemed to be vibrating. "Zekk had a lot to lose too, Patsy. He's been scraping by for years, but he sees himself as an entrepreneur. When Vanderhooven talked about the retreat, he probably promised him introductions to the bigwigs, just like he did with Beth Landau. You can see how that would appeal to Joe Zekk. So he comes out here, lives in isolation. Then suddenly Van-derhooven changes his mind, gives up his plans for the great re-treat, and decides on a monastery. Suddenly he can't be bothered with his 'friend.' He's spending all his time playing monk in his dome. Zekk's drinking; he's bitter, and he knows how to tie knots."

Patsy sat up straight. "Kiernan, Beth thinks he was the prowler. Suppose, Kiernan, he took the bottle from Beth's office, got Van-derhooven to drink some—"

"Maybe he left it on Vanderhooven's blotter with a note suppos-edly from Beth, saying she was willing to make up for being pissed off about the monastery—"

"And then he hangs the guy in his own church—what better revenge, huh?"

"And Patsy," Kiernan said, "Joe Zekk has no alibi for Wednes-day night."

36

ON THE WAY BACK to Phoenix, Kiernan stopped twice to call Joe Zekk's phone number. After the second set of unanswered rings, she considered and vetoed the idea of heading back into the mountains to question him face-to-face. She dropped Patsy off at her house, traded in the Jeep (for another automatic!), circled by Ben's Burgers, and brought dinner back to her motel.

She called Stu Wiggins. Not home. Joe Zekk, still not home. She pictured Zekk driving off as soon as she was out of sight of his house. The only question was to whom he was racing to report. Philip Vanderhooven? Despite his questionable financial connections, Vanderhooven hadn't killed his son. He was in Hawaii then. And the Rattlesnake feud had taken place thirty years before he had wintered in Phoenix. Without much hope, she dialed the rectory for Bishop Dowd.

Dowd wasn't home either. But Mrs. Johnarndt, his housekeeper, was, and she was worried. As Kiernan sympathized and coaxed, she found herself picturing her childhood priest's plump, white-haired housekeeper, holding the receiver slightly away from her ear and nervously wiping her hand on a purple flowered apron. Finally Mrs. Johnarndt took a deep breath and broke into sobs. "I was standing in the hallway. Bishop walked right past me. Like I wasn't there. It's not like him . . . go rushing out like that . . . and not tell me what to say."

"Do you think he could be with a parishioner?" Kiernan asked gently.

"No. No one here," she said, clearly making an effort to control her outburst. "The call was long distance. Collect."

"This call, Mrs. Johnarndt, when did the bishop get it?"

"Right before he left. About an hour ago."

"Do you have any idea who it was from?" Kiernan asked.

"That Joe Zekk, up there in the mountains. Collect, like all those other calls from there."

"What did Zekk say?" Kiernan held her breath.

"I don't know. Bishop didn't say. He didn't say *anything*. He just walked out."

Kiernan exhaled deeply, angry at Bishop Dowd for the pain he'd caused his housekeeper, frustrated at her own helplessness, and furious that she'd discovered just enough to know she didn't know enough. She offered a few more words of comfort and hung up.

Grabbing a pair of jeans and a clean blue oxford-cloth shirt, she headed into the bathroom. She took a shower, penciled on eyeliner, and rubbed some pink stuff over the circles under her eyes. But no cover-up could mask the effects of the last three days. However, Dowd, if she found him, was hardly likely to notice. With what Zekk would have told him, Dowd would have plenty on his mind.

She stopped at the motel desk and checked for messages. There was one from Stu Wiggins: "3 of Austin V's lg. dist. calls to monastery in CA. Taking archdiocese law. to dinner. Call you A.M. Stu."

Pocketing the note, she walked to the Jeep. She rolled the window full open and felt the invigorating sting of the breeze on her face as she drove along Baseline Road toward the Pima Freeway. The night air felt surprisingly cool. The thick smell of grease from the chicken takeouts and burger joints in the shopping centers mixed with exhaust fumes from pickups and bursts of music that were too tantalizingly short to recognize.

She pulled onto the freeway and then off before the Gila River Indian Reservation.

Had Vanderhooven been calling that monastery in California for advice? Or had he planned to connect his own monastery with whatever order ran that one?

She pulled around the corner by the blue-and-yellow gas station, open but empty, as it was on the night she arrived in Phoenix. Beyond it, the houses of Azure Acres Homes were dark. The night of her arrival she had been taken aback by the stark whiteness of the mission church, and by Bishop Dowd with his faded chestnut hair and tightly arched eyebrows. But tonight the courtyard lights merely served to emphasize the darkness within the church itself. There was no light in Vanderhooven's house either.

She climbed back into the Jeep and headed into town.

It was nearly eleven P.M. when she pulled up in front of Dowd's rectory, a two-story Spanish-style house on the outskirts of Encanto Park, one of the most desirable downtown neighborhoods. The porch light was burning. But the carport was empty.

She checked with Dowd's housekeeper (who looked just the way Kiernan had imagined, except for her apron, which had an Indian design). Dowd hadn't returned, Mrs. Johnarndt said. Father Simmons and Father Bastent were at a retreat in Tucson. Monsignor Valdez was visiting his sister, who was dying. Bishop Dowd hadn't called; no one else had called.

Kiernan headed back to the freeway, back to Mission San Leo. At twelve-thirty she pulled up in front. Both the church and the rectory were still dark inside. "Damn!" she muttered. Where was the man? She could drive to Dowd's residence once more. She could call Mrs. Johnarndt again. Sighing, she fingered the steering wheel and pondered.

If Vanderhooven built a monastery on the land but no retreat, Dowd had good reason to want him dead. But why now? Dowd had had plenty of time to see the danger his underling posed. If he was going to kill him, why hadn't he done it earlier? Or why not wait till later? Vanderhooven hadn't been contacting his financial backers for a year. Nothing was happening with the building project. Why kill him now? What was happening now?

Kiernan slapped both hands on the steering wheel in triumph. John McKinley was dying now, that's what! John McKinley was waiting for Vanderhooven to return something. What? Surely not McKinley's will. If he had changed his mind about the will, all McKinley needed to do was make a new will. But who would make a new will for him? The 1937 will had been drawn up by a lawyer. So chances were that McKinley would have had a lawyer handle this one too. But McKinley never left Rattlesnake. No lawyer came out there. So who would carry the forms? Certainly not Zekk. No, it would have been the one man McKinley was waiting for, Austin Vanderhooven. If John McKinley was waiting to sign the will, that would explain why he had been refusing the morphine.

Kiernan extricated McKinley's will and read over it. Then she drove to the gas-station phone booth. Behind her four teenaged boys moved around a pickup truck, yelling back and forth. She pulled the door shut, amazed at the relative quiet within the booth, and dialed Stu Wiggins.

This time Wiggins was home. "Let me tell you about my buddy, the archdiocese lawyer," he began before she could speak. "The man can't chew and think at the same time. He's so busy shovelling in, it's hard to get an answer to anything, much less—"

"Stu, I'm at a gas station."

"Then don't waste time making small talk, tell me what you want."

She told him. In the twenty-seven minutes before Wiggins called back, the teenagers clambered into the pickup, to be replaced by one after another payload of adolescents. On the street, cars whizzed by in all eight lanes.

Finally the station emptied, and almost immediately the phone rang. She pulled the phone-booth door shut and listened as Wiggins said, "You owe me. I've talked to Gilbert Hayes and he did indeed draw up a will for John McKinley. Kerry, you know what it's like to get ahold of a lawyer at one A.M. on a Sunday morning? He could have been drunk. He could have been 'entertaining.' Fortunately, Gillie's the type who's in bed by ten. But I'll tell you, Kerry, that didn't make him a mite happier to hear from me at this hour. Do you know how much fast talking I had to do to get him thinking about a will he drew up for an old man he never saw? His father drew up the last one, and old Gil's been dead for twenty years. 'Course Gillie read over the original will before he drew up this one. He also wouldn't tell me what's in it."

"That's okay for now. I just needed to know a new one existed. Did he tell you when he drew it up?"

"A week ago last Monday. And Kerry, here's a little boon for you. You know who carried McKinley's requirements to Gillie, and who picked the will up?"

"Austin Vanderhooven?"

"Smart lady! Vanderhooven picked it up from Gillie that Friday. He was supposed to bring it back the following Monday, but he called to say McKinley wanted more time to go over it. Said the old man didn't read any too good to begin with, and what with being in a lot of pain, he needed time. Said he'd get the signed document back to Gillie the following Monday."

A green Chevy convertible pulled in by the self-service pump. The radio blared Willie Nelson. Kiernan put her free hand over her ear and shouted. "Austin Vanderhooven planned to go to Rattlesnake yesterday. And take the will to Hayes tomorrow!" The radio stopped. In the relative silence, Kiernan said, "It's almost comical, Stu. Vanderhooven's killer is searching frantically through the rectory and Vanderhooven's dome, and all the time the will is still down in Rattlesnake with the McKinleys."

"Reckon we could be safe in saying our killer doesn't know that."

"Reckon we could, Stu."

"Right. But Kerry, that's not the boon I was offering you."

"It's not?" Nervously, Kiernan eyed the Chevy driver, a longhair in cutoffs and a T-shirt with a picture of a foaming beer glass and "Wet Arizona" on it. He was holding the gas nozzle but eyeing his silent radio. "Come on, Stu, what?"

"Well, Gillie Hayes is a stickler for having everything above question. Gillie's good on paperwork, but he's no ball of fire in court. He's lost cases a first-year law student could have won. He knows it. And he goes out of his way to make sure there are no loose ends. You get the picture?"

"Right, Stu." "Wet Arizona" turned the nozzle end up and hoisted it back into the pump.

"So, Kerry, you can imagine what state poor Gillie Hayes is in when he gets handed the will of a client he's never seen, an old mountain man who could have a brain of mush for all he knows. Gillie sees himself walking into a court challenge with a will witnessed by a couple of bumpkins who are related to the inheritors, and he's worried. You can picture that, right?"

"Stu, it's going to get noisy here in a minute."

Clearly undaunted, Wiggins said, "And then Gillie realizes he's got an educated man available, a priest of the Roman Catholic Church. It's a miracle. Or as close to a miracle as an officer of the court is likely to come. So what do you think he does?"

"If he's been worrying as long as you've been keeping me in suspense, he's too weak to do anything. What, Stu?"

Swallowing his laughter, Wiggins said, "He tells Vanderhooven it's essential that he be one of the witnesses. And what that means for us—"

"Is that Vanderhooven was not an inheritor in the new will, right?"

"Right. How 'bout them apples?"

All the tension of the day bubbled up; Kiernan threw her head back and laughed. "Wet Arizona" stared at her, then flipped his radio back on full-blare. He revved up the engine, sending gusts of black exhaust toward her. And when he pulled out the screech of his tires drowned out the radio.

Kiernan stood a moment watching the exhaust float up and around the booth. Then, taking advantage of the quiet, she said to Wiggins, "So what Vanderhooven was 'returning' to McKinley was what McKinley had allowed him to use all along—what McKinley had given him in an earlier will so the gift would be legal when the old man died . . ."

"The retreat land?"

"No, that he had deeded over years ago. Besides Vanderhooven wanted the land for his monastery." She grinned. "No, Stu, now let's see how you handle being strung along. What could Vander-hooven return to the villagers that in itself would assure that the retreat land could be used for a monastery but not for a fancy retreat?"

Stu didn't reply.

"A fancy retreat with a swimming pool, Stu, with seventy-five rooms and seventy-five showers—"

"Ah-hah!" Stu laughed as loud as Kiernan had.

"I thought as a veteran of water-right battles you'd appreciate that one. Am I correct in assuming that without Rattlesnake's water rights, the church could build nothing more than a small self sustaining monastery?"

"You are. You are. They could drill down to the underground aquifer and get enough water for a couple dozen monks, leastways monks who didn't wash too often. But that's it."

"And the great retreat would be gone forever. Unless they could kill Vanderhooven before he witnessed John McKinley's signing of the new will."

"And they did!"

"Right. And what they were looking for was the new will!"

"They? Who? You got an idea?"

"I'm going to make another stab at finding Dowd."

At Mission San Leo nothing had changed in the last hour. Frus-trated, Kiernan jumped down from the Jeep and headed through the courtyard gate around the side of the church, toward the house.

There was an odd smell. Something burning? She stopped and stared back at the church. A hazy, dim light wavered behind the stained-glass windows. It hadn't been visible from the street. Of course it hadn't; the church had no windows on the front. But she didn't find that reassuring. Moving more quietly, she climbed the steps and pushed the brass handle on the big wooden door. It didn't budge. She pushed harder, but the massive door stood firm.

If Bishop Dowd was in the church, he would have entered through the sacristy in the back.

Careful to move quietly, Kiernan hurried around back. A date palm stood near the sacristy door, its fronds blocking out the moonlight. Kiernan tried the door—locked. She fished out Vanderhooven's keys and tried two before one worked.

The sacristy was dark. The acrid smell of incense hit her. She made her way carefully across the room and felt along the wall for the door to the chancel and pulled it open. Clouds of incense poured through the doorway. She leapt back and shoved the door shut. She felt around for one of those robes she'd seen hanging here earlier, ripped off a wide strip of cloth, and, holding it over her mouth and nose, opened the door again.

The whole church was filled with incense. She coughed. Her eyes were watering. Her nose filled with the harsh smell. The dry heat pricked at her skin. She felt for the light switch and flicked it on. Nothing happened. Four blurs of light came from the rear of the altar table. The altar candles? She moved toward them, but even close up they gave off little light. Beyond, lines of lighter gray might have indicated windows—she couldn't tell.

"Hello?" she called.

No answer. She pulled the nearest candle from its holder, dripped wax on the marble surface of the altar table, and stuck the base of the candle in it. The metal candlestick was eighteen inches tall. Too heavy for a protective weapon, but it would have to do. Carrying it by the top, she moved slowly, silently forward to the far side of the chancel. Again she stopped, listened. Again there was no sound. "Anyone here?" No response.

The incense was not coming from the altar but was flowing

forward from the pews and the deep shadows by the heavy wooden doors beyond them.

The heat made it hard to breathe. It was like being in a forest fire. She squeezed her eyes shut.

"Bishop Dowd?" she called. "Your housekeeper is very worried about you." Still there was no indication of a listener. She felt her way down the chancel steps into the nave. Ahead were the wooden pews, barriers that could hide an army of silent watchers. To the sides were the two small side altars.

Pressing the cloth to her nose with her left hand, she inched forward till her hip touched the first pew and made her way in front of the pews to the side aisle. The incense was thicker, stronger, the air hotter. She started down the side aisle, looking down the length of the first pew, knowing anyone could be hiding at the far end, hidden by the thick fumes. Unable to stop herself, she coughed. Her foot hit something hard, and hot ash sprayed over her ankle. She jumped back, grabbed her ankle, brushing away the stinging ash.

She felt around with her foot. A large dish on the floor was filled with burning coals and incense. The hot heavy smoke filled her mouth; she gagged and swallowed hard. Forcing back a cough, she listened for a footfall, a clearing of the throat, any human sound. Nothing.

Sliding her feet, she moved toward the next pew and came up against another dish on the floor. She squeezed her eyes shut for a moment, squatted, and looked down the pew. Nothing moved. How many of these dishes were there?

Giving up on the pews, she made her way to the small side altar opposite the one where Vanderhooven's body had hung. There was one candle on it, smaller than those on the main altar. It stood so far back that its flame nearly licked the wall, and its light was enclosed by the altar pillars beside it. She peered at the altar. The paint on the statues was streaked with brown.

The fiery heat rose from the floor, reverberated off the walls. Her shirt stuck to her back. Her face felt as if it was about to crack.

Something shifted in the middle aisle.

Sweat rolled down her face. She gripped the candlestick and inched forward, avoiding the dishes of incense, stepping softly, listening. Another noise—a footstep. From the center aisle? Peering into the darkness, she tried to make out a figure, but the smoke was too thick.

"Bishop Dowd?" she called.

No answer.

She started through the pew toward the center aisle. Her foot smacked something hard—the kneeling bench. She lurched forward. The candlestick fell. It hit the floor with a resounding clang. She dropped down and searched for it frantically, but the candlestick was gone.

Ahead, feet hit the floor. Coming closer. She froze. The steps were clearer now; two or three pews away. She ducked down, grabbed the kneeler, and carefully folded it up out of the way. The footsteps were closer. Keeping down she inched forward. The center aisle was less than a yard away. She wanted to peer over the edge of the pew but didn't dare, not this close. She reached the end of the pew. With her head not twelve inches from the floor, she peered into the aisle, just in time to see a leg disappear into the pew across the aisle.

She stood up and squinted into the dense smoke, but she could make out only a dim blur from the candle on the other side altar, the altar where Austin Vanderhooven died. The footsteps were moving toward it, away from her, moving faster.

She followed. For the first time she heard a low moan, coming from the altar. She moved closer. In the candlelight, she saw a dark form at the right end of the altar. Bishop Dowd! Blindfolded, he was standing on the altar, tottering at the edge, with his hands bound behind his back and a noose around his neck. She rushed toward him.

She heard the footsteps coming behind her just before she felt the blow on her head.

37

KIERNAN FELL SIDEWAYS, over the back of a pew. Her eyes shut against the pain of the blow. She could hear her assailant running off. Furious, she forced her eyes open, but it was too late to see a figure through the clouds of incense. Waves of pain washed through her head. "Can't pass out!" a voice said. Smoke filled her nose and throat. Weakly, she coughed.

Another voice moaned.

Her eyes stung. She closed them and sank farther down into the pew. The sacristy door slammed.

Her stomach felt awful. She was going to throw up. She jammed her teeth together.

A gasp came from the altar. Slowly, she opened her eyes and looked toward it. Miraculously, Bishop Dowd was still balanced on the edge. He looked as if he'd been drugged.

She lurched up and braced herself against the pew. "Don't move! I'll get you down!"

Dowd swayed forward. The rope went taut. He gagged. She shoved him back. "Keep your knees stiff!"

He swayed back from her push. His face was blank.

She pushed the candlestick to the far end of the altar, away from Dowd, grasped one of the columns, and pulled herself up onto the altar. Dowd swayed to the side. She grabbed his arm and pulled him back. "Don't move a muscle!" Releasing his arm, she loosened the noose and lifted the rope over his head. He swayed again, more violently. She caught him, this time around the chest, and pulled back. His knees buckled; he slid down till his feet slipped off the edge of the altar. Momentarily, he balanced sitting on the edge, then slid to the floor.

She jumped down beside him; the pain exploded in her head. Her legs gave way; she fell forward and lay on the floor until she could breathe again.

Dowd lay groaning at the foot of the altar. Slowly, she knelt to untie his hands. The light glinted off something shiny on the floor next to him. Kiernan reached for it—a tiny bottle, an airline liquor bottle, like the ones that littered Joe Zekk's house. She stared at it, enraged.

Dowd moaned. Kiernan turned back to him, coaxing him into a sitting position with his back against the altar. He coughed, wiped ineffectually at his eyes, and coughed again.

Finally, she got him standing unsteadily and half-walked, half-dragged him out of the smoke-filled church. The fresh air outside revived him briefly. He walked, mostly under his own power, to the rectory and, as if finding safety on Vanderhooven's couch, he sighed and passed out.

"Damn!" she muttered. The man was breathing, his color was as good as could be expected under the circumstances, his pulse was reasonable. "Lucky not to have a heart attack." Sighing, she dialed 911, wishing there were a way to call an ambulance and the fire department without alerting the sheriff.

The medics arrived moments before the first fire engine. She passed on the essential information. As they clustered around the bishop, she edged out of the room and across the hallway to the kitchen. Outside a siren shrieked and died. The medics wheeled Dowd along the hallway and out the front door. Kiernan raced out the back, let herself out the gate, and walked quickly down the alley. When she reached the street she slowed her pace and joined the gaggle of neighbors already heading toward the front of the church.

All the windows of the church were open now. Firemen scurried back and forth. Kiernan slithered along behind the onlookers, away from the church, hurried across the street to the Jeep, and drove slowly out of Azure Acres Homes.

Her head throbbed. It was going to take more than Alka-Seltzers this time. Goddammit, Joe Zekk would not get away again. He had half an hour's lead. But he wouldn't be expecting her to follow him. He'd be home, rooting through his piles of stuff, yanking out this and that to take with him. If he pictured her at all, it would be in the hospital battling the effects of smoke inhalation. Or in the morgue.

It was already after four A.M. Begrudging the time it took, she stopped at the first gas station, filled the tank, the spare can, and the water bottle. Next door, at the 7-11, she downed four Alka-

Seltzers and picked up a couple sandwiches; she climbed back in the Jeep and headed onto the Pima Freeway.

For once the freeway was nearly empty. Only a few red taillights dotted the blackness ahead. The seemingly endless sky was thickly splattered with specks of white. As she veered onto the Superstition Freeway the streaky white of headlights was visible across the divider. The cool night air brushed her face and neck, but it did nothing to cool her anger. She squeezed the steering wheel harder and thought of Joe Zekk.

The whole operation would have been so easy for him. He was virtually a sentry for the town of Rattlesnake. He must have seen Austin Vanderhooven go down there two weeks ago, when John McKinley gave him the instructions for his new will. Then Zekk would have seen Vanderhooven go down that winding road on Saturday—eight days ago now—with the will itself. Had Austin been frustrated and angry when he came back up empty-handed? A four-hour drive for nothing? Had he been angry enough to complain to Joe Zekk? Had he told him about the will but stopped short of telling him where it was. And had Zekk realized the money-making possibilities in murdering Vanderhooven and possessing that new will?

Night was just beginning to fade as she started the climb into the mountains. The sharp hills and craggy peaks seemed to suck the black into themselves; they stood ominous against the paling sky. The stars that had crowded the dark expanse minutes earlier had faded to invisibility against its dark gray.

With the will unrecorded, and John McKinley dead, the retreat was still viable. Had Zekk offered that hope to Bishop Dowd? Planned to sell him the will?

Already the sky was lighter, no longer a battleship gray but a pale gray. The crags had lost their sharp points and gone fuzzy, as if they were covered with velvet.

Sylvia Necri? As a buyer for the will? Or a full-fledged accomplice? When he sabotaged the retreat, Vanderhooven had snatched away her professional chance of a lifetime. The retreat meant at least as much to her as it did to Dowd.

A jolt drew Kiernan's attention back to the road. Both hands on the wheel, she eyed the straight strip ahead and then let her gaze rise back up to include cloudless expanse above. As she watched,

the color of the sky shifted from gray to beige. The road curved to
the left; palo verde trees and ocotillo crowded near the sides. She
passed jojoba bushes and the squat barrel cacti with their bright
orange flowers.

Bud Warren? The longer the church or Sylvia Necri controlled
the water rights, the better off he was. He needed three years to
show off his process. Kiernan could picture him buying the will.
She could see him shrugging off the murder if he thought he could
get away with it. But she couldn't see him as a co-planner. The
vicious sexual humiliation involved in Vanderhooven's murder
reeked of revenge. Bud Warren had no reason for seeking revenge.
That kind of revenge fit Sylvia Necri. Or Beth Landau.

Beth Landau. She had the Culiacán. She was the only one likely
to know the significance of that liqueur. The peace-offering ritual
was not something the closed-mouthed Vanderhooven would have
told anyone. And she had the revenge motive in spades. But she
gained nothing financially.

"Damn!" Kiernan muttered. "Nothing quite fits."

Over the top of the hills a strip of orange sun poked up. Sprays
of blinding yellow turned the hillside gold and caramel and brown.
Without thinking, Kiernan slowed down. Beams of light glistened
off the tops of the paloverdes and the saguaro cacti like stars on a
Christmas tree. And then the sun rose quickly and poured light
over crest of the mountains. The trees and jutting rocks reclaimed
their shapes, the sepia tones vanished from the landscape, and the
mesquite and the paloverde trees stood pale green in the golden
mist of morning.

She shook her head sharply to break the spell. It was easy to see
how the high desert seduced people. Just as easy to see how those
people drove their Jeeps off the road.

The metal Z that marked Joe Zekk's road came up on the right.
She turned onto the unpaved road, driving too fast for even the
Jeep's suspension. What had Zekk said to Dowd at nine-thirty last
night to lure the bishop to Mission San Leo? Had he threatened to
expose his part in the Rattlesnake massacre? Or had he lied and
told him he had the will?

The mesa came into sight. Zekk's house sat, castlelike, on the
edge. At the far end of the mesa she could see the small round rise

of Vanderhooven's dome, and from this angle, that giant forearm and fist of rock that hung over the end of the valley.

She looked back at Zekk's house. The land in front was empty. Zekk's green panel truck was gone.

"Damn! Oh, hell! Damn, damn, damn!" She pounded her fist against the steering wheel. She slammed on the brakes and stared at the offending building, then rolled the Jeep forward and parked in front of the house.

If Joe Zekk wasn't here, at least his house could be useful. She grabbed her water bottle, extricated Austin Vanderhooven's keys, and headed in through the kitchen door.

The vaguely sweet smell she had noticed yesterday was stronger now. Was it from the sticky soda cans on the counter?

The kitchen looked no different than it had yesterday afternoon. The potential avalanche of dishes in the sink seemed just as precarious, the pile on the counter just as architecturally amazing. She pulled open the refrigerator door and found the contents unchanged: beer, soda, butter, a raw steak—nothing that smelled.

She walked slowly through the living room. It, too, looked as bad as the previous day. As bad, but not lots worse, as it would if Zekk had rooted through the piles for things he wanted to take with him.

Disgusted, she checked the dresser and the closet. No empty drawers or hangers. In the bathroom the medicine cabinet appeared untouched. A dry toothbrush hung in its holder.

She walked back to the kitchen, looked at the sink once more, and edged her water bottle in under the tap.

Zekk's truck was gone, but none of his things appeared to be missing. Or was he gone?

Of course, Zekk hadn't left for good. What he had to sell was McKinley's new will. And that was at the bottom of the hill in Rattlesnake. Zekk wouldn't leave without it.

But how could he get it? The McKinleys were hardly about to let him wander down the switchback road. They had shot at her yesterday; they would shoot at Zekk today. He would never get near the will.

If Zekk planned to steal the will, he would have to wait till after dark. And be very clever, very quiet, and very, very lucky.

38

KIERNAN PULLED the Jeep against the west side of Zekk's house
and settled in the shade to wait for his return. She ate a sandwich,
kept an eye on the switchback road, watching for angry McKinleys, and reviled Joe Zekk for keeping a house that smelled too bad
for her to wait in. From time to time she found herself catnapping.
Every couple of hours she ventured in to the bathroom. Twice she
swallowed more Alka-Seltzer. By noon she had reconsidered her
premise about Zekk a dozen times. Maybe Zekk would not return
after all. Maybe he had abandoned the will and fled. He could be in
L.A. by now. Maybe she was sweating in the middle of the desert
for nothing. She considered walking down to the dome. But the
last time she had been in there it had been almost as hot inside as
out. Instead, she doused herself in water and refilled the bottle. The
Rattlesnake River looked tantalizingly cool below. By three in the
afternoon she was ready to admit that the day had been wasted.
Zekk had to come back to Rattlesnake at night, but there was no
reason to assume he would return before then.

But now it was too late to leave. She longed for ten minutes in
Zekk's shower. She yearned for a cool spot, even a merely *cooler*
spot, to wait in.

It had been morning when she was inside the dome yesterday.
Maybe it was cooler in there in the afternoon. She didn't believe it,
but after eight hours of waiting, any diversion had its merits. From
there she could hear Zekk's truck approaching.

She drove to the far side of the high adobe wall, walked to the
gate, opened it with one of the keys on Vanderhooven's ring, and
walked inside the enclosure.

The stench was overwhelming! How had she not smelled it outside? Maybe the air flowed up from inside the walls. Maybe . . .

She stared slowly around the garden. Cacti, succulents, hard red
dirt. Even more slowly, she walked toward the dome itself.

The door stood open. On the floor, a triangle of light from the
skylight stood out against the darkness. It took a moment for her

eyes to adjust. She stepped closer, into the doorway. The first thing she spotted was the blowflies, hundreds of them. Then she saw Zekk. She jammed her teeth together and swallowed hard.

Joe Zekk lay on his side. The back of his head had been blown away. Blood and brain and skin and hair stuck to the dome walls, the floor, the sheets on Vanderhooven's mat.

She spun around and raced outside, swatting at the flies as they buzzed around her nose and mouth. Through her teeth, she breathed in, pulling the fresher air into her lungs. It wasn't like the autopsy table here. There you knew it was coming. Here . . . Christ! What kind of gun had the velocity to blow the back of a man's head off?

The bullet that did that kind of damage had to have been hollow-tipped, a shell that would explode on impact and break through the brains like an electric mixer blade. Or a thin-jacketed shell, the type used in high-velocity rifles. Varmint rifles. Rifles like those the McKinleys carried.

She shivered at the thought. A wave of sorrow shook her as she remembered Zekk, sitting amid the piles of clutter on his sofa, his short dark hair swept so carefully back and the corners of his mouth quivering under his baby-fat cheeks because she'd hurt his feelings. Would she be the only one to feel a stab of grief for his wasted life?

The blowflies kept after her. As she fanned them away from her face, she recalled the fly-ridden animal carcass she had seen on the dead tree below the cliff edge. The blowflies had had a short trip to Zekk's body.

She hesitated, letting herself wonder what had happened after Joe Zekk called Bishop Dowd at nine-thirty the previous night. Who had had enough of his threats? Or who decided he knew too much? Had that person banged on Zekk's door as he hung up the receiver? Or had he, or she, waited till the early hours of the morning to kill him?

She swatted at the blowflies. She knew she was putting off what had to be done. Taking a last breath in the outside air, she covered her nose with her hand and made her way carefully into the dome.

The blowflies completely masked large portions of Zekk's head. They buzzed in flight and resettled. The smell of death filled the room. Zekk lay on his right side. He was wearing the same teal polo shirt and blue deck pants he had had on yesterday afternoon. Now they were flecked with bits of his head.

Swatting the flies away with her left hand, she bent down and felt Zekk's arm with her right. Cold. Not cool, but cold. She wished she had a thermometer and was simultaneously relieved she didn't. She tried to flex his elbow. Solid.

On his face there was already a white caking in the blood. The first stage of maggot eggs.

The flies were all around her nose. She swatted with both hands. Stooping quickly, she looked at Zekk's abdomen. The first hint of green was visible. Decomposition. Already. Probably accelerated by the heat?

She stood. The flies buzzed madly then reclaimed the body. Kiernan moved away and looked quickly at the top of the wooden chest. Nothing there at all. With a cloth she lifted the lid. Books inside, still lying there as they had been the last time she looked. No clock beside the bed. On the floor, no footprints in the blood. The killer must have stood in the doorway.

She turned and walked outside, forcing herself to make a slow circle around the courtyard, checking for threads caught on cacti, for vomit, for any clue.

When she found none, she went back in and looked at Zekk's body again. Things didn't add up right. But she could worry about that outside. She glanced up through the pink skylight. Zekk had thought that light was blue, of course, because he had seen it only from the outside. Had he looked up before he was shot and seen it was pink? Or were she and Beth the only ones still alive who shared that small secret?

But, of course, they weren't.

Aware of the shakiness of her arms and the queasiness in her stomach, she walked out, relocked the gate, and gratefully inhaled the clean, death-free air.

She moved slowly around the high wall, for the moment concentrating only on placing one foot in front of other. What was it that didn't fit? She passed the Jeep and kept on, walking out along the rocky forearm that hung over the valley. There was something comforting about its presence there, despite its precarious position, as if it had maintained itself by will alone. She walked toward the fist of red rock, staring at the dead tree in front of it. Dead as Zekk, dead as Vanderhooven, but somehow, not so dead. Dirt skidded across the yard-wide peninsula of land and dropped off the edge. Despite her years of training in the gym, practicing balance day after day, she felt a shot of terror. She grabbed the dead tree and shut her eyes against the fear.

She shook her head sharply, and opened her eyes. She took a breath and forced herself to look down at the rocky peninsula on which she stood, down over the side, down the side of the sheer cliff. The remains of the dead animal that she had seen there the previous day were almost gone. Most of the flies had deserted it. Deserted it for the more appetizing banquet of Joe Zekk.

She let go of the tree and walked back, carefully, across the rocky forearm to the Jeep, climbed in, and sat.

Joe Zekk had called Bishop Dowd at nine-thirty. Sometime after that he came to the dome and was killed. That just did not fit.

Zekk's skin was cool for a hot place like this. He had not been killed this morning—he wouldn't have cooled that quickly in the daytime heat. He had to already have been dead in the night when the temperature was thirty degrees lower. "Not enough," she muttered. Body temperature was notoriously unreliable as an indicator of time of death.

Rigor was set. All that that told her was that Zekk had been killed before she set herself up outside his house this morning.

But the maggot eggs. She had seen flies laying their eggs, she'd seen that white crusty material spread hour by hour. She'd seen it on training films, in lab tests, on bodies left outside. The flies wouldn't have laid eggs till daylight. The crust of maggot eggs on Zekk's face was too great to have formed in a mere nine hours' time. But if the flies had laid those eggs before dusk, a full ten hours earlier . . .

Still not enough. Not if she had to go to court with it.

But add the decomposition that was starting in the abdomen. That discoloration would not have been noticeable only fourteen or fifteen hours after death. It took longer.

Enough? Maybe not enough to go to court with. Still, it did explain why Zekk's house had looked the same as it had the previous afternoon. It explained why that steak that he would logically have cooked for dinner last night was still thawing in his refrigerator. It explained his wearing the same clothes. It explained the drop in body temp.

It said that Joe Zekk had been killed not this morning, not late last night, but before dusk. He was dead before Bishop Dowd got his long-distance call. Someone else had used Zekk's phone to call Bishop Dowd last night. Someone, not Zekk, had dragged the bishop into the church, hauled him up on the altar, and left him to hang. And that person had attacked her there.

She thought of the skylight. She recalled someone mentioning Vanderhooven's *pink* skylight. The village boy considered it blue. Only someone who had been *inside* would see it as pink. The killer. Now the pieces of the puzzle did fit together.

Kiernan looked down over the cliffside and shivered. How many rifles were there down there? High-velocity varmint rifles. The will was down there. There was no way to avoid going down there again.

39

KIERNAN DROVE the Jeep back by Zekk's house. As she had learned to do in the autopsy room, she pushed from her mind the grief she had felt for Zekk and concentrated on working out her plan. The killer would arrive after dark, intending to sneak into Rattlesnake, get the will, and destroy it. The sight of her Jeep abandoned at the top of the road would only increase the pressure to rush down there. And down there she'd be waiting, with the McKinleys and their rifles to back her up. They *should* help her. They benefited from protecting the old man's will. But how to get to them, convince them, without getting shot first—that was the question.

The sky darkened from khaki to brown. The wind picked up. Dust began to swirl. She closed the vents but there was no way to keep out the gritty dust. Choosing the lesser of evils she headed into Joe Zekk's house to wait out the storm. The one last night had been over in half an hour.

Briefly she had wondered if the killer knew the will was down there. But one look around Zekk's house reminded her that the house had not been searched. The killer had not bothered to root around there for the will; pointing a rifle at Zekk and demanding the information had been easier. She didn't waste time debating whether Zekk had talked. In those circumstances anyone would talk, and Zekk faster than most.

Had the killer gone down into Rattlesnake last night to get the will? Not after driving to Zekk's with the lights on, which would have alerted the villagers. No one would venture down there without the element of surprise.

She herself would have just a few minutes at dusk to get down into Rattlesnake and ready the trap. Any earlier and she would make a clear target for the McKinleys as she moved back and forth across the switchback road, like one of those metal silhouettes in a boardwalk sharpshooting concession. After sunset it would be too late.

Wind smacked hard against the windows. It spit dirt across the mesa. The sky grew darker by the minute, the air thicker. It masked the Jeep outside. She looked at her watch—4:41. Plenty of time . . .

The sky flashed white, and thunder broke over the mesa. It echoed back from the far cliffs. Rain, thick as the dust had been, filled the air. Kiernan stood by the window, watching it bounce off the hard-baked dirt.

She could convince Frank McKinley to help, she assured herself. She had done the McKinleys a favor already, showing Frank how to give his father the shot. She would remind him of that. *If* she had the chance to talk.

The sky grew darker still; rain slashed down in sheets.

After half an hour she accepted the conclusion she had been avoiding. This might not be a passing thunderstorm. It could rain all night. It might not stop for days.

After dark, in the rain, the switchback road would be too treacherous. *The killer wouldn't dare wait till nightfall.* Neither could she.

Lightning spiked the sky and thunder rattled the windows again and again. She thought fondly of the Jeep. A Jeep could make it down that switchback road. What would Rattlesnake be like, down at the bottom of the gorge? Stu Wiggins hadn't been exaggerating, she knew, when he talked about sudden walls of water.

But those little wooden houses in Rattlesnake had withstood many years of monsoons. No flash floods had washed them away.

She looked out at the Jeep. She could barely see it through the rain. The Jeep probably would make it down the hill to Rattlesnake. But it would never make it back up the hill.

With a last look back at the dry, safe house, she stepped out the front door and ran. Rain slapped her head, pressing her thick short hair against her skull, pulling the curls straight.

The road looked like an amusement park water slide. A channel of mud ran down the center, rounding each cutback and heading down the next straightaway with renewed force. At the bottom, lights were on in houses and the street was empty. The swollen Rattlesnake River flowed fast, bubbling into whitecaps, rushing over its banks. No wonder they had flash floods here when rivers swelled this fast.

She pushed off and headed down the steep, muddy road. She tried to hug the inside walls, but it was impossible to stay out of the growing stream of mud. Rain slapped in from the north; water streamed down the hillside, swelling the stream in the roadbed. A few yards ahead lightning cracked the air. Almost immediately thunder reverberated off the sides of the canyon. By the second switchback, she was soaked. Her running shoes felt like cement boots. She wiped the rain from her eyes and rushed on, leaping foot to foot, squishing into the mud, smacking the hard surface beneath.

Another flash of lightning seared the color from the road and the cacti and the tombstones. Everything looked dead. Thunder shook the hillside.

At the bottom of the road, she looked toward the village. The river had leapt its banks; it fanned over the village street, gathering broken branches and debris; it lapped at the steps of the houses. On his porch stood Frank McKinley, rifle pointed.

She started into the street toward him. Water rushed over her ankles. An ocotillo branch slapped against her shin. The air was almost too thick to breathe. She was halfway across when Frank stepped to the edge of his porch.

"Pa died last night," he yelled. The cold fury in his voice cut through the drumming of the rain. "I gave him the shot, and he died!"

Despite the steamy rain, she shivered. No men came toward her this time. *Because* no one was going to haul her into the house this time. Because Frank was going to shoot her. Frantically, Kiernan sought for questions—keep him talking. The will? But of course the old man had signed it. That's what the two witnesses Frank had called were for. Frank gave him the shot only after he'd signed the will.

"Run!" Frank ordered.

She didn't move. Rain pelted her shoulders.

Lightning crackled, and a crash of thunder bounced off the cliffs, slamming against her ears. Against the dark porch Frank McKinley's face shone granite-white, unyielding.

"Run!" he yelled. "I like a moving target."

"Frank—" There was no cover on the switchback road, nothing

to protect her from the McKinleys, or from Vanderhooven's killer, who'd be coming down into her "trap."

He aimed and shot. The bullet hit the water by her feet, spraying her legs. "Run. Woman."

She turned and started back toward the road, wiping at her eyes as the rain streaked down her face.

"Faster," he yelled.

She reached the switchback road and broke into a trot, pushing her feet against the muddy surface. How much of a cat-and-mouse game was this with McKinley? Would he shoot her here, or wait till she was close enough to the top to think she might live? Close enough for Vanderhooven's killer to pick her off first.

Lightning flashed, the thunder almost upon it. The picture of Joe Zekk's splattered head filled her mind. She started to run, looking up the hill for a rock big enough to shield her. None. The cemetery, maybe—

A great crash shook the air, like a hundred thunderclaps—but no lightning had preceded it. Rocks tumbled down the hillside, bouncing off the hard undersurface of the road and over the edge, down the hill. She raced on past the switchback over the broken ground toward the cemetery.

Below her men yelled. She kept running.

Another crash cut through the air. An explosion! The hillside shook; boulders leapt into the air, avalanching down, knocking others loose in their path. Kiernan flung herself, panting, behind a gravestone. In the village below, figures were running toward the houses, yelling. Frank's porch was empty. She looked up at the top of the road where the explosion came from. No one was in sight.

Explosions weren't part of her plan. How had . . . ? She thought of the rocky fist overhanging the end of the valley. Her body went cold. No wonder the McKinleys had let her go; they had a much greater danger to deal with.

Water rushed down the hillside, slewing around the gravestones. She started up the path between the two halves of the graveyard, where she'd sat with the boy only yesterday. The rise was steep and her feet slipped on the mud. Thrusting her weight forward, she grasped the top of a gravestone and pulled herself up. The stone gave. She fell back, landing hard.

Through the pounding of the rain and the smacking of the rocks rolling down the hillside she could hear shrill voices from the village. How soon would one of the McKinleys remember her and assume she was connected with the explosions? She grabbed at another headstone and pulled herself up.

Another explosion resounded from the top of the canyon. Rocks crashed down to her right. If boulders dammed the valley, the fast-running Rattlesnake River would soon put the whole place under water. Veering to the left, she climbed upward, planting a foot, and pushing off before it had time to slip. How long would it take to set the next explosion? Two minutes? Less? She reached for an out-cropping of rock. Her hands slipped; she slid backward. She hooked her fingers around ocotillo, ignoring the thorns, pulled, grabbed another just as the first snapped.

The canyon top by Zekk's house was twenty feet above her now, but the wall was sheer. Somehow she found a toehold, then another. Her breath was coming in quick pants. Near the top was a boojum tree, a single, succulent stalk. She grabbed it, swung herself around it, and planted her feet.

The edge was five feet above her head. She caught an outcropping of rock halfway up, pulled, braced her feet, and looked up, ready to reach for the edge.

Bud Warren stuck a hand down. "Kiernan!" he yelled over the roar of the wind and rain and the river below. "I saw you down there. Thank God you're safe. Can you reach?"

His hand was too far away. She felt a wave of panic. "Bud, come closer."

He leaned toward her.

Keeping hold of the rock, she reached beyond his hand and grabbed his sleeve.

He jerked back, ripped his arm free, and lunged at her shoulders. She went flying backwards, butt over head in the mud, and smacked into the boojum tree.

Mud filled her mouth and nose. She spit and spit again. Her feet slipped. She clutched the tree, barely aware of the sharp spines cutting into her hand. Half-dazed, she looked with blurred eyes down to the village, watching the splotches of color that had to be people rushing out of houses. Rocks tumbled down the hillside, crashing below. Bud Warren would still be up at the top of the hill, behind her. She wiped the mud from her eyelashes, pushed herself up, and turned around.

Warren was gone!

Or had he just taken a couple of steps backward, to get better leverage for a shove that would send her crashing down through the gravestones to the boulders below?

Holding on to the tree, she leaned back and tried to see over the canyon edge. No hand or foot was visible. Cautiously she continued up the hillside, digging her toes in farther, making each hold deeper. She grabbed a root right below the edge, leaned in against the wet hillside and listened. The dull roar of the rushing river was broken by the staccato clacks of rocks smacking together and the frantic yells of the people below. Over it all, like a thick drape, was the thrumming of the hard rain. Bud Warren could be right above her. There was plenty of noise to muffle any sound he might be making.

She planted her feet, pushed off, and swung herself up and over. Warren wasn't there.

Her hands stung; the skin was ripped. Her head throbbed, and her arms and thighs ached. Forcing herself to run, she headed to the side of the house and made her way around it to the front. She stopped and listened, then looked down the length of the plateau in time to see Warren move behind the dome wall.

She ran, pressing her feet into the soft earth, forcing herself to move faster across the wet ground. She flung herself, panting, against the dome wall.

Was that a noise inside the dome wall? Warren could be in there. He certainly knew how to get in. He'd been in "Austin's little prayer dome with the pink glass window"—both he and Beth had used those words—often enough with Beth. Hoisting herself up, she peered over the wall. The door to the dome was open. Zekk's feet were visible. But there was no sign of Warren.

Beyond the dome was nothing but the narrow peninsula that led to the jagged outcropping of rock. The giant fist of rock. Kiernan's body went cold. One explosion there and those huge rocks would crash down, setting off an avalanche that would dam the canyon. The flood waters would fill it faster than the villagers could clamber up the slippery hillside. It would form a lake over Rattlesnake, the McKinleys, the old man's will, and over her own corpse.

She raced around the dome wall, stopping just short of the narrow arm of the peninsula. Fifteen feet long, a yard wide, slick with rain. Beneath it nothing but the canyon bed. Warren was out at the far end near the rocky fist. He was right in front of the dead tree. His dark hair flopped in his face. He was bending, planting wires. Explosive wires.

He stood up. Mud sprayed over the edges of the peninsula into nothingness. He stared at her, his face etched with fury. He raced forward. Still on the mesa itself, she leapt to the side. His momentum propelled him on.

Desperately, she looked at the dome. There'd be no safety there. Warren was twice her size. There was only one place she would have a chance, where her agility could save her and she could use his size against him. *If* she could get him to move fast enough.

She ran out the narrow arm to the fist of rocks. The dead tree was behind her. Inches away on either side of her the ground dropped off. Rain pelted her face, ran down her body. It bounced off the muddy ground into the abyss. She turned to face Warren. Stooping, she yanked at the wires. Her feet skidded to the side. She hung on to the wires and scrambled to pull her feet back from the edge.

Face red with rage, Warren started toward her, striding more slowly now, confident in his physical advantage. His dark hair clung to his face; his soaked work shirt outlined his muscular body.

She backed up against the trunk of the dead tree. She could thrust her arms behind her, and she could hang on.

One chance, she thought. Just one. Got to make him move faster. She reached down for the wires, and pulled.

"Leave them," he yelled.

She yanked again. The ground gave. Dirt and mud and water shot over the edge of the outcropping into the empty air below. The wires lifted, almost free.

Warren raced across the muddy ground toward her. She flung her arms back, grabbed tight around the tree behind her. He was four feet away, coming fast. She let out a yell. He lunged at her. With both feet, she kicked. Grazed his hands. Slammed her heels against his eyes. Instinctively, he grabbed his face. He stumbled back. One foot skidded to the side. He scrambled for footing, fell forward. Kiernan watched his fingers slip through the mud as he clawed for a hold in the wet ground. Slowly, he slipped over the edge.

His scream reverberated off the canyon walls.

40

WAYLON JENNINGS was singing "Ladies Love Outlaws." Every table in the tavern was filled. The smoke was so thick you could cut it. The whole place reeked of beer. Dusty men in faded jeans and boots bellied up to the bar rail. Each one held a beer—the round of beer she had bought. Patsy Luca was in heaven.

"What do you think of it, Stu? It's great, isn't it?" Patsy yelled over the beat of the jukebox.

"Great," he muttered.

"See the guy at the end of the bar, the one in the 'Outlaws' sweatshirt? He's the one who gave me the tip on that old Packard I traced last year. And the guy three down from him—"

"So what're you going to do with your earnings, Patsy?"

Patsy grinned. "I've got my eye on a Winchester four-ninety. Guy who owns it wants way too much. But I'll get him down. What about you?"

Wiggins leaned back in his chair, momentarily balancing on the back two legs. The jukebox stopped, but the noise level decreased only slightly. He waited till Patsy leaned in close enough so he didn't have to shout. "Well, you know, I've been thinking that a few days on the beach might not do an old codger any harm. Don't have to worry about the sun ruining my looks." He laughed. "And now that we've got this invitation to San Diego . . ." He shrugged.

Patsy stared, amazed. She thought the world of Stu, she really did. But sometimes the man got strange ideas. To throw away his money, to *pay* to leave Phoenix . . . Especially now, when the word among her sources was that there was a hot-car ring operating out of a house on East Ellis Drive in Tempe. Maybe if he had another beer . . .

41

A LONG, EASY RISE in the gray-green Pacific surf swept up to an arc, poised motionless a breathless instant longer than seemed physically possible, then spilled raucously over the edge and crashed down on the rocky beach. Above, Kiernan sat on her deck, her feet on the rail. The afternoon sun was still hot, but she hadn't been out long enough for her stomach to be red, even the part not covered by Ezra's gray furry snout. Ezra was snoring.

Kiernan scratched the wolfhound's head. Eyes closed, he moaned with pleasure. In his excitement he had been up most of the night. But now, his kingdom in order once again, he was sleeping the sleep of the satisfied. Kiernan leaned back, noting how welcome was the cocoon of home after a case like the one she had just finished. And yet she missed the intensity. She picked up the phone and started to dial Stu Wiggins's number. But no, the case was over. She compromised and dialed Sam Chase.

"Chase here."

"Hi, Sam. It's Kiernan. I'm back."

"I figured you might be. I just talked to the archbishop's office. They're not pleased about your fee. If you want to see red silk fly . . ." He laughed.

"I take it that means no problem, for us."

"Oh no. They're not pleased, but at least the murderer wasn't one of their own. And so far, the media hasn't mentioned the seamier details of Vanderhooven's death. Their focus is on Warren planning the murder to protect his water rights."

Kiernan leaned back in the chair. "That's lucky for them. Warren was after the water rights, certainly, but with him there was also a touch of revenge. Maybe he'd spent too many nights lying under the stained-glass window in Vanderhooven's meditation dome listening to Beth Landau complain about Vanderhooven."

"Nothing like righteous indignation to put a better face on greed, eh?"

From the kitchen came the sound of the broiler door opening. "Five minutes," Brad Tchernak called.

Eyes half-opened, Ezra lifted his brown head, stretched, and dropped it back on Kiernan's stomach. To Chase she said, "He was Beth's lover, which also meant he had access to her key to Vanderhooven's rectory, to her office at Hohokam Lodge, and to the Culiacán. He was the one person who could take that bottle and put it back in the drawer a couple of days later. And the peace-making ritual Vanderhooven and Beth had, Vanderhooven would never have mentioned it, but Beth did. You can just picture her lying there in the dome, telling Bud Warren about it. So he knew that if he left the bottle on Vanderhooven's desk, Vanderhooven would take a drink, for old time's sake. Vanderhooven would see that peace offering as Beth's accepting his idea of the monastery. Vanderhooven would be drinking to his ultimate triumph. His last triumph. You can see how the idea would appeal to Bud Warren."

"But what about the autoerotic asphyxia?"

"For Beth's boyfriend there was a wonderful irony to it, don't you think? But it had a very practical purpose, to divert attention until John McKinley died. All Warren needed was for Rattlesnake to be isolated long enough for the old man to die without signing the new will."

"Four minutes," Brad Tchernak called from the kitchen.

"What's that?" Chase asked.

"Dinner. Brad's broiling the bluefish and tomatoes I had flown in from Jersey. You see what a decadent life I'm leading, Sam."

"That's pretty blue-collar decadence." Chase laughed. "Well, bon appétit."

Kiernan hesitated then replaced the receiver.

The smell of broiling fish floated through the door. Ezra cocked his head expectantly. Below, a huge wave arched and crashed, sending three bodysurfers speeding toward the rocky shore. Kiernan watched them hold form till they were within seconds of being smashed into the rocks, then twist back under the surf. Last week when Chase had said she was not unlike Austin Vanderhooven she hadn't asked him why. The question had gnawed at her all week. Vanderhooven had died in the rising wave of his obsession. And she'd been lucky enough to see her obsession peak and crash like the waves. Like the surfers, she could duck under and float back out.

The phone rang. Irritably, Ezra barked, yawned, and returned his head to its perch. "Kerry. It's Stu. How're you doing out there?"

"As well as can be expected for someone who is virtually buried under wolfhound. How about you?"

"It seems kind of dull here in Phoenix without you stirring things up. You know you left enough ruffled feathers to fill a heap of pillows."

"Who are those feathers attached to?"

"For starters you've got the Vanderhoovens fussing because they can't bury the body until the coroner's inquest comes up with a real death certificate. The one Necri signed is gone—not that it would have been legal anyway. Necri seems to be gone too. Can't say I'm surprised."

Kiernan could picture Stu, settled much like herself on the porch of the house she'd imagined for him. His boots would be on the railing, a beer in one hand, an empty Ben's Burger bag beside him. "What about Sylvia Necri?"

"Well, no doubt about it, Sylvia's in a heap of trouble. Once the sheriff heard about her giving Bud Warren access to the retreat's water rights, he didn't take long to ask 'in return for what?' "

"For updates on the status of Rattlesnake and McKinley's will? Information that Bud Warren got from Beth Landau, who got it from Vanderhooven, right?"

"Right. I don't know what-all the D.A. could have done with that, but what he is doing is using it as leverage. So between that leverage and the forgery charge, Sylvia's talking a mile a minute. On the other hand, Bishop Dowd isn't talking at all. Under psychiatric care is the official word. And what I hear is that Dowd is showing no improvement. Considering all the charges the D.A. could bring against him, that could be a right smart move on his part. Only thing he did let slip was that there are Sheltons in L.A. and Florida."

"How'd that sit with the archdiocese. I can't imagine the Sheltons would get much from the McKinleys, but from the Church . . . ?"

"Make one helluva lawsuit. But it'll never go to trial. Bishop

Harrington is making it his business to find the Sheltons and take care of them. Harrington's an ethical man; he wants to do the right thing by them. He'll get a lot of support on that. The Catholic community here is really getting behind it. The Sheltons won't be wanting for much."

"So, Stu, are you taking it easy now?"

"Easy! Kerry, I'll be running my bow legs into the ground for the next month paying off all the favors I begged for you. You're going to have to hire me to help you out on a case out there just so I can get away. You know, I've got connections all over."

Kiernan smiled. "I'll bet you do, Stu. But for now, you stay put. I've got some Jersey bluefish on the way to you, and if Federal Express has to leave them on your stoop, you're going to be real sorry."

"One minute to dinner!" Brad Tchernak called from the kitchen doorway.

"I heard that, Kerry, and I know better than to stand between you and your fodder." The phone clicked dead.

"You ready?" Tchernak stepped around the doorway. His sun-bleached hair stood out in all directions after their swim in the inlet. On his deeply tanned chest the thatch of hair was nearly blond now. One of those grins that transformed his face slowly took hold. "Kiernan, you know it's great to have you back." His smile widened; he dropped into a three-point stance, grunted menacingly, charged across the room to the deck and scooped her up. Ezra barked and resettled himself.

Nuzzling her neck, Tchernak said, "Lineman's greeting."

"That's how you handled the defensive line, huh?"

"Well, on the field we got penalized ten yards for holding. And we didn't end with a kiss."

"Ten yards? A small price to pay." She grinned, reached a hand around his back and palpated his gluteus maximus.

ABOUT THE AUTHOR

SUSAN DUNLAP has been called the "leading proponent of gutsy, non-traditional women who nimbly tread in he-man territory" and "one of the best of the new crop of mystery writers." She is the author of ten novels, including *Too Close to the Edge* and *A Dinner to Die For*. She lives near San Francisco and is working on the next Kiernan O'Shaughnessy novel.

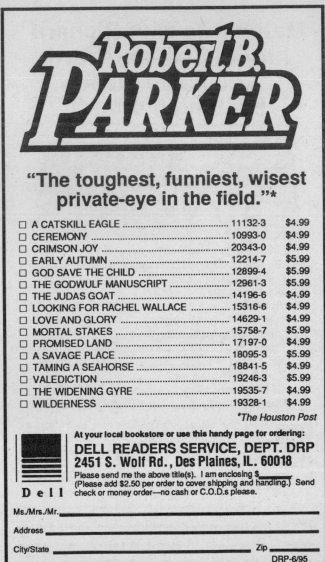